The Chronicles of Finn Stonefist

&

The Staff of Jotunheim

By Quin Folkestad

Table of Contents

Prologue 3
Chapter 1 11
Chapter 2 27
Chapter 3 36
Chapter 4 46
Chapter 5 68
Chapter 6 74
Chapter 7 79
Chapter 8 96
Chapter 9 106
Chapter 10 117
Chapter 11 124
Chapter 12 138
Chapter 13 160
Chapter 14 169
Chapter 15 184
Chapter 16 201
Chapter 17 218
Chapter 18 233
Chapter 19 261

Prologue

Was it late or early? Tove couldn't tell anymore. It seemed like driving was all she had done for days. Her eyes burned from exhaustion as the gray Alaskan sky brightened and the sun climbed above the horizon. This wasn't new to her. The summers were always like this, but if someone weren't paying attention, they could lose track of time.

Tove rolled the window down and let the crisp morning air whip across her skin and through her hair. She loved the peninsula; the air was clean and cool. She looked across the seat from her at her brother, Erik, asleep against his window, mouth open with drool sneaking out the side of his mouth. Next to her, the whole reason for the impromptu trip from Denali stirred: the infant in his seat, buried in so many blankets, his face was bright pink from the warmth. Tove used her thumb to push a blonde curl out of his face, then gently stroked his cheek. The babe seemed to recognize this touch and immediately settled down. Tove forced the tears back that were threatening to break free. She knew what she had to do, but it terrified her to think about it too much. She was afraid it would overcome her. She swallowed her emotions and returned her gaze to the road.

As Tove's rusty old Chevy rounded the bend, the all too familiar pull off known to the locals as Black Water Bend came into view. She had spent many summers as a child here, playing in the river and surrounding wood. It held many happy memories. Now it would hold its first sad one. As she pulled the old pickup in, she noticed the coffee shop wasn't open yet. It still had "closed for the season" signs on the windows, and had shades drawn, making it look dark and forbidding. As she put the truck in park, Erik woke up.

"We're here?" he asked as he wiped the drool from his cheek.

The teenager looked as exhausted as Tove felt.

"We're here," Tove answered, and she got out of the truck.

She walked to the front and leaned on the hood facing the woods. The heat of the previously running engine felt nice on her back after hours of driving with little sleep.

"Almost there," she muttered to herself.

Erik joined her at the front of the truck just in time to see Tove remove something from her jacket pocket. It was a jade figurine of an eagle. Its wings spread wide, and it posed its feet as if it were about to snatch a great fish from the water.

"Where did you get that?" asked Erik.

"A friend," said Tove as she cupped the figure in her hands and brought it close to her lips where she whispered something to it.

Erik strained to see what she was doing, but before he could, Tove tossed the little green eagle into the air as if she were releasing an actual bird. The air cracked with thunder, there was a green flash, and the little figurine transformed into a great bald eagle. His great wings covered the sky as he hovered above them, staring at Tove for a moment, then turning and flying into the woods. As the magnificent bird disappeared, it let out a call that echoed around them. Tove let out a sigh and leaned on the truck's hood.

Erik turned to her. "Now what?"

Tove looked into his eyes. "Now we wait." And with that, she turned and got back into the truck.

She removed the infant from his car seat and nursed him. Erik had no desire to be in the truck while his sister breast fed the baby, so he slumped to the ground next to the truck, resting his head on the bumper. The eagle was out of sight, but he swore he could still hear its call.

***

The sun was high when Tove woke with a start. The babe was in his seat, sound asleep. After checking on him, she panned the surrounding wood. Something had woken her. Her heart pounded in her chest as she got out of the truck and walked to the front where she found Erik on his feet, eyes wide, armed with a single bladed pocketknife not even big enough to sword fight an angry pixie.

Tove gently put her hand on Erik's. "Put that away. It won't help, and we don't need it, anyway."

Erik lowered the knife but refused to holster it. He lived by the philosophy that you never know what's coming. Also, more to the point, he was afraid of lopping a finger off trying to close it.

There it was again, a low gentle rumble coming from the forest where the eagle had flown to. It wasn't loud, but it was haunting.

"Maybe it's an earthquake," said Erik hopefully.

Tove didn't bother looking at him. "It's not an earthquake."

Again, the rumble; this time it was closer and more intense.

"There!" shouted Erik, pointing to the forest directly in front of them.

The trees were shivering like something had them by the root and were trying to rattle every pine needle from its branch. Again, the rumble, much more intense this time. Tove felt it in her chest. The grass in front of the trees rolled like waves on the oceans. And then a man emerged from the trees.

Not a large man or tall man; just an average man wearing a flannel shirt and jeans. Middle-aged with light gray hair on his temples. He carried a large walking staff and had a large buck knife hanging from his belt. The man-made eye contact with Tove and smiled. And the second he smiled; the rumbling stopped.

The man made his way over to Tove and Erik. He had a limp and used his staff to stay upright. Once he reached Tove, he embraced her with all the intensity of a father finding a lost child. Then he pushed her back and turned to Erik. "Who is this strapping man?"

"He is my brother Erik," replied Tove.

And with that, the man snatched Erik into a bone-crushing bear hug.

Erik imagined he would die in the man's embrace, only to be released just before losing consciousness. Once he had regained the full function of his lungs, Erik turned to Tove. "So, you going to explain who this old guy is?" He was still trying to get over the fright he'd felt by the rumbling.

Tove chuckled at the exasperated boy. "This is Anders Stonefist; my father-in-law."

Erik looked like someone had just told him a joke. "This is the great Anders Stonefist? This waif of an old man?"

Anders ignored the boy. "Tove, tell me why you are here. You wouldn't have sent Heimdal for me unless it was important."

Tove went to the cab of the truck and retrieved the infant. "This is Finn. Finn Stonefist, your grandson."

"Grandson?" The old man's eyes lit up with pure joy. He hefted the babe from Tove's arms and brought the child close to his face and breathed in deep. "My son must be so proud. But where is he? Why isn't he here?"

Erik suddenly became still, and all the color drained from Tove's face.

"Tove, where is he? Tell me!"

Tove swallowed hard and her voice felt weak. "There was an attack on the keep."

"An attack? By whom?" Anders asked.

Tove opened her mouth, but nothing came out.

Erik stepped forward. "It was Rathgar," he said coldly. "Rathgar and his thugs blasted their way into the keep. Einar rallied the troops, and there was a battle. I just made it to the inner keep before Rathgar barricaded it shut. Einar pushed me, Tove, and the baby into an escape tunnel before turning to face Rathgar. There was an explosion and the tunnel entrance to the inner keep collapsed."

Tove interrupted as she choked back her emotions. "It wasn't until we were about halfway here that we learned Rathgar had seized control and Einar was dead." Then she couldn't hold back any longer. She let the tears come.

Anders handed the baby to Erik and pulled the sobbing girl to him. The events of the last few days overcame her, and she would have collapsed to the ground if Anders hadn't held her up in his arms.

"Calm yourself, daughter. You will come with me now," whispered Anders.

He looked at Erik and told him to gather their things from the truck. Then, leaving the truck behind, Anders guided them up the path into the woods from where he had appeared earlier.

The path up to Anders' house wasn't long but, it was rough. Erik was more than grumpy by the time they got to the gate. He had all their bags on his back and baby Finn on his front. It wasn't fair, but he kept his complaints to himself.... mostly. Finally, they reached the gate just outside Anders's front yard. The house was a small trapper shack made from logs that looked like someone had felled them, then just stacked them on top of each other with no regard for size or shape, giving the hovel a crooked look. There was a river rock chimney on one side that appeared to be built with as much care as the cabin. The remaining forest was close, and it gave the surrounding grounds a dark, damp feel.

"This is it?" said Erik, not trying to hide his disappointment, though after the trek they'd just made, he'd been hoping for more.

Anders looked over his shoulder and smiled while gripping his staff with both hands as he pushed the gate open. Almost at once, Tove and Erik felt a blast of warm air and sunlight.

"Welcome home. Welcome to Troll's Rest," said Anders as he gestured for them to enter.

As they passed through the gate, Tove and Erik couldn't believe what they were seeing. The air was warm; the sun shone bright. The yard was full of soft green grass and fragrant trees lining the edge of the property. In place of the shack was a two-story log cabin whose beams shone brightly in the sun with lacquer. The top floor had large windows and a small greenhouse on the upper deck. The lower deck had a porch swing and two rocking chairs to the side of the front door. To the left of the cabin was an orchard in full bloom. The air carried the sweet fragrance of blossoms. In the orchard's front was an enormous garden where Tove and Erik could see the spring's first sprouts. Humming filled the air, which came from a set of six beehives to the right of the house, about twice the size of a normal beehive. Busy bumble bees about the size of robins buzzing from one oversized wildflower to the next.

Erik looked back and could see the forest behind them. It was still dark and damp and forbidding.

"Anders, how did you manage this!" asked Tove.

"Oh, an old friend helped me," said Anders. "Now come into the house. I have stew ready, and we can discuss what's next."

***

Later that night, Tove lay in her soft bed and listened to the breathing of Finn, who was asleep in the crib next to her. For the first time since it had happened, she processed the last few days. She had lost her home, her family, and the only man she had ever loved, but she still had Finn. She got up and crossed the room to the window and opened it, letting in the cool night air. She looked up and could see a sky full of stars and prayed Einar was watching her from one of them.

Suddenly, a shadow moving in the surrounding wood caught her eye. Fearing that her enemies had found her, she closed the window and hurried to Finn's side. She hadn't even picked him up when there was a loud, thunderous crash from outside. Tove dared to look out the window, staying low to the ground. There was the shadow, smashing its fists into the protective grid of wards that surrounded the property. She couldn't let this creature get through. She kissed Finn's face and raced downstairs. As she pulled the heavy wooden door open, a stench of brimstone and burning wood struck her. She stepped out and crossed the yard to the gate where they entered earlier. She heard something behind her and looked to see Erik on the porch.

"What are you doing?" he called.

"Go back inside!" Tove yelled.

Just then, something growled outside the gate. Tove turned towards it.

"Do your worst demon, but you will never have my son!" she yelled into the darkness. She pulled the gate open and stepped out.

"Tove!" yelled Erik and ran towards her. "Come back!"

Tove looked back at him and tried to give him the most comforting look she could. Then a sword appeared in her hand, glowing green. She turned back to the darkness and let out a deafening roar of her own as she charged into the night. Erik ran as fast as he could, but he couldn't seem to move fast enough. In front of him, he could hear roaring and trees breaking. There was a smell of charcoal and death in the air, and then nothing. The forest beyond the gate fell as silent and as still as before.

"Tove!" he yelled, but there was no response.

Anders appeared by his side. "Come, my boy, she is gone, and she would not want you to waste your life to save hers. That babe needs us. We must protect him now. We must protect the next king of the Giants."

***

Chapter 1

6 AM. The alarm clock was carrying on with its monotone drone. Finn peered at it with one eye and pulled his pillow over his head, hoping no one else was awake yet. No such luck. He could hear someone clanging plates together downstairs, and the smell of freshly brewed coffee had made its way into his room. With a groan, he emerged from his sanctuary of pillows and slapped the clock into silent submission.

"Finn, time to get up. You're going to be late!" called a female voice from downstairs.

"I'm up, aunty, I'll be down in a minute," Finn called in reply.

With a noisy and rather involved stretch, he retrieved a shirt from the floor, smelled it for freshness, and, satisfied with the odor level, donned the shirt and made his way downstairs. In the kitchen, Finn's grandfather Anders was already there, sipping on a mug of coffee and gazing at the table in front of him. He was deep in thought, and Finn knew better than to disturb his grandfather before the mug in front of him was empty. Finn took his place to the right of Anders and greeted his uncle Erik. Erik looked up from his plate of eggs, bacon, and toast just long enough to respond. Then his face was down again on his plate, like it was going to be stolen from him if he didn't devour its contents that instant. Erik worked as a wildlife officer with the Alaska State Troopers and was often away from sunup to dark. It wasn't often Finn saw him at the breakfast table. Finn noticed his uncle had shaved his normal stubble and was wearing his dress uniform.

"What's with the get up, Erik?" Finn asked.

Erik stopped to swallow, check his uniform, and replied "Oh, I have court today to see if we can get a criminal team assembled for this string of poaching cases I have." Erik looked at his watch and jumped up like someone had bitten him. "I got to go; I am going to be late." Then he rounded the table to face his wife, Hilde. She was a tall, dark-haired woman with olive skin and big brown eyes. She came from a small native village not far away called Nanwalek. Erik had met her as a rookie while working a case in her village. She was very kind and patient, but Finn knew better than to cross her. Behind her gentle eyes was a storm just ready to explode, should someone mess with her family. Aside from being an excellent cook in Finn's opinion, she was also very adept in using herbs, berries and wild plants and had many times come up with the perfect remedy for several ailments for Finn and the family over the years, from sore muscles after football practice to colds and flus.

She was holding a travel mug full of coffee for Erik, but charged him a kiss before letting him grab it and dash out the door.

Turning to Finn, Anders said, "Birthday this weekend, right?"

"Yep, on Saturday." Finn replied.

"How old are you?" asked Anders.

"Seventeen." Couldn't his own grandfather keep his age straight?

Hilde put a plate of breakfast in front of Finn. The smell of bacon drifted up to his nose, consuming his mind.

"We need to have a talk tonight, Finn," said Anders.

"Tonight?" asked Finn. "I was going to Bishop's beach with my friends after school."

"When you get home then, but it must be tonight," said Anders.

Finn thought about arguing but caught a look from Hilde from behind her coffee mug that said, "Let it go." So he did.

"Fine, but it might be late." Finn was hoping this would dissuade the old man and give Finn carte blanche to stay out all night. It wasn't just the eve before his seventeenth birthday. It was also the last day of the school year.

Anders simply sipped his coffee and said, "I'll be in the garden waiting."

Conceding defeat, Finn shoveled down his breakfast and shot upstairs to get ready for school. Hilde met him at the bottom of the stairs with his lunch in hand. This cost Finn a kiss as well but, on the cheek. He grabbed the bag and turned to go. But in his path, Anders stood with a serious look on his face.

"Be careful tonight, my boy." He cupped Finn's cheek in his hand.

Finn was a little taken aback by the earnestness in the old man's eyes.

"I will, grandpa, I'll see you tonight." And with that, he slipped past Anders and out the door.

The forty-minute bus ride Finn had to endure into town every morning was typically uneventful, but this morning was even worse. It was a particularly chilly morning for May, so the bus driver had the heat turned up to broil, causing the windows to have a thin film of condensation. This meant watching the world speed by was out. Finn would have to settle for staring at the back of the seat in front of him. He slumped into his customary seat in the back and pulled out his phone, donned his ear buds and cranked his music, hoping this would broadcast a message of leave me alone to anyone who would talk to him or worse, sit with him.

The bus glided to a stop in front of the high school, and a blast of cold air hit Finn as the driver opened the doors. Finn stood, took a deep breath, and muttered "almost there" to himself. After stowing his phone and ear buds in his backpack, he climbed the steps to the school, barely reaching the top when a high-speed mass practically tackled him, reeking of chlorine and cheap deodorant. It was Erik and Hilde's son and Finn's cousin, Arna, who was a year younger than Finn but about the same size. Arna liked to go swimming in the mornings for exercise, so often drove himself in town early to have the school pool to himself. They played on the varsity football team together, both on the defensive line, since they were bigger than most of the other kids in their school. When they could get side by side on the line, they would create what everyone in the league called "THE WALL of STONE." It was a move that was yet to be defeated and no one could stand in its way.

"Last day of school, cousin!" said Arna. "Hey, you're coming to Bishop's Beach tonight, aren't you?"

"Ya, but gramps wants me home early," replied Finn.

"What for?" asked Arna.

"I don't know, man, he just said he needed to talk to me." Finn tried to act like it was no big deal. But deep down, he knew it was a big deal. He wasn't sure why, but he knew.

"Well, you can't go home too early. Tallis will be there," said Arna as he jabbed an elbow into Finn's side.

Finn smiled and pushed his cousin to where he almost fell down the stairs in front of the school. As the boys entered the school, a fellow teammate greeted them with a shout of "THE WALL!" and a fist in the air.

Finn Stonefist

Finn gave a half wave back while Arna had his fist high in air screaming, "You know it, baby!"

Finn could only laugh as he watched his cousin do an impression of Rocky that he was pretty sure Sylvester Stallone would take issue with. Just then, he felt a light touch on the back of his arm.

"Hey, big shot, got any time for us little people," said a gentle voice.

Finn turned to see his long-time girlfriend Tallis Nightfeather standing there with her twin brother Talon brooding behind her. He was in Finn's class but had failed his driving test, so he had to deal with being driven around by Tallis.

"Oh, I think I think I could fit you in," said Finn, feeling rather clever at his coy response.

"Oh brother," grunted Talon, rolling his eyes before walking off.

Tallis and Finn had only been dating six months, but the two had known each other most of their lives. Tallis was slightly shorter than Finn, with a slight build and long, brown hair. Finn often thought she was so small that he might break her if squeezed her too tight. Her eyes were his favorite; green with flecks of gold. It was those eyes that mesmerized him at the Winter ball last year. Tallis slipped her hand into Finn's and hugged his arm.

"So, are you coming tonight?" she asked.

"Oh probably. Marcy Dugnar asked if I was going, so I should probably show up," he said with a grin.

Tallis pinched his bicep and said, "You jerk, you've never had it so good."

Finn knew she was right; he had never had it this good. School jock star, great girlfriend, good grades. It was those

~ 15 ~

things that made the meeting with his grandfather weigh so heavily. He decided not to tell Tallis about it. He figured he would come up with some excuse about why he had to leave and promise her a beach walk the next day.

***

That night at Bishop's Beach was a sight of pure adolescent revelry. Down the bluff from the parking lot sat a huddled mass of kids watching the group of boys who had taken to dancing around the enormous bonfire. Leading the charge was a shirtless Arna, covered in blue and gold paint in true school pride. He was doing a combination of arm flails and hip thrusts to the beat of the music that was playing from a stereo balanced on a piece of driftwood.

Finn sat next to Tallis on a log in front of the fire. She hugged his arm as they sat in silence. "I don't want this to change, ever," she finally said.

"What do you mean?"

She pointed in the party's direction and said, "To me this is happiness, good friends, good music, a beautiful place and not a worry in the world."

Finn knew what she was talking about. The closer he got to his senior year, the more it weighed on him that things would change. Tallis turned to face Finn and pulled his gaze from watching his crazy cousin dance half naked around fire.

"Hey," she said, and like coming out of a daze, he seemed to see her for the first time that night. The fire light caused her green eyes to sparkle and the gold flecks in them to shine. Tallis leaned in for a kiss, and when their lips met, Finn recognized the familiar butterfly feeling he always got when they kissed, but this time there was something else with it. It was almost like a burning that started in the deepest part of his stomach and radiated out. Then a feeling of electricity that shot through his limbs. Finn jumped back, almost calling out, but stifling the yelp.

"Are you okay?" Tallis asked.

The feeling subsided, and Finn got control of himself. "I'm fine," he replied, and leaned in for another kiss. He felt the electricity again, but this time only in his hand. He snuck a look and noticed his hand was about twice as big as it should be. Again, he jumped back, knocking himself off of the log. As he picked himself up off the sand, he looked down. Now both hands had doubled in size. Finn jumped to his feet and stuffed his hands in his jacket pockets, praying that Tallis hadn't seen.

"Um, I'm not feeling very good. I need to go," he stammered.

Tallis put a hand on his forehead. As she did, Finn could feel the electricity moving up his arm. He could feel his arm pushing against the fabric of his jacket.

"You don't feel warm," said Tallis.

"It's a stomach thing, very sudden," said Finn, already trying to make his way back to his car.

"Do you want me to drive you home?" asked Tallis.

"Oh, no, I wouldn't want you to miss the party," said Finn. He was desperate to get out of there. He turned to go. He could feel the surge of energy moving up to his shoulders and into his neck.

"Are you sure?" Tallis shouted to his back.

He turned in frustration and shouted, "I've got it!" But it wasn't his voice. It was incredibly loud and made the air rumble. It not only shocked Finn and Tallis, but everyone was looking at them now. Finn covered his mouth and ran.

In the safety of his car, the pain was getting worse. Finn felt his clothes getting tight. He was afraid he wouldn't make it home. His hands were huge on the steering wheel, like it was a toy. To steady them, he took a few deep breaths. It seemed to work. He started his car and drove off. The entire way home, in between waves of pain, his mind wandered to the shocked look on Tallis's face. He couldn't believe he'd yelled at her. But he could deal with that later. Right now, he had to get home and get to his grandfather. His grandfather would know what to do.

Finn's little Subaru came to a halt in the gravel drive outside of his house. As he jumped from the car, the searing pain shot down both legs, causing him to stumble and fall. This time, Finn didn't hold back and let out a yell of pure agony. Only this time, like at the beach, his voice was incredibly loud and deep, like a beast was trying to claw its way out. Suddenly the door to the house was flung open and Auntie came rushing out with Anders limping as fast as he could behind her.

"My boy!" said Hilde. She kneeled at Finn's side.

Seeing her gave Finn hope he might live through this. Hilde pulled a small round object from her pocket and placed it against Finn's forehead. The talisman was cold on his skin and, almost instantly, the pain dissipated. Anders caught up with them and came to an awkward kneeling position next to them.

"Tell me boy what happened, were you attacked?"

With the pain subsiding, Finn could once again think clearly. "What? No, no one attacked me. I was at the beach with Arna and Tallis and when I kissed her, this happened." Finn raised his hands.

"Oh, thank the gods," said Anders.

Hilde sat back in the gravel in shock. "The shift," she whispered.

Finn's eyes got wide and the panic from before threatened to return. "The shift? You mean the actual shift, like becoming a giant for the first-time kind of shift?" He couldn't keep the panic from his voice.

"That's sure what it looks like," said Anders.

"That's impossible. I'm too young. I have at one more year before I am supposed to go through the ritual. How can this be happening now?"

They both sat there in silence, staring at him. Hilde looked like she was going to cry, and Anders appeared to be searching for the answer.

Anders finally turned to Hilde and said, "You had better call Mick and tell him to bring the healer."

Hilde nodded and went to the house.

"Why do we need Tallis' dad?" Finn asked. "And why the healer?"

Anders turned and Finn could see for the first-time genuine worry on the old man's face. "Giants who shift without proper preparation and the ritual can undergo what we call a malshift where the energy that allows your giant form to come through can overwhelm you and you could die."

The panic was back. Finn's hands tingled. His grandfather's face seemed to get very distant, along with his voice. Then darkness.

***

As Finn opened his eyes, his mouth felt dry, and his head felt like it was going to split in two. As he scanned the room, he recognized it as his. He was on his bed, but he didn't remember how he got there. As a matter of fact, he couldn't remember anything after the driveway. Sun came through the window, but it was still low on the horizon. At the foot of his bed stood Anders with another man. Their backs were to him and they hadn't noticed he was awake.

"Gramps?" muttered Finn.

Anders rushed over to his side. The other man, Dr. Terrance, the family doctor, hurried to Finn's other side. But why would Anders have brought him into this? Finn didn't want to become some military experiment because a human discovered there were giants among them.

Dr. Terrance leaned forward with a stethoscope and Finn pulled away.

"It's okay Finn, you know Dr. Terrance," said Anders.

"Ya, but we both know this isn't a medical problem," said Finn with a look of "please know what I am talking about."

"Oh, my boy, that couldn't be truer," said Dr. Terrance as he stood back up. "You are shifting into your giant form and prematurely, I might say."

Finn, dumbfounded, just stared at the spindly man like he was from outer space. "You know what I am?"

"I should hope so. I've been treating you since you were a baby," the doctor replied. "Not to mention..."

At the words, Finn noticed something different about his old pediatrician. There was a faint glow about him.

"... I'm half elf, half giant. My father was a giant," explained Dr. Terrance. "Now that you started the shift, you may notice something different about me."

"You're glowing!" said Finn.

"That's my aura. Unlike you, when I shift into my true form or elf form, my physical appearance doesn't change much, but those who have undergone the shift can see a faint glow."

"Why didn't I know this before?" asked Finn.

Anders piped in with the answer. "Until one goes through their first shift, they may not know who else in the community is one of us. Now, doctor, what can we do about Finn?"

"Well, we have applied a stronger talisman," said Doctor Terrance, pointing to the round jade talisman on Finn's chest just over his heart. This was the first time Finn noticed the coaster sized disc that was on his chest. It was green, jade, cool to the touch and etched with an outline of a man with a bigger outline of a man around it. The edge had Nordic runes etched into. The whole thing seemed to hum, and though there were no bands or thongs, it held itself in place on his chest.

Finn reached to lift it off, but Anders grabbed his hand and said, "If you do that, the energy from last night will return and it could kill you."

The words "kill you" were all the convincing Finn needed to leave it be.

Anders turned back to Doctor Terrance and said, "We both know this is not a permanent fix. He is too young for the shift. We must find a way to stop it until he is ready."

Doctor Terrance shook his head. "I know, but this is beyond me. He is too far into the shift for me to do anything. There is only one place that can give you the answers you seek but you won't like it."

Anders narrowed his eyes. "No. That's not an option. The cost is too high," he said and left the room.

Finn did not know what that was about, but he didn't get the chance to ask Dr. Terrance. The doctor gathered his things, gave Finn a look of sadness, and followed Anders out the door. They left Finn alone in the room with no answers or even a plan of how to fix this. He rolled onto his side and fell asleep to the faint humming of the talisman on his chest.

Hours later, he woke to the sounds of voices downstairs. Finn got up from his bed, dressed only in his underwear. His body was sore and ached everywhere and was still in a half-shifted state. That ruled out regular clothes. He grabbed the sheet from his bed and made a toga out of it before heading for the door. Walking was hard since he had grown over two feet in a night and his legs were two different sizes. He banged his head on the top of the doorjamb and made his way to the top of the stairs. They seemed very far away and tiny. His feet were about fives sizes bigger than before. There was barely enough room for him to put the heel of a foot on the step. Then it happened. He missed the next step and down he went. A rolling mass of misshapen body parts came to a crumpled heap at the bottom of the stairs.

"Oh, my!" said Hilde and rushed over to his aid.

As she helped Finn to his enormous feet, she gasped.

"I know I'm hideous," said Finn, only to notice she was looking behind him. He turned to see that apparently his pride wasn't the only damaged thing to come from falling down the stairs. Every stair from where Finn had fallen at the top all the way to the last was crushed and splintered, including the landing under his feet. He looked back at his grandfather with a look of apology. Anders looked at the boy, then started laughing, not a small chuckle but a full-on belly laugh that made his entire body shake. Tears rolled down Anders's cheeks. He was laughing so hard he had to lean on the table to steady himself. That's when Finn noticed everyone else in the room. There was Hilde, Erik, Dr. Terrance, Arna, and to Finn's surprise, Tallis and Talon were there as well. They were all laughing hysterically. Finn didn't know whether to be embarrassed or angry. His face felt hot, then he realized his toga had come loose during his travels down the stairs and he was in his underwear for all to see. Horrified at this realization, he snatched the sheet from the floor and turned to run from the room. Only he had forgotten his newly gained height and he crashed into the large oak ceiling beam separating the dining room and living room, knocking himself to the floor and out cold.

Finn Stonefist

When Finn came to, he faced yet another person. It was Mick Nightfeather, father of Tallis and Talon. Mick was average height with a broad chest and a twinkle in his eye, like he was secretly laughing at you.

He was leaning over Finn and chuckled. "Quite a mess you're in."

Finn was growing tired of being the center of comedy hour. He sat up. His head was throbbing, and he felt a large goose egg on his forehead with his hand. He looked up and saw a noticeable dent in the large wooden beam. Finn dragged his misshapen body to the couch only a few feet away. The sofa groaned under his weight, and Finn feared it would be the next victim of household damage.

"Well, Mick, is there anything to do?" asked Anders as he walked into the living room.

Mick stood in front of Finn with his hands folded. That's when Finn noticed that besides the fact that the hula shirt Mick was wearing was considerably colorful, he too glowed just like Dr. Terrance.

"Wait," said Finn, "You're an elf too?"

"Half elf and half forest troll," replied Mick.

"So that means that Tallis is a..." Finn's voice trailed off

"Is mostly elf, my wife is full elf. The bit of troll makes us more durable if you ask me."

Finn turned his gaze to Tallis. He could see her aura, too. It was a faint glow of gold that seemed to cover her entire body. It was by far the most beautiful thing he'd ever seen in his life.

"Did you know I was a giant?" Finn asked her.

"Yeah. Elves can shift and detect our kind from birth," she said.

~ 23 ~

"Why didn't you ever tell me you knew?" asked Finn. "Here, I thought I had to keep this enormous secret from you. Do you realize how hard that was?"

"Because it's against the rules," Tallis said. "To reveal ourselves to those who haven't gone through the shift yet."

"That makes no sense." Finn felt like they had excluded him from the coolest secret ever.

Hilde sat on the couch next to Finn and put a gentle hand on his knee. "Do you remember the stories we've told you over the years?"

"Some of them," Finn muttered.

"Well, those stories are more our actual history. Especially the one about when the humans rose against us. To make a long story short, the five races, Giants, Trolls, Elves, Dwarves, and the Fae were to be protectors and guides to the young human race but, there those of us who thought the humans should serve us, so they enslaved the humans and did undeniable evils towards them. Eventually, the humans revolted and overthrew their enslavers and vowed to kill any of our kind; so we had to hide our true form."

"And we wrote none of our history down so it couldn't be used against us," blurted out Erik.

I tried to make sense of everything, but it was a lot to take in. "So you're saying—"

"If it helps, this is all new to me too, cousin," butted in Arna. "I didn't know you were dating a Trelf until now."

Then Mick seized Arna by the throat and hoisted my cousin clean off his feet. To make matter worse, Mick started growing, easily getting to eye level with Arna.

"What did you call my daughter?" roared Mick, who was now nearly large enough to fill the vaulted ceiling of the living room.

Arna's eyes were bulging from terror, and his face was turning a weird shade of red and purple. He struggled to free himself from the grasp of Mick's enormous hand.

Erik shifted in size to match and bellowed, "Release him!" so loudly that the house shook.

Mick seemed to wake up from a daze, shook his head and dropped Arna. Arna collapsed to the ground, gasping for air, but otherwise unhurt.

"I apologize for my outburst, it's just that name is very offensive to us," Mick almost growled. Slowly, he shrunk until he got back to his regular size.

Erik got right in his face. "If you ever touch my boy like that again I will kill you."

That was certainly not something to say if he wanted to ease tensions.

"I do not doubt you," muttered Mick, and backed away to stand by Tallis and Talon.

The entire exchange made Finn wonder about power struggles between the various races, but he figured now wasn't the time to ask.

"Can we get back to Finn's problem?" said Anders.

Erik turned and faced Anders. "You will not like it but, Dr. Terrance is right. Take him to her. She will know what to do."

Finn had enough of the cryptic talk. "Take me to who?" he asked.

"The Norn," sighed Anders. "A creature of fate. Her and her sisters can travel between all the realms of Yggdrasil at will. They can see past, present, and future and will tell you anything you want to know for a price. Many times there are strings attached to their visions and they typically have dire consequences."

That certainly didn't make it seem very appealing.

"Well, if the Norn can help, then you should take Finn to her," urged Tallis, taking a seat next to him on the couch.

Had she not just heard the part about the dire consequences?

Hilde said, "It has to be Finn's choice. And Finn, you need to understand that you have to pay the Norn's price, or the consequences will be worse than anything she can ask for."

Finn sat quietly, all eyes on him, waiting for his response. Worry. Anticipation. Love. It all hung there in the room as the talisman gently hummed against his chest.

"Can't I just use the talisman?" Finn asked.

Dr. Terrance stepped forward. He looked gray and older suddenly. "Finn, that talisman is only a stopgap. It will fail."

"And when it does?" Finn asked.

The doctor swallowed hard and said, "Because you shifted too early and you haven't done the proper preparations and the ritual of the shift; when the talisman fails, the energy of the shift will overcome you and it will destroy you."

Hilde cried and buried her face in Erik's chest. Tallis hugged Finn's arm tightly, like she was afraid he was going to float away. But to Finn, the answer seemed clear.

"So my choices are doing nothing and die, or ask this Norn lady for help and possibly write a check my ass can't cash, or find out she can't help, and I die anyway?" He let out an enormous sigh. "Where does this Norn live?"

Chapter 2

Finn couldn't remember falling asleep, but Anders woke him by jabbing at him with his walking staff.

"Get up boy, it's time to git," Anders snapped.

Finn rolled off the couch and got to his feet. He was a little steadier standing, but his head felt like it was floating. Then that familiar warm burning in his throat happened. He was going to throw up. He desperately looked for a large enough receptacle. Suddenly Hilde appeared at Finn's side with the ash pot from the hearth. Finn snatched it from her at the last second. When he finished, he lifted his head and thanked her. She grimaced and took the nearly full pail into the bathroom. Finn scanned the room. Erik was barking at Arna, who'd been quite sheepish since his brush with death, to hurry and pack. As Mick rose and crossed the room, Arna and Erik kept a close eye on him.

"Ah man!" said Talon from in front of the fireplace, where he stood covered in soot from the neck up. In her hurry to get Finn a bucket, Hilde hadn't paid very good attention to where she tossed the ashes that were in the bucket, so subsequently Talon caught the full load in the face. Tallis hopelessly tried to dust off her brother, but Talon swatted her away and stomped off to the bathroom to clean up. Finn mouthed the words good morning to her and coyly waved hi from her sleeping bag.

Finned turned to Anders and asked, "When do we leave?"

"As soon as you put pants on," said Erik.

Finn looked down, horrified that he had forgotten he was practically naked. He tried to cover himself with his hands, which he was thankful were still huge. Just then, Anders caught his eye and signaled for him to follow to the hall closet. The hall was just big enough for Finn, but he squatted so Anders

~ 27 ~

was closer to eye level. Anders opened the closet and told Finn to hand him a large wooden box from the top shelf. As Finn handled the box, he could tell it felt empty and the light wood hummed just like his talisman. It was about the size of a shoe box and had a figure of the world tree, Yggdrasil, carved into it.

"It is made of Asgardian wood and exists in this realm and in the realm of Asgard simultaneously," said Anders.

Finn felt a sudden reverence for the little box.

"When our ancestors came to Earth, Thor gave each family one of these and blessed them that as long as they were worthy of Asgard's help, these boxes would give it to them," Anders said. "Take it in your hands and think of something you might need for this journey."

Finn took the box and felt the gentle humming. The only thing he could think of was clothes that would fit him. Suddenly a light shone from between the lid, and the box jerked like someone dropped something heavy in it. Upon opening it, Finn saw exactly what he needed: a pair of jeans and a dark blue T-shirt.

"Of all the things you could ask for and you asked for clothes?" said Anders. But then he seemed to notice Finn's enormous size again. "Oh, I see. Excellent choice, my boy."

Finn returned to the living room with the box and pulled the clothes out. The pants were a perfect fit, like they had been tailored for only him. Finn put the T-shirt on, and it too fit, like the pants, perfect. But the box wasn't empty. Inside, Finn found a pair of generic tennis shoes and a pair of socks, both of which were also made to fit his large and misshapen feet.

"That's better," said Tallis, and she wrapped her arms around Finn's chest to hug him.

Finn Stonefist

As she stepped back, the talisman that was holding itself securely to Finn's chest hummed louder and louder. It drew the attention of everyone in the room. Suddenly the humming stopped, and the talisman drop to the carpet from under Finn's shirt.

"Gramps!" called Finn, wondering if he should pick it up or leave it be.

Anders appeared and saw the talisman on the floor. "What did you do?"

"Nothing! I just hugged Tallis and it fell off!" said Finn.

Just as Anders was about to ask another question, the T-shirt Finn was wearing glowed with the same light that came from the box. When it faded away, a replica of the talisman appeared like an iron-on print. It had replaced the top rune with a symbol that looked like Thor's hammer Mjolnir. The symbol was printed in gold and was warm against Finn's skin.

"I guess the Gods are watching," Mick said. "This is a good sign."

"How do you feel, my boy?" asked Anders.

"I feel better, actually. Steadier," Finn replied. "And I don't hurt."

But Anders didn't seem convinced. He looked Finn up and down like he expected him to explode.

Erik came up and put his hand on the old man's shoulders. "Mick said this is a good sign. That the Gods are with us!"

"Humph, why the Gods are so interested in our little venture?" said Anders.

But nobody had an answer to that.

Outside, Erik and Hilde were arguing about how the vehicle should be packed, and Tallis and Talon were scuffling over who had to sit in the middle seat. In the end, age won, and

Erik conceded to his all-knowing wife. As Finn stepped out of the house, he realized he would not fit in the car.

"So, where do I sit?" he asked the group.

Erik approached him with his hands up. "Well, that is going to be a little hard to explain," he said. "You, my boy, are going to have to sit in the trunk. It's the only place with enough room to accommodate your... condition."

Finn peered over Erik's shoulder and eyed the trunk space. He could already feel the claustrophobia but, he sighed and muttered, "So be it" under his breath. Finn climbed into the trunk space and folded his enormous limbs in around himself the best he could.

Once he was settled Hilde, piled in sleeping bags and pillows in any space, she could find. When she finished, she stood back admiring her work and asked, "Comfy?"

"I feel like the family dog," grunted Finn.

She smiled and pulled the hatch down. Once latched, Finn watched everyone else climb in. Erik was driving with Mick as the navigator. Hilde and Anders were in the next row, and Tallis, Arna, and Talon shared the third row with the remaining gear that Hilde couldn't fit in with Finn.

"Now what?" asked Finn.

"First, we have to go to Homer to see a friend," said Mick. "He works for the electric company and travels the state working on remote power lines. If the Norn is in Alaska like I suspect, then he'll know where she's at."

While they waited outside the electric company, Finn took this opportunity to get some answers from his grandpa.

"Grandpa, why did I mal-shift?" Finn asked.

Anders twisted in his seat so he could face Finn a little better. "Honestly, I don't know. Mal shifts are so rare, and they typically have some kind of external cause to them, be it a congenital defect or a magical curse. I have never heard of a mal shift happening on its own. They almost always happen during the rite of the shift."

Finn mulled this over in his mind. "Well, since I was perfectly healthy, and I wasn't doing the ritual, it must be some kind of curse."

"That is very possible," said Anders.

"Who would want to curse me, though?" asked Finn.

"I can think of one person," said Erik from the front seat.

"Quiet you!" barked Anders.

But Finn would not let that go. "Who?"

Anders didn't say a word.

Finn looked at his uncle. "Who, Erik?"

Before Anders could stop him, Erik said "Rathgar."

The name seemed to ring through the car, causing silence to fall over them.

"Why does that name sound familiar to me?" Finn asked.

"He's the man who killed your parents and is currently sitting on the throne of giants," said Erik. Anger seethed under his skin.

"He is also my son and your uncle," said Anders so quietly that Finn barely heard him. "He has been power hungry his whole life and has never agreed with hiding ourselves from the humans. He thinks we should rule like in the old days."

Finn could hardly breathe. "Why would he curse me?" asked Finn, terrified of the answer.

"When Rathgar attacked, your father, Einar, was the current king of the giants," said Anders.

"So that means I'm a... I'm a prince?" stammered Finn.

"It also means you are the only living heir to the throne as King of the Giants," said Anders.

Finn's head got really light. "What happened to my parents?"

"We don't know for sure, but all accounts say your father fell while fighting Rathgar's forces, and later Rathgar sent a demon, and it took your mother," said Erik, allowing a tear to escape down his cheek.

His own uncle had done that. That meant he would stop at nothing to kill Finn.

Just then, the passenger door opened, and Mick appeared. Looking at the sullen group, he smiled and asked, "Yeesh guys, who died?"

Tallis shot him a glance, and he silently got in the car without another word.

"What did your friend have to say, Mick?" asked Erik.

"He said he wasn't sure, but most of the reports said she is near Gun Sight Mountain."

"That's at least a day's drive," Erik said. "We better gas up."

"And get snacks," chimed in Arna. "Lots of snacks."

After about a couple of hours, Finn was literally aching and needed out of his confinement to stretch his enlarged limbs. Erik found a secluded spot on the backside of a place called Summit Lake. It was high in the mountains that separated the Kenai Peninsula from the rest of the state. Those who didn't mind got out to relieve themselves and stretch out while the rest took the car to a lodge nearby and used "civilized facilities" as Tallis put it.

Finn found a log next to the lake large enough for him to sit on. As he stared out over the calm water of the lake, Arna appeared next to him, clambering on to the log and straddling it to face Finn. "Hell, of a day," he said.

"Understatement of the year," Finn said.

"What are you going to do about it?" asked Arna.

"I don't know, I really don't know," said Finn.

"I'll tell you what we will do," Arna said. "We'll get shoulder to shoulder like we do on the field and we will plow through all this, leaving our problems broken and hurting in our path."

"We, huh?" said Finn, smiling at his cousin.

"Absolutely! We are the Wall, and the Wall is undefeated!" shouted Arna, getting to his feet. He balanced on the log and raised his arms in the air yelling, "THE WALL!"

"Come on, say it with me," Arna said, kicking Finn's large arm.

Finn tried to wave him off, but Arna wouldn't have it. Finally, Finn got to his feet, lifted both misshapen arms in the air and yelled, "THE WALL!" but his cheer caused a flock of birds to take flight in terror.

"Are you idiots trying to get us noticed?" hissed Erik. "Now everyone's back. It's time to go." He motioned for them to follow.

The boys looked at each other and laughed.

After the break, the feeling in the car was a little lighter but, the closer they came to their destination, the more Finn felt the dread building inside him. When the group finally stopped for the night, they were in a small area known as Glacierview. It was in a vast valley surrounded by mountains and, yes, glaciers. Erik selected a secluded area off the road for them to camp.

The woods were sparse, but Erik found a small group of trees to camp among for a windbreak and to hide their presence. Mick walked into town to talk to the locals and find out if they knew where the Norn was. It wasn't long before Hilde had a large pot of beef stew bubbling over the fire. The smell was intoxicating, and Finn didn't realize how hungry he was. A couple of hours later, Mick reappeared with good news. The Norn was close. It was about a five-mile hike to her hovel in the forest.

"You leave at first light," Anders told Finn.

Wait what? That sounded completely wrong to Finn.

"Me? Like alone? Aren't you coming with me?" asked Finn, but he kind of already knew the answer.

"My leg can't do that kind of hike, and you will need to move quickly. You will take Erik with you."

So many thoughts went through Finn's mind. He was sure his grandfather was going to be there when he faced the Norn. Erik was okay, but his grandfather was older and had way more experience.

Anders put a hand on his shoulder. "You'll be fine, son. Just stay true to why you are there and listen carefully to every word. And make no agreements without talking to your uncle first."

Unable to speak, Finn just nodded and turned to face the fire.

***

What only felt like moments later, Erik was shaking him awake. "Finn, wake up. It's time to go."

Finn hadn't even remembered falling asleep. He stirred and groaned as he hoisted himself off of the ground and to his feet. Erik handed him a day pack with water and some simple snacks made by Hilde. The straps were too small for his left shoulder, so he would have to carry it awkwardly.

As the two made their way out of camp, Hilde and Tallis greeted them. When Tallis hugged him, worry filled her eyes. He hugged her close and tried to comfort her.

"You boys be safe and come back to us," instructed Hilde.

"No heroics," said Tallis, pointing a finger into Finn's chest.

Finn looked at her in feigned disbelief. "Me? I am the picture of humility," he said, smiling and walking past her.

She glared in return, then smiled.

He just hoped there would not be a need for heroics.

Chapter 3

As Erik and Finn exited the grove of trees, it gave way to a vast and open valley nestled between two immense mountain ranges. The highest peaks still covered in snow, and wind that came off the summits, were cold and smelled of snow. Finn pulled the hood of his jacket up and shuddered. He could see the forest's edge in the distance on the other side of the valley, dark and very uninviting. Finn couldn't imagine why anyone would want to live there.

Their pace was quick, but Finn had to watch that he didn't go too fast. With his new, longer legs, his normal step was twice as long as Erik's. Erik kept up and didn't complain, but Finn could tell he was getting tired. They stopped for breakfast at a little stream about halfway through the valley. The day was warm, and the sky was clear. Finn closed his eyes and let the bright sun warm his face. He could hear the bubbling of the stream and the wind gently brushing the low growing tundra. The cry of an eagle sounded out, and Finn opened his eyes to see a bald eagle soaring overhead. Finn had always imagined how free it must feel to soar that high above everything. He looked to his uncle to share the moment, but Erik paced anxiously. He stood and packed up his snack and shoulder his pack.

"We need to leave now," said Erik.

Finn quickly packed his things. As he shouldered his pack, Erik was already moving.

Finn caught up. "What's wrong uncle?"

"Eagles," said Erik, hurrying his pace.

They were at a trot now, and Finn was getting more worried.

"What's so bad about eagles?"

"Stop talking and run!"

Finn looked up and saw that the single eagle from before was now joined by two others. They were still in a circular holding pattern, but they were slowly spiraling down. Erik and Finn came to the remnants of an old tree, and Erik dove over it, quickly burrowing. But there was no way Finn could fit. The eagles were even lower now. All three were enormous and locked on to Erik's and Finn's position. Finn looked down at where his uncle had hidden himself; Erik was nearly completely under the tree now.

"Get down Finn!" Erik shouted.

Finn panicked. His half giant state made it impossible for him to fit. The eagles were much closer now. Finn could hear the wind ruffling their feathers. He did the only thing he could think of. He dropped to his knees next to the tree and curled into the tightest ball he could manage in his state. Then he did something he hadn't done in years. He repeated a prayer to Thor that Auntie had taught him for when he got scared. "Thor is with me; I am not afraid of thee," he repeated.

He could hear the eagles' cries. They sounded like they were just above them.

"Thor is with me; I am not afraid of thee," he repeated faster.

Just then, the symbol on his T-shirt hummed loudly, and it felt hot against his skin. Then he began sinking into the earth.

"Finn, what are you doing?" shouted Erik as the two sank deeper into the earth.

The earth filled in until it completely entombed the two. When everything had gone quiet, Finn could hear the eagles still, but they sounded muffled and distant. But despite this, he could tell they were on the ground and felt them scratching at the spot where he and Erik had disappeared. Finn looked down at his uncle and realized his uncle looked much smaller than before. He was in a half fetal position under Finn's chest.

"Uncle, you shrank," said Finn.

"Actually, you grew," said Erik.

Finn inspected what he could and realized his uncle spoke the truth. Not only had he grown again, but the parts that didn't grow the first time matched the others. He was now completely twice his normal size, based on his biceps and chest, since that was all he could see with the faint glow of the symbol on his shirt.

After what seemed like hours, the sounds of the eagles faded and so did the symbol's light. Finn took this as a sign that danger had passed.

"I am going to stand," he said.

Erik nodded in agreement and shielded his face from the buckets of dirt that rained off Finn's back. Finn stood and stretched, inspecting his new body. He was enormous, at least ten feet tall, and had a body that "The Rock" would be jealous of. It suited him. Erik pulled himself from the dirt and brushed himself off. He saw Finn admiring his new body and punched him in the thigh.

"Hey lunkhead, take a picture. We need to get going."

Finn knew he was right and grabbed his bag, which was much too small for him now. With the sky clear of eagles, their pace was quick, but not exhausting.

"Hey, do you think Tallis will like my new bod?" Finn asked, flexing his biceps.

Erik looked up at him and laughed. "In your current state, if you kissed Tallis you would break her face."

Finn's smile faded. "Oh. Really?"

"You have a lot to learn," said Erik as he came to stop at the edge of the forest.

Finn had been so interested in his new physique he hadn't noticed they'd reached the forest until he nearly stepped on Erik. Finn's heart quickened, and suddenly he didn't feel so big. The forest was dark, and he couldn't see the other side of it. But they had no choice. They had to enter it.

Finn took a deep breath. "Here we go."

He took a few steps forward and noticed Erik hadn't moved.

"Uncle, let's go." Finn waved at his uncle, who just stood there looking at him with a pained look.

"Finn, you must go alone. Whatever the Norn has to say is for you." Erik looked like he was going to cry.

"What? No. I can't do this on my own. I don't know what to ask," said Finn.

"Trust in yourself and everything we have taught you," Erik said.

"Uncle!" Finn took a step toward Erik when the trees in front of him suddenly closed ranks. Finn could no longer see his uncle. He pulled and thrashed against the wall of trees, but despite his new strength, everything he pulled off only grew back. He sank to the ground in frustration, then let out a monstrous roar while punching the ground. Around him, pine needles fell in droves.

"That is quite the temper," said a voice from just behind him.

Finn jumped to his feet. "Who's there?"

"No one dangerous to a giant," said the formless voice.

"Are you the Norn!" demanded Finn from the darkness.

A chuckle filled the air and made Finn shiver. "the Norn? Oh no, young one. Just a humble servant of she who holds all the answers."

"I demand you show yourself and take me to the Norn," said Finn. He tried to make himself appear as intimidating as possible, drawing himself up to his full height.

Just then, a figure edged into the dim light that crept through the wall of trees. A young woman not much older than Finn, with a slight build, dark hair, and bright green eyes. There was something oddly familiar about her. Finn shook himself and tried to look as stern as he could in the dark.

"Will you take me to the Norn?" he asked, a little less demanding this time.

The girl smiled and motioned for him to follow her into the woods. She seemed to glide along the forest floor, not disturbing as much as a pine needle from its place. Finn was quite the opposite. He crashed into every low hanging tree limb and kept tripping over every root. His shoes hadn't survived the growth spurt, and so he was barefoot and constantly picking stickers from his feet. The farther they went into the forest, the trees were farther apart. The air was cool, and it seemed to hum like the symbol on his shirt. They came to a clearing devoid of trees except for one large pine tree in the middle. It was so tall Finn couldn't see the top, and the lowest limbs were ten feet above his head and about three feet around. Finn was so in awe of the tree that he failed to notice that the girl had vanished.

"Anyone there?" he called, weakly praying no one would answer.

Just then, the giant tree groaned, and an opening appeared in the trunk. Golden light poured from it and filled the clearing. Another figure appeared in the light.

"Come forward and state your purpose," said the figure.

"I am Finn Stonefist, and I am here to speak with the Norn," Finn stated as officially as he could.

Finn Stonefist

"Are you now?" asked an unfamiliar voice.

Finn spun around. There behind him, where he had been a second before, was another woman who was laughing so hard she was an odd shade of purple.

"You giants are so jumpy. That is fun to do every time." She wiped the tears from her face while catching her breath.

She did not impress Finn with her sense of humor.

"Oh, come on, honey, when you have lived as long as I have, you find very few things funny, but that never gets old," she said.

"You are the Norn then?" Finn asked, keeping a careful eye on the woman.

Like the girl, she was slight but had short gray hair and wore blue jeans, a plaid shirt, and hiking boots, making her look very woodsy.

"I am." She waved her hands, and a tree stump pushed up from the ground, which she promptly sat on.

"I am told you can help me," Finn said, motioning at his body. "I have entered the shift too early and without the ritual."

The Norn folded her arms and studied Finn. "Why aren't you dead then?"

"Well, some of it was quick thinking of my grandfather and Auntie, and some is this symbol on my shirt," Finn explained.

The Norn stood and walked over to Finn. She motioned for him to get on his knees, so his shirt was level with her. Then she said, "Powerful magic here."

"Can you help just until I get the ritual done next year?" He hated to sound desperate, but this was his life on the line.

She ran her finger around the outer runes of the symbol and came to a stop on the one shaped like Thor's hammer. Her eyes suddenly darted between the rune and Finn's face.

"What did you say your name was?" she asked.

"Finn, Finn Stonefist."

She quickly lurched backward like something had tried to bite her.

"Einar or Rathgar?" she asked quickly.

"Einar is my father."

"You shall know the one when the son shall come," she muttered. "You are the son of the king."

"Yes, I guess so, but that doesn't solve my problem," said Finn.

"Convergence," the Norn muttered. Her focus snapped back to Finn. "You must leave," she said, pushing him back the way he'd come.

"What? You haven't helped with anything," cried Finn.

"You must go!" she shouted.

Suddenly, Finn felt an enormous force lift him from the ground and launch him toward the sky. The branches whipped his face and suddenly he came flying through the top of the canopy and began falling to the ground. Finn rolled end over end as he careened toward the earth. He could see the ground hurtling toward him, and he thought to himself, "This is it; this is how the not-so-great Finn Stonefist will die." He closed his eyes and waited for the end, but it never came.

Finn carefully opened one eye and then the other and found himself face down, hovering over the ground about ten feet up. Erik walked beneath him and looked up. The symbol on the T-shirt was glowing again like it had when the eagles attacked.

"By Thor's hammer, someone is looking out for you, kid," Erik said.

Just then, the symbol's light went out. Finn dropped the remaining distance and landed with a heavy thud. Finn was grateful to be alive, but had he really needed to land face first on a rather moist pile of moose scat? Someone was not looking out for him, or else they had a terrible sense of humor.

He rolled over and sat up, scraping the moose excrement from his face. Erik, who had avoided being squashed by his oversized nephew by just a nanosecond, handed Finn a rag he had soaked in some of their water.

"See what happens to young giants who try to land on their uncles," he chuckled.

Finn snatched the rag and cleaned the remains of the moose dung from his face and hands. He grumbled something, but it wasn't even words to him.

"So was the Norn helpful?" Erik asked.

"Not a damn bit." And he explained what happened.

"So she said nothing helpful?" Erik asked.

Finn thought about it. "She said one thing just before she tossed me out, but I don't know if it's helpful."

"Well, let's have it," Erik said.

"She said you will know the one when the son shall come. Then she tossed me out," Finn replied.

"The one?" Erik repeated. "Well, maybe Anders will know what it means."

The hike back was fortunately eagle-free and uneventful. It was dusk by the time they reached the grove of trees where they had camped the night before. Hilde ran and threw her arms around Erik's neck.

"We were so worried when you took so long," she told Erik.

"Things didn't go according to plan, but mission accomplished," Erik said.

Then Finn entered camp. Everyone stopped talking and stared at the teenager's new size.

"The Wall!" Arna said. "Now that's what I'm talking about!"

Finn couldn't help but grin. No football player would ever have a chance of getting past him again.

Tallis came up to him and hugged him awkwardly around the waist.

Anders looked him over with wide eyes. "Well, let's have it. Let's hear what happened to you."

The group huddled around the campfire and Finn retold the day's events without skipping a single detail. When he finished, silence filled the surrounding space.

Arna was the first to speak. "So when the Norn said she would know the one, did she mean like some kind of chosen one? Because that's the last ego boost you need," said Arna with a smirk.

But pain was moving through Finn again. "Can we just figure out some way to make it stop hurting?" he asked.

Anders seemed to consider this. "I know someone who might help us."

"Well, we can't do anything without sleep, which is what we need to do now," said Hilde.

Everyone stood and moved to their respective sleeping areas except Tallis, who seemed intent on staying next to Finn.

"Tallis, let's go," said Mick, motioning for her to follow.

She reluctantly got to her feet, kissed Finn, and followed her father and brother to their tent. Finn no longer fit in a tent, so Hilde gave him the two spare sleeping bags plus his own and he made a kind of nest next to the fire. It wasn't too uncomfortable, and the fire felt good on his back. As Finn drifted off to sleep, he felt the gentle humming of the symbol and the all too familiar knot of panic working its way to the surface.

"Thor is with me; I do not fear thee," he muttered to the darkness.

A few brief hours later, Finn awoke to something striking his forehead. He sat up and panned the camp. He could hear the distant snoring of Mick and his grandfather. Again, something struck him. He looked in the direction it came from just in time to see a figure dart behind a tree.

"Who's there?" called Finn.

The figure peered from behind the tree, then darted back again.

"I won't hurt you. Just come out into the light," Finn urged.

The figure stepped out from behind the tree and into the firelight. To Finn's surprise, it was the girl from the woods.

"You!" he said.

She quickly came forward and put her small, gentle hand over his mouth.

"Quiet!" she said. "I have come with a message from the Norn. You need to go to the place where Thor struck the mountain."

"Why?"

"It is in that place you will get many of the answers you seek." With that, the girl stepped back and disappeared into the darkness again. Finn stood to follow, but realized it was pointless. She was gone.

■■

Chapter 4

The next morning, the camp was busy. Hilde and Erik made breakfast over the fire and everyone else packed up camp. Finn sat in the place where he slept, going over his midnight encounter, trying to figure out if it was a dream or not.

"Sleep well?" Erik asked, coming over to sit next to him.

"I had a late-night visitor," said Finn, catching the attention of everyone else in camp. "That girl from the woods came last night with a message from the Norn. She said if I wanted answers, I was to go to the spot where Thor struck the mountain. Where is that?"

"Gunsight Mountain," said Erik, pointing up at a nearby peak.

"They say the mountain insulted the great god, so he struck it on the peak with his thunder hammer and now there is a perfect shape of the hammer left in it," said Mick.

"Well, that's where I need to go," Finn said, standing up.

Arna stood next to him. "That is one heck of a hike. But I'm in."

"Not me," Mick said. "And I doubt Anders will be up for it either."

Anders grumbled something in response but didn't disagree.

Erik and Hilde both had their own excuses, but Tallis and Talon were already grabbing their bags. About an hour later, the four teenagers geared up and got ready for the hike.

Finn approached Anders. "You have been very quiet, grandpa."

"I am worried. Anything that can scare a Norn is extremely worrisome."

"It will be okay, gramps, I promise," said Finn. He hoped he was telling the truth.

"May the gods be with you, my boy," said Anders.

Finn gently clasped the old man's shoulder with his enormous hand and stood to leave. Tallis and Talon hugged their father and Arna pried himself from his sobbing mother. Finn looked one last time over his shoulder at his grandfather with a feeling that he might not see him again. Then they were off.

With his new size, Finn stopped often to wait on the others to catch up. It was midday when they reached the foot of the mountain and agreed it was a good place to rest and eat some lunch before starting their climb. The group sat and ate in near silence. Finn felt more anxious than scared. He wanted answers, and he didn't know what he would do if he didn't get any; then again, he didn't know what he would do if he got the answers he was looking for. Either way, his life would never be the same. Finn looked across at his friends and didn't know where he would be without them. He couldn't let them get hurt.

He straightened himself and said, "I think I should go up alone."

Tallis, Talon and Arna looked at him like he had just said the dumbest thing ever.

"Listen, your highness, we came this far. We are not stopping now because you think it's the noble thing to do," said Arna.

"He's right, Finn, we are friends and there is no shaking that. Sorry babe," said Tallis, patting his knee.

Finn looked at Talon. Talon put up his hands. "Hey, I'm just here to make sure your cousin behaves himself and that Tallis doesn't die or something, so if she goes, I go."

Finn could see their looks of determination and knew there was no talking them out of it.

"Fine. But we should go. It's getting late," said Finn as he stood.

The group packed up their things and began their ascent up the mountain. The lower part of the mountain was mostly forest and made for easy climbing, despite the steep terrain. But as they neared the top, the terrain became very rocky, and Finn found it difficult for his enormous feet to find good footing. The last half of the hike took as long as all the travel that day. Finn was constantly causing small avalanches, sending rocks and boulders down on his friends, so he finally hung back some and let them go ahead of him. As he reached the top, he saw the other three clamber over the edge and disappear. Finn, exhausted, he heaved himself over the edge of the top. He rolled onto his back to catch his breath.

He had just about recovered when Arna called to him, "You need to come see this dude!"

Finn rolled over and came to his feet. What he saw was unbelievable. The top was flat as a board and nearly as smooth, with only a thin layer of dust and gravel covering it. To the left and right were enormous walls of stone. They were at least a hundred feet high and flat and smooth like the floor. On the other side, the top just dropped off down the back side of the mountain.

Talon peered over the edge. "Wouldn't want to fall off of that," he said and slowly backed away from the edge.

Finn turned around and faced the way they came. He could see the entire valley, and in the distance, he could just make out the grove of tree where his grandfather waited for him.

Finn walked over to his friends near the middle. "Now what?" he asked the group.

Arna shrugged. "Did your midnight visitor tell you someone would meet you here?"

"No, just that I would find answers here," said Finn.

He backed up a little and called out, "I am Finn Stonefist, and I am here for the answers promised me!" His voice was so loud it echoed off the immense walls on either side.

The group stood silently, but the mountain remained quiet except for the wind.

"Now what" asked Tallis.

Just then, the mountain shook and nearly knocked the group off their feet.

"Earthquake!" screamed Talon.

There was nowhere to take cover. Lightning struck the tops of the great stone walls, sending enormous boulders down toward them. Finn grabbed his friends and shielded them with his enormous body. Stones hit his back, but they didn't hurt. The mountain shook harder, and more lightning struck. Rocks fell all around them, and Finn was sure it would bury them alive. Then the shaking stopped, and the lightning quit. Once Finn was sure it was over, he heaved himself up, shrugging off the remaining boulders. He looked around and saw huge car size boulders littering the area.

"Is everyone okay?" he asked, helping Tallis to her feet.

"My hero," she said, brushing herself off.

He reached to help Talon, but Talon slapped Finn's hand away and stood on his own. Arna was already up and standing on a nearby boulder to survey the area.

"Some answers," grumbled Finn.

"Uh, Finn, you need to come and see this," called Arna.

Finn went over and looked in the direction Arna was pointing. At the far end of the flat top stood a figure in a dark cloak.

"Who do you think that is?" asked Arna in a whisper.

"Only one way to find out," said Finn as he climbed over the pile of boulders. As he got closer to the figure, he saw it was a tall man with long red hair, a thick red beard, and blue eyes that seemed to pierce Finn's mind. "Who are you?" Finn asked.

The man didn't answer.

"Are you the one sent to give the answers I seek?" he asked.

The man stood there silently, like he didn't hear Finn's questions.

"Listen bud, if you aren't here to help us then I am assuming you are here to hurt us, and I can't have that," said Finn.

The man didn't budge.

"Don't say I didn't warn you," said Finn.

He balled his fist and swung as hard as he could at the man's chest. Suddenly, the man flinched. He swatted Finn's fist like he was swatting a fly and struck Finn in the chest with something hard and metallic. Finn grunted and flew clear back into the pile of boulders, sending several of them skittering across the flat top. Finn's chest hurt, but he was alive and angry. He got to his unsteady feet and locked eyes with the man.

"You asked for it now, bubba," said Finn through gritted teeth.

"Finn don't," pleaded Tallis.

But Finn ignored her. There was something about this man that egged him on. It was impossible to back down. Finn let out a deafening roar and charged the man. Finn could have sworn that he saw the man smile as he produced the metallic object he had struck Finn with before. Finn rolled to avoid another blow, grabbed the man by the shoulder, and threw him as hard as he could, sending him crashing into one of the stone walls. Finn stood breathing hard, watching the pile of rubble where the man landed.

"Holy cow, cuz. I guess you showed him," said Arna.

Just then, the rubble moved, and the metallic object came flying towards Finn like a missile. It was a rectangular block of metal which veered off course, heading straight for Arna.

"Arna move!" screamed Tallis.

Everything seemed to move in slow motion. Finn shoved Arna out of the way just in time to take the full impact to the chest again. This time, it pinned him against the stone wall and held him there. Despite Finn's best efforts, he couldn't pull the thing off his chest, and he couldn't move off the wall. Arna, Talon, and Tallis ran over and tried to pull it off, but to no avail. Just then, the man emerged from the rubble. He started walking toward Finn and his friends, but he was laughing and clapping. He made his way up to them, laughing and clapping the entire time. When he reached them, he had a huge grin still on his face.

"You have great heart, young giant," said the man.

"Who are you" asked Finn, straining under the object.

"If I let you go, then we are done battling, and I will give you the answers you seek," said the man. "Agreed?"

"Fine, just let me go," said Finn. His blood was boiling, but he needed answers.

The man reached out with his hand, and the object flew backwards into the man's hand, where he took it by the wood handle Finn hadn't noticed before. Finn dropped to knees, rubbing the spot on his chest where he'd been hit. Tallis came to him and helped him up to his feet.

"Now explain yourself. Why did you attack us?" Finn pushed.

"Well, you actually attacked me," the man said.

"Finn, don't you know who this is?" stuttered Arna.

Finn let all the pieces of the puzzle come together. The lightning, super strength, the red hair, the hammer. No, that couldn't be right. It couldn't be.

"Thor?" he said.

Thor removed his cloak to reveal a plain tunic, leather pants, and an ornate belt around his waist. He wore leather boots that laced halfway up his calf with the pants tucked in them. His face was battle-hardened, but there was happiness in his electric blue eyes. His hair and beard were long, and most definitely red. He was tall and not an ounce of fat on him. He hung his hammer from his belt, which Finn assumed was Mjolnir, the hammer of legend, and directed the group to sit with him near a heap of boulders.

Once settled, Thor turned to them and asked, "First off, I thank you for the fight. I have found that you learn a person's true nature in battle, and you showed great courage and love for your fellow man. If I meant you ill, you would be dead, young giant. So, Finn Stonefist, what do you want to know?"

Finn was still in a state of shock as he realized he had battled the legendary God of Thunder and lived through it. Once he had caught his composure, he started. "Look at me. I shifted nearly a year too early. I didn't think that could happen until I was eighteen?"

"Tell me, Finn, what do you know of your ancestry?" asked Thor.

"Just what my grandfather has told me. He said that thousands of years ago our people had to flee our home world of Jotunheim because of some disaster."

"That's right." said Thor.

Finn saw the happiness in his eyes fade and the great God looked pale and sad.

"Thousands of years ago, your world was nearly destroyed because of my brother Loki. He had convinced a family of giants that they should rule Jotunheim and all of its inhabitants. He helped them construct a weapon that froze the heart of their world. It covered everything in ice and forced everyone living there to flee to Midgard, or Earth, as you call it. The thing was, the weapon had an unknown side effect; it also froze the hearts of the giant family, turning them into Frost Giants. Realizing they were betrayed, they raged against the people of Jotunheim and Loki. Not knowing Loki's treachery, my father, Odin, sent me with his army to create a portal for the people to escape and to stop the giants from getting through to this world and destroying it too. I was successful and found the weapon. It wasn't until after I had destroyed it I learned that without it the giant family would remain frost giants and I couldn't heal them or Jotunheim. I sealed the portal and Odin forbid anyone from ever going to Jotunheim again, thus trapping the Frost Giants."

"Okay, but that still doesn't explain why I am shifting early," said Finn.

"I'm getting to that," said Thor. "On Midgard, man was very young so, I charged all the races that escaped Jotunheim to be protectors and teachers of humans, and for thousands of years man and giants, elves, trolls and all the other Asgardian races lived harmoniously. The races even intermarried and had children, but there were some who thought the humans were lesser beings and should serve them and not be equals. This same group thought that marrying outside of their race was an offense against the gods.

"Earth has always had race issues," said Talon.

"Where do you think man learned it from?" asked Thor. "Now eventually the humans had had enough of their tyrannical masters and started a resistance with some other like-minded Jotuns but, the rebel Jotuns needed to hide their true selves to work more covertly. They pleaded with the gods for help and typically we try to say hands off and let things progress naturally. But since the Jotuns were on Midgard because of unnatural means, my father Odin thought it was prudent we help. He created an elixir I gave the rebels to allow them to take human form and hide their true selves and they could shift between their true form and human when they needed to. What we didn't expect was that the elixir took on a life of its own and bound itself to the life force of Midgard. The result was glorious. Then, the elixir affected a certain number of Jotuns with abilities that would only come after years of growth and training. They were faster, stronger, smarter and could access parts of their ancestry."

"What do you mean, access to part of their ancestry?" asked Finn.

"Well, Finn, they are called Sammeloper," replied Thor. "It's like if a Jotun was elf and troll, then their true form could be a troll or an elf. The confluence of two great rivers. Many times, a Sammeloper would shift sooner than others and couldn't control it at first without help. It is just too much energy for a young one to handle. There is no way to detect one before their first shift and so many don't survive." Thor turned and faced Finn. "You are obviously a Sammeloper."

Finn Stonefist

Finn looked like someone had just slapped him across the face. He sat with his mouth open, staring at the God of Thunder.

"That's impossible. Our family is pure blood giants," said Arna.

"Oh, that is not so true, young one, and there is nothing wrong with that," answered Thor. "You are descendants of one of the greatest giants houses in all of Jotunheim, but you are not pure. You have elf uncles and troll grandparents and fairy cousins going back generations. Finn, the only time a Sammeloper appears is when Midgard feels the need to restore balance to the magic that keeps all the realms alive and connected. Something must have happened, and you being the rightful king of the giants, Midgard chose you to set things right."

Finn finally finding his voice. "What happened?"

"I don't know, but my scouts say something is going on in the giant's keep under Mount Denali near to here."

"That's where my uncle lives," said Finn through gritted teeth.

"Well, whatever he is up to, it is throwing this world into chaos," said Thor.

Finn's mind spun from all this information. But it had changed nothing. Not really. "This is great and all and very informative, but you haven't told me anything about how I can fix my current situation."

"Ah yes, as you train you will learn to control the shift but, until then, so you don't explode from energy overload, because that is very messy, you will want to wear this at all times." Thor reached into a pouch on his belt and pulled out a medallion that looked just like the jade talisman his aunt put on him when this first started shifting.

Finn saw it and his heart sank. "We tried that, but the first time I had a surge, it cracked and died."

Thor grinned and flipped the medallion over in his palm, showing it off. "Yes, but that medallion was made of jade. This one is made of dwarven silver from Asgard. It can absorb untold amounts of energy and give access to it by the wearer. With this you should be able to shift safely and train as you need to so you can put the world back on track."

Finn took the pendant and put it around his neck. It hummed and felt warm to the touch like the other, and as soon as it touched his shirt, the symbol on the shirt faded away and the pendant hummed louder for just a second. Finn looked down. He was still half giant.

"It didn't work!" he said.

"Close your eyes," said Thor. "Picture what you looked like in human form and focus on it."

That was easy for Finn. It seemed like that was all he had been thinking about for days. He heard the pendant hum loudly, and he felt warmth cross his body.

"Finn, open your eyes." said Tallis.

He carefully opened one eye, then another. The first thing he saw was Tallis's face beaming with excitement. Then he looked down.

"It worked!" Finn was almost in tears.

"Now a few instructions," Thor said. "Until you gain control of the Sammeloper energy, you must wear this at all times or the troubles you had before will come again, and this time you won't survive." Thor tapped the pendant. "Also, the pendant will change as you master an additional part of yourself and eventually it will fall off when you have mastered everything that you need to. Oh, and one more thing. I have gifts for all of you from the All Father."

Finn Stonefist

    Thor then handed each one a wooden box similar in design to the one in Anders's closet.

    "Now these Asgardian wood boxes will help you on your travels, but don't open them until you have reached your family at the grove of trees," said Thor.

    Finn almost asked Thor how he knew where everyone else was, but then he remembers, this was a god.

    Thor stepped away from the group. "It is time for me to return to my father, but I will be watching Finn Stonefist. Oh, and tell Anders that I'm still looking." With that there was a tremendous flash of lightning, and the Great God was gone as fast as he had showed up.

    "Well, that was interesting," Arna said, which summed up the whole encounter pretty well.

    After that, the hike down the mountain was quiet. Finn felt like his head was going to explode. For every answer he'd received, he had a dozen more questions. And what did Thor mean by still looking? Looking for what? Or who? Finn could only hope that his grandfather could shed light on all of this. Before Finn knew it, he could smell the campfire in the grove of trees. He looked up and could see his aunt, uncle, and grandfather sitting silently around the fire. Hilde looked up, and the fire glinted in her eyes as she caught Finn's gaze. She jumped to her feet and practically hurtled the fire. Finn smiled to see her, but she blew straight past him and threw her arm around Arna.

    While the others reunited with their parents, Finn took their momentary distraction to recount the day's events to his grandfather. By the time Finn had finished everyone, had rejoined them at the fireside and Anders was sitting silently gazing into the fire. After a minute or two, Finn couldn't take the silence anymore.

"Grandfather, what does it mean?" he asked. "What is Thor looking for?"

"Your uncle has always been jealous of your father," said Anders. "I always tried to love both of my sons equally, but I failed. When Rathgar was young, he fell in with dark elves and started practicing dark magic. He believes humans should serve us and that we shouldn't have to hide our true selves from them. He didn't understand that humans had lost their connection to the magic of Midgard, and as a result have become violent and skeptical towards anything different from them. His ideology became actions, and he spent all of his time seeking weapons of significant power to subjugate the humans with. I, as king, did what I could to thwart him. I would find the items first and destroy them if I could or dismantle them and hide them if they couldn't be destroyed." Anders stopped. His voice was weak. Even in fire light Finn could see he looked pale.

"What is it grandpa?" Finn asked softly.

Anders sighed. "On the night of the summer solstice many years ago, we were having a glorious celebration in the great hall of the Keep. Everyone was there, your parents, uncles, aunts, cousins, and your grandmother." Anders paused.

Finn had never heard him talk about her before. He never knew what happened to her, just that she wasn't around.

Anders continued, "As was customary, the five great families would present gifts to your grandmother and I as a tribute for a prosperous year. The night had been full of a procession of well-wishers and gift-givers, and then someone showed up I will never forget. The Norn entered the hall. I remember the entire hall fell silent in her presence. She approached the throne and kneeled before us. I begged her not to kneel and bade our family kneel before her. As we kneeled, she spoke. She said she had a gift for the solstice. She produced from her robes a great silver staff with a large blue stone on the top of it. I recognized it at once. It was just like the paintings I had seen of it as a child. It was the very weapon used by Loki to freeze Jotunheim. I knew she meant us harm, and I jumped at her, but she knocked me back without so much as touching me. She cackled and walked towards my family. She grabbed Anna, your grandmother, by the wrist and vanished in a flash, leaving the staff on the floor. I tried to stand, but my leg was broken. Then I saw the true plot. Rathgar stood and in his hand was the staff. I begged him not to use it. He told me it was the only way to make the humans fear us. Einar, your father, attacked him, and the battle ensued. Rathgar had many more supporters than I had thought, but in the end, your father won. Rathgar was imprisoned, and I made your father king since I could no longer lead." Anders sighed and slumped against a log like a tremendous weight had lifted.

"So I'm guessing Uncle Rathgar didn't stay in prison and now he wants revenge," asked Arna.

Erik stepped forward. "True, Rathgar is in power, but he doesn't have the love of the people, and he does not have the staff. Einar dismantled and hid it. Rathgar will want that before he makes a move on the human world and he will want to get rid of you, Finn. You are possibly his only threat."

That wasn't an honor Finn was excited about, but there wasn't much he could do to change the facts. "So, the thing Thor is looking for is Grandma, isn't it?" asked Finn.

"It is. She was payment for her part in your uncle's betrayal. The Norn in known for taking slaves as payment, and she knows if I get a hold of her, I will serve her up to Thor on a silver spike," said Anders.

"So, what's our next step?" asked Finn.

"I don't know about you guys, but I say we pop the tops and play with our new Asgardian weapons," said Arna as he jumped off a log and removed his box from his backpack.

With everything Anders had said, Finn had nearly forgotten about the box the God had given each of them. Finn's box had his family crest on the top: a clenched fisted under the Nordic rune for strength. Tallis plopped down on the log next to Finn with her box in her hands. The top of hers had the Nordic symbol of healing, which looked like a very pointy capital "B." As she ran her fingers over the symbol, it glowed gold and the little box hummed. The top popped open like it was spring loaded, and Tallis removed a small round jar that looked like it was made from the greenest jade anyone had ever seen. The lid to the little jar had the same healing symbol on it, and when Tallis opened the jar, a foul odor emanated from it.

"Smells like the gods gave you a jar of Arna's toe jam," choked Talon.

Tallis next pulled a small book out of the bottom of the box. With a leather cover and bound with what looked like the sinew of an animal. The healing symbol was repeated on the book's cover with the words *The Salve of the Eternals*. She opened the cover and read aloud the first page:

"To the bearer of this salve, know that the gods have truly smiled upon you. With this salve, you can heal most any wound inflicted in battle on man or beast. It can neutralize any poison, break any fever, and mend any broken bone. What it cannot do is bring back those that have already entered the great hall of Valhalla, and it cannot mend wounds of the mind. Take heed to this warning that should you try to use it for these purposes, then you shall bring the wrath of the gods down upon you and your victim."

"No pressure," said Talon.

Tallis glared at him and turned to the next page, which was the table of contents:

Table of Contents
1. Wounds
2. Poisons
3. Bones
4. Fevers
5. Miscellaneous ailments

As she thumbed through, it amazed her to see the unbelievable amounts of things that could happen to the human body. It also broke each chapter down into human, beast, or other various Asgardian races.

"The book doesn't seem big enough to hold this much information," she said. And yet it was all there at her fingertips.

"Alright your turn Talon," said Mick.

Talon pulled his box to his lap. It was as long as his thigh, but only about four inches wide. In the center was a runic wheel that resembled a wheel of pitch forks. It too glowed gold and hummed when Talon touched it. When the humming ceased, Talon could slide the top of the box off with ease. When he looked inside, his eyes narrowed.

"What is it, boy?" asked his father.

"A stick, the gods gave me a stick." Talon lifted a dowel of wood the same color as the box. It was about a half inch around and had the same wheel rune on it. "What the heck do you think it does?"

Just then, his thumb grazed the little rune on the stick, causing it to hum loudly.

"Talon, drop it!" shouted Mick.

"I can't!" Talon jumped up from the log and desperately tried to shake the stick from his hand, but to no avail. Suddenly Talon's arm holding the stick shot straight out in front of him and the little stick grew straight down until it touched the ground. On the top it sprouted an orb of a blue crystal with the wheel rune etched on it. When it was all over, Talon stood holding a staff that came level with his eyes. Talon looked afraid to move.

Suddenly, Mick laughed. Everyone looked at him like he had lost his mind, including Talon.

"Do you know what this is, my boy?" Mick asked, nearly giddy.

Taking everyone's blank stare as a "no," he continued. "It's a Vegvisner or way finder. With this you can find your way to anywhere and I mean anywhere."

"So, the gods sent me GPS?" Talon looked at the staff suspiciously. "I already have a phone."

"You don't get it. This can literally show you the way to anywhere the gods have been," said Mick.

"Even (some place)?" Talon asked.

"Even (that place)," Mick said.

Talon shrugged, then sat down.

"Alright, Arna, open yours," said Hilde.

Arna's box was by far the smallest. It was not bigger than a jeweler's box for a watch, but that didn't seem to discourage him. He gently touched the horse and wolf emblems on the top. The top slid off, and inside he found two items. The first was a small jade figurine of a horse with eight legs and next to it in the box was a length of chain that seemed too small to do any good. Arna looked down at his gifts and then up at his parents. "Any ideas?"

Hilde took the little horse in her hands and studied it.

"May I see the chain?" asked Anders.

Arna handed it to him. Anders stretched it out to its full length of about two feet, studying every link.

"It can't be," he muttered.

"What?" asked Arna.

"This is a length of Gleipnir, the chain made of seven impossible things to bind Fenrir the wolf. The dwarves of Asgard made it. The poets say it is as thin as a ribbon but stronger than anything ever known. More than likely it will grow to any required length needed."

"I've got it!" said Hilde.

They turned to Hilde, who was still handling the little jade horse. "Arna, this is Asgardian Jade carved into the shape of Sjleipnir, a steed of the gods. See, that's his name on the saddle spelled in runes." She pointed to nearly microscopic runes.

"So, it's a jade toy?" asked Arna.

"It's not a toy, it's a totem. With this you can summon Sjleipnir himself, and as a steed of the gods, he can cross into any realm, ride on water or air just as easy as he can on the ground, All you need do is call his name while you hold the totem and he should heed your call."

"Wow, that's a nice toy," Arna said, taking back the gifts.

"You going to try it?" Finn asked.

Arna didn't answer. He sat with his mouth open.

"Well, there is a sight I never I thought I would see: Arna Fjellson speechless," said Talon.

"That leaves just you Finn." said Anders. "What did the gods give you, my boy?"

Finn looked down at the box on his lap and gently touched his family crest that was etched on the front. The crest glowed, and the top slid off just like the others. Inside, Finn found a large gray stone that took up nearly the entire interior of the box. Finn had to tip the box to get the stone out. It was heavy and cold to the touch. Setting the box down, Finn took the stone in both hands and turned it over, studying all sides of it.

It was smooth except for his family crest etched on one side. He looked at his grandfather for answers.

Anders looked like he had seen a ghost.

"Grandpa?" Finn asked.

Anders just stood there, staring at the stone.

"Grandpa!" Finn said louder this time.

Anders seemed to snap out of his trance. "Sorry my boy, I just never thought I would see it again."

"What is it?" said Finn.

"It's the King's Stone," Erik said. "Only the true king of the giants could possess it and control it. It used to sit above your grandfather's and father's thrones, but when Rathgar took control, it vanished. I assumed it was stolen. They carved it from the very mountains of Asgard by Odin himself and given to the first King in Midgard."

"And this being given to you, Finn, means the All father wants you to restore the balance of Midgard and that you have his confidence," said Anders.

"That also means that Rathgar has fallen out of favor with the gods, which means he's bound to be furious," said Mick. "Rathgar is going to be looking for you."

Talk about good news and bad news. But with everything else that had already happened, it seemed like just one more thing. "So what are we supposed to do now?" asked Finn.

Mick smiled like he'd just solved a puzzle. "Well, you have a Way Finder, so you're supposed to go somewhere, and you have an Asgardian steed, so wherever it is, it is far, and you need to get there fast. You have a healing salve, so it will be dangerous, and you will probably get hurt or worse. And you have the Kings Stone. The one thing that can unify and protect the people." Mick was practically giddy. "Touch the symbol on it."

Finn Stonefist

    Finn looked down at the symbol as he gently touched it. Almost at once, the stone seemed to dissolve into granules of silver sand and swirled and climb up his arm. Finn jumped to his feet. The silvery mini sandstorm continued to climb his arm up to his shoulder and stop.

    "My arm is stone!" Finn shouted.

    He looked back to Mick, who looked ecstatic. "Not solid stone, just covered in stone. The King's Stone is also the King's Armor. It is alive with Asgardian magic and can sense your needs. Try punching something."

    Finn looked around and saw a large tree that had fallen long ago. He walked over and punched it with his new stone covered hand. His arm went straight through it, shattering the log and sending splinters of wood all over the camp and its occupants.

    He turned and face the group, who were busy pulling wood splinters from their hair and clothes. "Did you guys see that? I have superpowers!"

    Anders looked both proud and sad at the same time. "As long as you are worthy. If you do anything to offend the Gods, the stone will leave you and find the next worthy heir," he said.

    It was good advice to keep in mind.

    "Okay, so we have to go somewhere dangerous and unite the people, and I might need to smash some stuff. But how do I get it off?" asked Finn.

    "That's easy. Just hold out your hands and say 'Return!'" said Mick.

    Finn held out both hands and in the most commanding voice he could muster he said, "Return!" The stone dissolved and swirled down his arm, reforming the large brick once again. He returned the stone to its box.

Anders made his way around the fire until he was in front of everyone. Then he cleared his throat. "For many years now, we have hidden in fear, not from man, but from our own kind. What Rathgar did, what my son did, is unforgivable, and I thought I would never live long enough to get the chance to fix all the damage he has caused. Then I met Finn, the boy who escaped Rathgar's terrible wrath. The boy that lived through that horrible day. I know it is no small part to those of you around this fire tonight but, tonight, hope surrounds this fire. A hope I haven't felt in a long time. I know we have a long road ahead of us and you children will have to learn and train in things this summer that most of us would take lifetimes to learn but, but I know the gods are watching and they have chosen to help, for that we are fortunate. In the morning, we will return home and each of you will train and learn how to use your gifts. We will restore the balance. We must." With that, Anders wandered into the dark.

Finn started after him, but Hilde put a hand on his arm, and he stopped, knowing he shouldn't follow.

***

The next morning, everyone was quiet as they broke camp. During the long drive home, while physically more comfortable for Finn, he was in knots on the inside. He left the mountain with so many questions. His entire future had changed.

Despite the amount of daylight, it was late when the vehicle bearing the weary party came to a stop outside of Ander's homestead. The front door was a jar.

"We did not forget to lock up," Erik said. He drew his service pistol and motioned everyone to stay at the car. Mick took a fighting stance in front of the car and shifted his arms into his troll form, making them about three times larger than normal. Erik disappeared into the house. It felt like an eternity before he reappeared, holstering his weapon.

"It's all clear, but you had better see this, Anders," he said.

Inside the house, it looked like someone had sprouted the most perfect forest garden. Ivy covered the walls, that shimmered silver and green, and the floor had been replaced by moss so soft it felt like a cushion. The air was heavy with moisture but cool to the skin and sweet to the smell. Small trees and bushes with fruits and berries blanketed the downstairs, and the staircase that Finn and shattered before the trip had been replaced by a gentle waterfall ending in the middle of the room where a blue, crystal-clear pond settled surrounded by large quartz stones that hummed and glowed a faint light. Finn turned a looked at his grandfather. Anders looked nearly purple with rage.

"You!" he shouted as he shoved his way past everyone, making his way towards the pool. He reached the edge of the pool, dropped his staff, and awkwardly kneeled beside it. Anders thrust his arm into the pool like he was trying to catch a fish by the tail. He pulled back with everything he had and yanked a girl by the top of her head clean out of the water and tossed her onto the soft moss floor. The girl had dark long hair and a dress the same color as the water. She screamed and sputtered. As soon as Anders let go, she clambered for the water, but Anders had hold of his staff again and was upright. He pinned her dress to the floor with it, making it impossible for her to return to the water. She ceased her struggle and turned to face Anders and the group.

...

Chapter 5

Finn made his way to his grandfather, who was standing like a mountain with the girl pinned under his staff.

"Grandpa, you want to fill us in on who this is and why you have her pinned to the floor?" he asked.

Anders just stood there in silence, staring at the wriggling teenager at his feet. There was an anger in his eyes Finn had never seen before.

"I know who you are," said Erik, stepping towards them. "She's Heidi, a Huldre. A kind of wood nymph known for their seductive powers, especially over humans. They thrive in nature, whether it's woods, water, or mountain. Heidi prefers clear ponds in the forest."

"So, why is she here? Why did she transform our house into a garden, and why does Anders look like he wants to split her in half?" asked Arna.

"Why she transformed the house is simple. She's hiding. Huldres will create sanctuaries when they need to hide from danger. This property is already warded against evil, but why she is hiding is a very interesting question," said Erik.

"And what's the answer?" asked Finn.

"Because Heidi is one of Rathgar's most trusted spies and helped in the coup that killed your parents," said Erik.

Finn felt heat rush to his face. His muscles throbbed, like they wanted to change into giant form right there and now and crush this creature. She'd helped kill his parents. He took a step forward.

"Why are you here, traitor!" shouted Anders, stopping Finn in his tracks.

The house shook, and dew fell from the moss-covered walls. Heidi coward into the smallest ball she could manage, and a small whimper came from her.

Mick jumped forward. "Anders, old friend, maybe a little more diplomacy here."

Anders looked at him like he was mad. "You can't trust anything she says. She is here to destroy us."

His grandfather was right. They couldn't trust this girl.

But Mick continued. "Trust is not the goal here, old friend, just information and you know that as part elf, I am more resistant to her charms. Let me talk to her. She won't scurry into the water again, will she, because then Hilde there might have to make the water boil with her in it." Mick motioned at Hilde, who glared at the water like it could happen at that very moment, then back at Heidi.

The nymph gave a small nod of her head.

Satisfied with this arrangement, Anders lifted his staff. Heidi gathered her dress close up against herself.

Mick kneeled down beside Heidi. "Now tell us why you are here and what you are hiding from."

The nymph sniffed. "I have left his service. He has gone so much farther than the old days of wanting pure families and domination over humans. He isn't just wanting to rule Midgard anymore. He wants all the races and the realms to bow to him, and he is killing anyone who opposes him. My father stood up to his madness, and Rathgar destroyed my village and killed my family. He seeks the staff Jotunheim." She nearly whispered the last sentence like someone might be listening.

Finn wanted to stay angry with her, but she painted such a sympathetic picture.

Anders scowled. "Finding the staff is impossible. No one knows where the pieces are. Not even me."

"He knows that," said Heidi. "That's why he did something so terrible I can't hardly speak of it."

"Well, come now, what is it?" asked Mick.

Heidi looked around the group and locked eyes with Finn. "You are Finn Stonefist, the one true king of the giants?" she asked.

With her enormous emerald green eyes locked on him, Finn stammered and stuttered.

Tallis jumped in. "What if he is? He is also unavailable."

Heidi smiled. "Don't worry. I didn't come here to steal your boyfriend. Finn, what if I told you that your parents are alive?"

"Alive?" Finn asked. That wasn't possible.

"Now wait just a minute. I watched Tove die," said Erik.

"Ah. You watched her get taken, but you never saw her die. And you never saw Einar die, either. Rathgar didn't kill Einar, but he captured him with dark magic. You know that all of us have a dark version of our true selves. For giants, if you take the life of an innocent, you become an ogre."

Anders burst forward. "What did he do? What did Rathgar make him do?"

Heidi squirmed under his gaze but held her position out of the water. "He didn't make them do anything. It's more what he made them believe they had done. He made your father believe he had killed you and your mother. The grief and belief were so strong that it invoked the Svartsjift in him, the dark shift. He turned into a terribly immense fire ogre completely under Rathgar's control. Rathgar then sent your father after your mother. When he captured your mother, he used the same magic on her, making her think she had done the same thing, but her change was so much worse." Heidi trailed off and closed her eyes.

Finn kneeled next to her and placed a hand on her shoulder. "Please tell me what happened to her," he whispered.

Heidi took a ragged breath. "Because of your mother's mixed genealogy, your uncle couldn't predict what would happen. She became what we call a Svart Sammeloper, a dark confluence. She can shift like you only into all the dark forms. She is incredibly powerful and even more dangerous."

Finn looked at Erik and Anders. Both men looked like they might get sick.

But Finn had to know if there was hope. "Grandpa, you told me there is no way to come back from the dark side. Is that really true?"

"Not exactly," Heidi said, answering instead. "Now we get to the reason you're still alive. There is a way to bring your parents back all around you."

"Not another word. I forbid it!" shouted Anders.

The last thing Finn wanted was more secrets being kept from him. "I deserve to know if there is a way to bring my parents back. I have a right to know. Now tell me." He held his grandfather's gaze, not backing down.

Anders finally sighed. "Very well."

"You can bring them back, Finn," Heidi said, excitement building in her big green eyes. "All you have to do is reassemble the three pieces of the staff of Jotunheim: the staff, the setting, and the stone."

That didn't sound like the most impossible task in the world.

"Where are the pieces?" Finn asked his grandfather.

Anders shook his head, but didn't seem like he really cared. "I don't know. I hid the pieces and then had the memories of everyone involved wiped of any knowledge of where the pieces are."

"Wait, what? Are you kidding?" Finn said.

"I'm not kidding," Anders said. "No one knows where they are."

"But you have to find the staff before Rathgar," said Heidi. "If he gets it before you, he can do the same thing he did to your parents, to the world in one fell swoop. That would throw all nine realms into chaos, killing the tree of life. Thus effectively killing all nine realms. You can't let that happen."

"I don't want to let that happen," Finn said. "But I don't know where to start."

"I think I know a way we can find out though," said Talon, holding out the box he had received from Thor. "My way finder can find anything anywhere the gods have been. I'm sure the Gods were paying attention when Anders hid the pieces." With that, Talon withdrew his staff and held it out in front of him. He cleared his throat and said, "Show me a piece of the Staff of Jotunheim!"

No one in the room so much as blinked. Even Heidi had stopped shaking enough to focus on the moment. Nothing happened. Talon felt silly standing there holding a stick like some Harry Potter wannabe.

"I don't get it!" he said. "Shouldn't it work for me?"

"It just may take some practice," said Mick, grasping his son by the shoulders.

Talon wriggled from his dad's embrace and sank onto a grassy knoll that used to be the sofa.

"Well, until we figure it out, we need to decide what to do with Heidi," said Erik.

"And how do I get my house back to normal? It's a damn forest!" shouted Anders.

Mick put both hands up. "If Heidi will undo what she has done to your house—because we know she can—we can give her a spot out by the barn where we can keep a close eye on her. She can enjoy the sanctuary that Troll's Rest affords all within its borders." Mick looked at Heidi, who was already nodding vigorously in agreement. "See Anders, she agrees. Now what do you say?"

Anders glared at her. "One misstep and I will crush her if it's the last thing I ever do. Thor, help me!"

Mick looked very pleased with his diplomatic solution. "Now, Anders, do you have any Asgardian wire?"

"A spool or two. But that only keeps things out," Anders replied.

"Yes, but I think with that and a little ingenuity, we can make a pen for our little guest. If she tries to leave, it will give her a shocking revelation," said Mick, with a wry little grin on his face.

They spent the rest of the day with Heidi undoing her handiwork under the very watchful gaze of Anders. Talon and Mick were in the backyard trying to figure out how to work the way finder. Everyone else spent their time stringing the Asgardian wire around a large square of the barnyard for Heidi's new accommodations. When all was done, Troll's Rest looked like its old self plus a new resident, and the old residents fell asleep where they sat.

...

Chapter 6

Anyone who's ever been to Alaska has heard of Mount Denali. It's a solitary peak in the middle of the great state that, though extraordinary, still resembles a normal mountain from the outside. But deep inside, the largest mountain in North America is the largest underground palace ever created. The Hall of the Mountain King has been home to the royal families of the five noble races: trolls, dwarves, elves, the Fae, and, of course, the royal family of the giants who also rule as king of all the Asgardian races. Normally, the hall is full of light and merriment, but tonight a figure moves with great haste to the throne room. The figure was Mir, a dark elf and high sorcerer to Rathgar, the self-appointed king. Mir reached the heavy doors to the throne room, which was being guarded by two orc sentries. At first they barred his entry because the king wasn't in there; it was the middle of the night.

"You must let me in!" he said, but the guards held their ground. "It concerns the fate of the king!" he shouted.

This gave the guards a reason to pause, and with a silent glance, they hefted the great wooden doors open just enough for Mir to slip through. Mir ran straight to the immense throne room where his fears were confirmed. The King's Stone was missing. Mir felt cold all over and sick to his stomach. Now he was going to have to tell the king that the gods no longer favored him.

Mir turned to the guards. "Get the king. It's a matter of life and death!"

Without hesitation, the guards ran to fetch the king. Moments later, the thunderous footsteps of the king could be heard and felt as the giant made his way to the throne room.

"You had better have a spectacular reason for summoning me in the middle of the night," Rathgar bellowed as he entered the room.

Mir shakily approached. Rathgar stood twenty feet tall. He was almost always in giant form, so Mir looked especially insignificant, which was the way Rathgar liked to view just about everyone.

"My Lord, something has happened. I can't explain it," Mir stammered.

"Well, spit it out" roared Rathgar.

"Your highness, dark elves everywhere are losing their magic, and if that isn't bad enough, it appears the gods have taken the King's Stone."

Rathgar cocked his head at the tiny dark elf as he tried to process the words.

"Look, my king, it is not on the throne." Mir pointed at a brick-shaped cavity in the headrest of the gigantic stone throne.

Rathgar stepped forward and rubbed a massive thumb over the now vacant spot. He turned his head upward and roared so loudly it shook the room.

Mir chanced stepping forward toward the furious giant. "Do you know what this means? It means the rumors are true. The child survived, and the gods have chosen him as king. They have given him the King's Stone."

"You don't think I know all that?!" bellowed Rathgar. Then Rathgar seemed to catch himself. He slumped onto the throne. His eyes darted back and forth like he was reading a plan being written in front of him. "He will still be a boy, maybe not even gone through the shift yet. He can't come for me until he can control the shift, let alone the stone."

"So we just wait him out, my Lord?" asked Mir.

"Oh no. We go to him now while we have the advantage," said Rathgar.

"But my Lord, we don't even know where he is; he could literally be anywhere."

"I know exactly where he is: Troll's Rest." Rathgar allowed a grin to tease his lips, but he cut it short and turned to Mir. "Bring me Einar!"

"Yes, my King," and with that Mir scurried out of the throne room.

A few minutes passed, and a rumble shook the throne room. It got closer until the doors burst open and a great ogre stooped low to pass through the doorway. Einar was in full form, standing nearly thirty feet tall with charred skin and red veins that ran the full length of his body, pulsing heat. The amount of heat put off by the giant fire ogre made everyone sweat, even Rathgar. Einar's hands and ankles were in manacles with glowing red runes carved into them. Without them, Einar would become a raging force of destruction that was nearly unstoppable.

"Big brother!" said Rathgar, standing from his seat.

Einar's face didn't flinch from the dead pan stare it always had.

"As always, brother, you are looking hot," chuckled Rathgar.

"I hear the gods have taken their stone back," said Einar smartly.

Rathgar looked back at the gap in the throne and let out a small growl. He turned back to Einar. "A small set back that will be rectified once you do a teeny tiny job for me."

"What is that?" asked Einar.

Rathgar sat back on the throne and folded his hands in his lap. "Well, it seems our father has found a young man that he is telling everyone is your son, Finn.. ."

Einar's chains rattled slightly at the news.

"It seems father wants to overthrow me, but you know as well as I do what really happened to Tove and Finn, don't you?"

Einar's eyes glowed brightly with fire.

"And what happened to them, brother? Tell me again?" asked Rathgar, with a wry smile on his face.

"I killed them in a fit of rage, but it was an accident," growled Einar.

"Accident or not brother, you ended not one but two innocent lives and thus triggering the dark shift, and you became the most magnificent and terrifying fire ogre ever to live!"

Einar's shoulders sagged and with a sigh he asked, "What will you have of me?"

With a voice that gave even the great fire ogre Einar a shiver, Rathgar said, "I want you to go to Troll's Rest and kill father and everyone else there. Take no prisoners."

With that, Rathgar touched a rune on Einar's neck manacle, causing the great ogre to roar and sending his eyes fiery red. The sweat steamed from his skin, and he breathed heavily. The manacles around Einar's ankles and wrists fell to the ground, leaving only the neck manacle. Rathgar smiled and stepped back to view his monstrous creation.

"Now go, brother, and do as I have asked. Rain fire on my enemies!"

Einar turned and made his way from the throne room down the main hallway. As he approached the main entrance to

Quin Folkestad

the mountain, he let out a roar and burst forth from the mount, gaining speed as he ran towards his quarry.

...

Chapter 7

Even though Einar's roar echoed for miles, Heidi heard it, as if he was standing right next to her. She woke with a shriek, covered in sweat. She needed to get the attention of the people in the house, but how could she do that from her barnyard pen? Although the sun was getting high in the Alaskan sky, it was still only about eight or nine in the morning. Everyone would sleep late after their journey, so the chances of someone seeing her were slim. Then it came to her. She planted her feet and let out a scream with everything she had. It was so loud it scattered the resting birds and her neighbors, the pigs, scrambled in confusion. She eyed the house just in time to see lights coming on and half-dressed, barely awake people stumble over each other to get to her.

Erik was the first to reach her. He had shifted his arms to about twice their normal size, thus making his service weapon look almost like a toy in his hands.

"What's the matter? Are you hurt?" he asked breathlessly.

The others gathered behind him in different stages of shifting. Even Finn had enlarged one forearm. Anders used his staff to shove through the crowd and approach Heidi. "What is the meaning of this girl?" he said, out of breath and leaning heavily on his staff.

Heidi's eyes looked wild and darted everywhere. Sweat matted her black hair to her head. Finn approached the fence and disconnected it. The humming stopped. He made a move to step into the pen when Anders grabbed his arm. "What are you doing? She is dangerous. This could all be a trick."

"She's terrified," said Finn, pulling his arm free of his grandfather's grip. He stepped toward her, and Heidi ran forward, grabbing his arms by the biceps.

"He's coming, he is coming," she cried.

"Who is?" Finn asked. He gripped Heidi by the shoulders and stared her straight into her wild green eyes. "Is it Rathgar?"

Suddenly the trembling girl became still and her eyes glowed bright green, like sunlight blazing through emerald pendants. She grabbed Finn by the head and kissed him. Tallis screamed his named and forced her way towards the two lip locked teenagers. Just as she reached them, Heidi released him, and Finn fell to the ground unconscious.

Tallis kneeled next to Finn. Hefting his head into her lap, she turned and shouted at Heidi, "What did you do?"

"I gave him what he needed," replied Heidi weakly. She was white as a sheet and looked like she might vomit. Whatever she had done had totally drained her. A lock of her hair had turned white. Erik and Arna hefted Finn up into their arms and hauled his limp body up to the house.

Anders turned towards Heidi and gestured with his large staff. "You did this and you will undo it."

"There is nothing to undo. He will wake on his own, in time."

But Anders was having none of that. "Hilde, take her up to the house, please."

At the house, Finn was laid on the couch. Hilde got to his side and looked him over. "He seems to be fine, just asleep. All we can do is watch and wait."

"Not acceptable!" Tallis grabbed a fistful of Heidi's hair and wrenched her head backwards. "He had better wake up soon, you harpy, or so help me..."

Mick jumped forward and wrapped his arms around his hysterical daughter. "Tallis! Calm yourself! He will wake, I promise."

Tallis released her grip on the girl and Heidi hid behind the nearest person which happen to be Arna.

Tallis composed herself and asked her father, "Do you know what has happened?"

"I think so. I believe she has given Finn a portion of her essence or life force. In the old days, Huldre would seduce human men as mates. If the men stayed with them, they would give a portion of their essence or soul to connect them to each other." He turned to Heidi. "is that what you did? Did you perform a sjeldele or soul sharing?"

At first Heidi said nothing but finally sighed and said, "I did." Tallis growled, so Heidi quickly added, "But not for the reason you think. The kiss is the only way to transfer my essence, but it isn't sexual. I had a vision last night and Finn is running out of time. Rathgar has sent Einar. He is nearly unstoppable and full of self-hatred from the lies Rathgar has fed him."

"That still doesn't explain why you gave Finn the Sjeldele," said Mick.

"I did it because, with my essence, he has more power to draw on. He will master his ability to giant shift almost immediately. He will, like me, be able to draw on nature to help him. He can control the elements and he might stand a chance against Einar," said Heidi. "It was a ton of power I transferred. His body will need time to recover, but when he does, he'll be stronger for it."

"Well, if Einar's really coming, we need to reinforce the wards around Troll's Rest and come up with something to give us every chance of surviving this encounter," said Mick.

With that, they dispersed to get dressed and start researching how to stop a dark fire ogre. Tallis kneeled beside Finn and held his hand. She gently kissed his lips as a tear escaped down her cheek.

***

The last thing Finn remembered was a blinding green light that seemed to come from Heidi and her lips, which were on his, soft and wet. The next thing he knew, the world was black, and he was filled with the sensation of falling. But from the darkness came a familiar voice. It was Tallis calling his name.

He reached into the darkness, calling her name in return. Suddenly, he felt as though he was rising far above the ground faster and faster. After what seemed like forever, he came to a dead stop, and when he looked down, he saw something that almost broke his brain. It was his body on the couch in the house and Tallis was holding his hand as she rested her head on his chest. He called her named, but she couldn't seem to hear him. Suddenly, he fell straight towards himself.

Finn's body jerked suddenly, and Tallis jumped up.

"Finn!" she cried.

Her shout was enough to draw the attention of Hilde, who rushed over. Finn opened his eyes. At first, all he could see was green, then it faded to real world colors. He looked over and saw Tallis and Hilde smiling at him.

"Am I dead?" Finn asked as their faces came into view.

"Oh, no, you are very much alive," said Hilde.

Finn sat up on the couch. As Tallis sat next to him, she asked how he felt.

"I feel fine except for that buzzing sound. Do you hear it?" asked Finn.

They shook their heads, but for Finn, the buzzing got louder. Finn stood and made his way to the back patio, where he nearly ran into Heidi.

"Oh good, you're awake. That took longer than I thought. You were asleep for hours," she said.

But Finn couldn't hardly hear her since the buzzing was almost deafening.

"Do you hear that!" he asked her.

"If you mean the buzzing, then yes. It is the power you absorbed from me. It will subside. It will subside faster if you shift," said Heidi.

Hilde and Tallis stepped out onto the patio. Heidi gripped Finn by the shoulders and the buzzing stopped.

"That's better," said Finn.

"It's only temporary. As soon as I let go, it will return. You need to shift into Giant form and then back into human form, so your body learns to regulate the extra amount of power," she said.

"I don't know how to do that. You saw me this morning. I barely enlarged my arm," said Finn.

"Things are different now. I gave you some of my power, so all you have to do is focus on what you want to be, and it should happen."

As she let go, the buzzing came back to Finn even louder than before. Covering his ears, he moved to the middle of the backyard. Heidi mouthed the word "Focus."

Finn closed his eyes and tried to focus on being bigger. The buzzing was so loud now he couldn't hear anything else. He dropped to his knees and focused as hard as he could on shifting. He let out a roar that shook the ground. Then he felt something. The buzzing dimmed, and a warm sensation covered him. It got more intense until his entire body felt hot. A cool breeze hit him in the back. When he opened his eyes, he thought he was levitating, only to notice his feet hadn't left the ground. He was getting taller, and all his appendages were swelling with muscle and length. When he finally stopped growing, he could see over the main house's roof. He looked down at the group of family that had gathered at his enormous feet.

"Look at me!" he shouted.

But his voice was so deep that it knocked everyone to the ground.

"Oh sorry," he whispered.

Mick was the first one to speak. "My boy, you must be at least thirty feet tall! That is unheard of for most giants, let alone a new shifter or shiftling. Most giants never get above twenty feet. Even your grandfather only reached twenty feet in his prime."

"Twenty-one," Ander said. "And how do you feel?"

"I feel fine, I feel strong. Like I could do anything," said Finn with what he hoped was a soft enough voice. It didn't seem to shake anyone, so that was good. "This is way better than last time."

The rune pendant around his neck was glowing bright blue and was about the size of a truck tire. It hummed loudly, then changed the rune to one he didn't recognize.

Heidi called, "Okay Finn, you need to shift back. Focus on your human form."

Finn closed his eyes and focused on what he looked like as a human. So much shorter. Suddenly there was a whoosh of cool air, and when he opened his eyes, he was back to his original size. He all at once felt dizzy and fell to the ground, fighting the urge to vomit.

"The first few times you shift, it may make you sick," Mick said. "Also, the longer you spend in giant form, the more drained your human form will be until you can control the flow of power. With practice you will shift with no ill effects."

After Finn had recovered, he stood up and hugged Tallis with everything he had.

"Thank you for being here," he whispered in her ear. He then turned to Heidi. "I still am not one hundred percent sure we can trust you, but I thank you for the help."

As the group made their way back to the house where Hilde had a large pot of her famous chili waiting, Finn felt a cold shiver run down his spine that stopped him in his tracks. He turned and saw Heidi staring at him with a look of worry.

"He's coming, isn't he, my father? He's on his way and he wants blood?" he asked her.

Heidi nodded.

"How long do we have?" asked Finn.

"Two days, probably less," she replied.

They entered the house and joined everyone at the table where Finn was filled in on the day's events. About halfway through dinner, Mick thumped the table, causing bowls and spoons to jump. "I know how we can stop Einar. Now Finn, you're big but you won't have the experience Einar will in battle, so we must out smart him. I know of an ancient rune that was used to bind criminals to a single spot. It lines the dungeons of the old Keep with them. A ring of staves with the rune carved on them should work. But. . ."

"But what?" said Hilde.

"There has to be someone in the middle of the ring to brand Einar with the binding rune to activate the trap. It's a big possibility that person won't survive the encounter." Mick sat back in his chair, eyeing the now silent group.

"Well, it's obviously should be me since I am the biggest and will probably last the longest against him," said Finn.

"No!" said Tallis.

"I will do it," said Anders, standing up from his chair.

"Anders, you can't even shift. How will you protect yourself?" asked Erik.

"Maybe not, but he is coming for me and he doesn't know that Finn—the real Finn—is here, and I want to keep it that way for the time being. That means Heidi and Finn will stay in the house while the rest of us will detain my son." Anders slumped back into his chair as if the gravity of his decision had just hit him.

Mick turned to Talon and said, "Son, I need you to go out to the yard tonight with the way finder and try to see where Einar is so we can have an estimate of how much time we have."

Talon nodded and got up to retrieve the way finder.

Mick continued. "Erik, I will need your help to make the runes on the staves, and Anders, if you're serious about this, I will need your staff."

"My staff?" asked Anders. "Why?"

"I will explain in the barn," said Mick.

With that, Mick stood and motioned for Erik and Anders to follow him to the barn. After they had left, Talon reappeared with the way finder in full form.

"Who wants to find a terrifying fire ogre?" he said wryly.

"And I guess I will head back to my pen," said Heidi as she stood.

"Oh, no you don't! You started this whole mess and you are going to help us be as prepared as possible," said Finn. "I still can't control the King's Stone, and something tells me we might need it and I think you can help with that." Then he blushed and said, "Plus I can't let you sleep with the pigs after you helped me so much." He glanced at Tallis, who, to his surprise, smiled in agreement.

"This doesn't mean I like you or trust you, but you can stay in the guest room with me," Tallis said. "And no more kissing my boyfriend. Or anyone." Then she turned and followed Talon out to the yard.

Arna just shrugged and followed them out.

"I think she's warming up to you," said Finn.

Finn went out and met up with the others, who were shortly joined by Hilde and a sullen Heidi. Talon held the Way Finder vertically in front of him and in an unnaturally deepened voice he bellowed, "Find Einar!"

The staff hummed and projected a blue aura around itself then, nothing. The humming ceased and the blue aura faded. They heard a light giggle from behind the group. They turned and saw Heidi trying to suppress another outburst of laughter.

"What would you do? I couldn't have been clearer about what I was looking for a path to," said Talon.

"Well, have you ever met Einar?" she asked as she made her towards Talon.

"No" he answered.

"Then how do you know what to visualize for the staff to work? Like Finn's stone, and yes, I knew you had it, but more on that later. Like the stone, the Vei Visner works on thoughts and emotions of the bearer. So, since you don't know what he looks like, think about what he might look like."

"That's clear as mud," said Arna.

"So, what does he look like? My father, I mean?" asked Finn. It wasn't like any of them had much experience seeing fire ogres.

"His movements will look like a wildfire on the move. So, picture the craziest, most out-of-control wildfire you can think of and that will most likely be him. The Way Finder will show you his true self," Heidi replied.

This time Talon stood in a sturdy stance holding the staff in front of himself, took a deep breath, and closed his eyes. In his regular voice, he restated his purpose and focused on imagining a raging fire. He opened his eyes, only he didn't see the backyard. He saw miles and miles of Alaskan wilderness zipping underneath him like he was flying. Just then he stopped over an area of forest and tundra, except that something clouded it with thick dark smoke and a large swath of land blazed in bright orange and red flames about a mile wide. It seemed to be alive and move in a straight line with a purpose. Talon focused on the front of the blaze and there he saw him. An enormous ogre at least thirty feet tall barreling at a full run through the forest. Leaving blazing wreckage in his wake. The ogre roared, and it startled Talon. When he opened his eyes again, he was back in the yard. He turned and described his vision to the group.

"From what you have described, we have less time than I thought, maybe twenty-four hours," said Heidi.

Hilde said, "I am going to check on the men's progress with the staves and tell them what we have learned. You guys go inside and Finn work with Heidi on the King's Stone. I know what your grandpa said, but we may need you." With that, she headed up to the barn, leaving Finn and the others in silence to ponder what they had learned.

They headed up to the main house, and Finn retrieved the box Thor had given him from his room. He opened it and removed the stone, holding it out in his hand. He could feel its faint hum. Heidi looked at it with wide eyes, like she couldn't believe what she was seeing.

"Rathgar never let me this close to the King's Stone. It's beautiful," she said.

"Would you like to hold it?" asked Finn and offered her the stone.

Finn Stonefist

At first it looked like she might take it, then she recoiled a little. "I shouldn't. Working with Rathgar, I have surely angered the Gods and would not want to touch anything they have touched for fear of the retribution that might come, but I can teach you how to use it, Finn."

"How do you know so much about it?" asked Arna.

"I was there when Rathgar learned from the dark elves how to use it. I paid attention, mostly out of curiosity, but after Rathgar burned my town, I had a feeling the Gods might be ready to give the stone to a new, more appropriate handler. That's when I sought Troll's Rest." Heidi focused her eyes back on the King's Stone. "Like the Way Finder, the stone works on thoughts and emotions. It can almost be mistaken for a living thing. It can be offended, and it lives to serve a proper master. So, if you are a righteous king and curry the favor of the gods, then it will continue to serve you without a fault. It can take any form it feels you need. A sword, a shield, or even armor. It will learn to anticipate your moves even before you consciously think of them. Now, take the stone in your dominant hand and think *armor*."

Finn took a step back from the group and held the stone in his right hand in front of him. He looked at the stone and thought about the word *armor*. The stoned hummed loudly and dissolved into gray silvery sand and climbed his arm. When it reached his shoulder, it split into three unequal pieces. One wandered back down his arm while the others worked their way to the middle of his chest and his left arm. There was a flash of light and when Finn opened his eyes, he saw Tallis and the others standing slack jawed and wide-eyed, staring at him.

"What?" he asked.

"Dude, you look awesome!" said Arna.

Finn looked down and saw the stone was now a breastplate and two bracers. The breast plate looked like polished silver that had solid metal straps connecting in the middle of his back. It etched the Stonefist family crest in the middle of it. It nearly covered his forearms in bracers of the same material, except they were studded with inch long spikes. Finn pumped his fist and said "Yes!" when suddenly the spikes shot from his bracer and flew fast as a bullet in all directions in the living room. Everyone hit the deck, trying to avoid being impaled.

"Whoa! Sorry guys. Are you all okay?" said Finn as he carefully examined his arm like he was looking at a high yield explosive.

The spikes had regenerated on the cuff. He looked around the room and saw the shiny shards stuck in the walls, furniture, ceiling, and floor all around him.

"Oh, Hilde is going to kill me!" he said.

As everyone picked themselves up from the floor, Heidi was laughing.

"That was awesome!" she said. "You have summoned the Guardian's Armor, very good for a beginner. It took Rathgar months to get this far, no joke."

"What happened to my living room!" yelled Hilde.

Everyone turned to see Anders and Hilde standing in the patio doorway. Hilde looked like she might murder every one of them, while Anders had a big grin taking up most of his face.

"The Guardian's Armor! Well done, my boy!" said Anders as he made his way over and clapped Finn on his broad armored shoulders.

"Everyone outside! No more practicing in my living room!" shouted Hilde loud enough to make even Anders jump.

In the yard Heidi continued to instruct Finn on how he could control the direction of the spikes, so he didn't have another "miss fire". Countless jokes derived from the terms "miss fire" abounded from Arna for most of the evening.

A faint yet sharp clang sounded out from the barn that caught the attention of Talon. He touched the rune on the Way Finder, and it retracted to the form of a stick no bigger than a drumstick and stuck in his back pocket. He left the group and made his way up to the barn. In the barn Talon found his father and Erik huddled around a homemade forge. Mick was pounding on an anvil. Upon closer inspection, Talon saw what he was hammering out looked like a strange wheel with spokes that has been bent and twisted into different angular shapes. Six spokes in all, each different from the next. Mick picked up the white-hot metal with tongs and quenched it in the water barrel. Steam hissed angrily from the water. As the steam cleared, Talon beheld a wheel of six runes joined at the center.

"Is that a binding rune?" Talon asked.

"Talon my son! Glad you are here. I wanted to show you this. This is the brand that will affix to the bottom of Ander's staff so he can brand Einar with it and hopefully capture him," said Mick.

"Won't it need to be hot like it was to brand him?" asked Talon.

"You would think, but because he is running so hot as a fire ogre, his skin is like molten rock. Anders need only push it into Einar's skin. The brand will connect with the others and do the rest."

"What staves are we using?" asked Talon.

"These!" said Erik and pointed to six diamond willow staffs leaning on the work bench.

Each stave was about five feet long and had two runes burned into them near the top. The top rune was a single rune from the wheel of the binding rune. The one below it was the complete wheel. They had sharpened the bottom end to a dull point. Six homemade wooden mallets with the same wheel of runes burned into the side of the head were laying on the worktable.

"Dad, I don't think these toy hammers are going to do much against a thirty-foot fire ogre," stated Talon as he hefted a mallet.

"No, I would expect not," chuckled Mick. "Those will hammer the staves into place, then you need only to grab the staff by the runes to activate it. Otherwise, we would have to stand there the whole time we want Einar bound."

"Is that going to work?" asked Talon.

"Absolutely!" said Erik.

"Well, probably," Mick said. "In theory, but these are rushed jobs, and we are using ancient and powerful magics. If we stick together and stick to the plan, we have a high chance of success."

Talon's face must have looked more worried than he thought because Mick took by the shoulders and said, "I won't let anything happen to you or Tallis. You know that, right?"

"I do," said Talon.

"Good!"

Just then a voice came from the barn door, "Michael Alastar Nightfeather!" Erik, Mick, and Talon turned to see a tall, slender woman with golden brown hair standing there with her hands on her hips.

"Mom, what are you doing here?" asked Talon.

"Well, since it has been days, and I hadn't heard from you or your father, I thought I should be concerned and hunted you down here. What in Midgard are you doing? You don't even call to tell me you and my only children are okay?"

"Well, that's a kind of long story," said Mick. "Why don't we go up to the house and I'll make you some nettle tea to calm my nerves and I'll tell you all about it?" Mick pecked her on the cheek in hopes this would soften her anger.

Mrs. Nightfeather dimmed her aura and followed her husband. Talon and Erik stayed behind to give Mick a moment alone with his irate wife.

"How much trouble is he in, do you think?" Erik asked.

"Tons. This maybe worse than the Cracker Barrel incident of 2011," said Talon.

"What?" asked Erik.

Talon just looked at and said "Oh! Never mind, it's just another time Dad got into this much trouble. He'll be fine, I think."

He jogged out of the barn to catch up to his parents, leaving Erik confused and alone in the barn.

"What a strange family," remarked Erik to himself and returned to finishing up the brand.

At the house Mick had managed to get his wife, Lorelei, to calm down enough to hear him out. He made her the promised cup of tea and as they sat on the newly shredded sofa in the living room; he explained everything that had transpired over the last few days in great detail to her. It took over an hour, but when he finally had her up to speed, he sat back and watched her now still and slightly shell-shocked face for any kind of sign that he was off the hook.

Finally, she spoke. "So you're telling me that hell fire incarnate is charging this way and your first thought was to capture it? That's nuts! He is a monster and should be treated as such!" She stood up from the sofa. "Do you know how much death he has caused? The only way to stop him is to kill him."

"Do you have any idea how to do that? asked Mick, standing to meet her gaze. He is a thirty-foot super charged fire ogre who thinks he is responsible for killing his wife and only child. You know as well as I do nothing fuels rage better than grief. So, unless you know a spell or rune that can kill him, we have to capture him and only then can we decide what needs to be done."

"But we can save him, can't we?" The couple turned to see Finn standing in the doorway, still wearing his armor. Tallis and Talon stood behind him.

"We could hear you arguing out in the yard," Finn explained. "Can we save him?"

"Oh sweetie, that's not what I meant," said Lorelei. "I just meant that no one has ever come back from the dark shift."

"Elves don't lie, and they certainly don't make vague comments. You always say what you mean, and you mean he is a monster and that we should put him down like a feral animal!" shouted Finn. "Well, you're wrong! He didn't mean to go through the dark shift. He didn't kill me or my mother. I have to believe he can be saved or what else is there? I am not killing my father! Not until every option to save him is exhausted."

Anders and Hilde had come into the room during the conversation.

"What is this I hear of killing?" asked Anders.

"No one is killing anyone, old friend. We are just having a spirited discussion on the merits of capturing Einar alive," said Mick.

"Oh Mick, you are acting like a fool. You both are. These children do not understand what cost the dark shift takes on a person. We do. We've seen the damage and heartache it causes. Death is a sweet escape for them and their families," said Lorelei.

    The roomed erupted into a flurry of arguments coming from Anders, Lorelei, and Mick. Finn couldn't believe what he was hearing. Was he going to watch the father he was robbed of; die on the very day they were re-united? Finn's head rang from the loud voices and the stress. His breathing got heavy, and the room spun. Finn turned around and ran for the backyard.

Chapter 8

In the backyard, Finn slumped to his knees and vomited. He wiped his mouth and fought the urge to vomit again.

Tallis appeared at his side. "Are you okay?"

"Why did your mom say those things?" he asked without looking up.

Tallis kneeled and put an arm around him. She rested her head on his shoulder and said, "She's just scared for us and what it means if we can reach the true Einar and bring him back."

"Why?" Finn asked, sitting back with his head still between his knees. He was still dizzy and was afraid of vomiting again.

"When my mom was a child, her older brother got in with the wrong crowd and they started playing with dark magics. One night, they had been partying and spell casting when my uncle cast a particularly nasty spell. It backfired, wounding him, and killing his girlfriend who had followed him to convince him to leave the group. She was innocent. So, it activated the dark shift in him and he became a dark elf. My grandfather tried for years to cure him with no luck. Eventually, the Elven council locked him away. It was in prison another inmate killed him. She said it broke her parents, and they were never the same after that. So you see that talk about curing dark ones is a sore subject because for years her family lived in hope of a cure but when it failed their sense of hope was destroyed."

"I am so sorry. I didn't know," said Finn.

"I know, that's why I am not angry with you, but my mother could have handled this whole thing better," said Tallis and kissed him on the cheek.

Finn Stonefist

"Now, let's go in so you can brush your teeth and you and mom can talk," said Tallis.

She helped Finn to his feet, and they started back to the house when Finn stopped and asked, "Do you smell hot tar?"

"Yeah, I do, but it smells more like . . ." she started.

"Fireball!"

They turned to see Arna, who had been on his way out to interrupt the love birds, frozen and pointing at the sky.

Finn and Tallis looked in the direction he was pointing and saw what looked like a mini sun hurtling towards them. Finn grabbed Tallis and shifted big enough to cover her body. The stone changed and created a metal dome over their bodies. There was a deafening explosion, but Finn felt nothing. No dirt, no heat, not even a shock wave. Finn stood and shifted back; when they looked up, and they could see a grid of blue energy fading back into the dark.

"Looks like your grandpa's wards held up," said Tallis.

Just then, two more fireballs came flying in on the same path as the first, only to be stopped by the grid and dispersed with a loud pop. After the second explosion, everyone else was in the backyard with Tallis and Finn.

"He's here!" trembled Heidi.

"What!" said Erik. "What happened to two days?"

"I said probably less," Heidi answered.

"FATHER!" bellowed a deep voice from within the forest on the north side of the yard.

"FATHER, WHERE ARE YOU COWARD?" it bellowed again.

Just then the trees trembled, and like chaffs of wheat they parted as an immense figure emerged from within.

"Einar," whispered Anders.

The ground shook as Einar stepped toward the yard. Finn nearly gagged again with the smell of brimstone and charred animal remains in the air. On Einar's shoulder, pine boughs smoldered, and Finn could see the remains of several birds seared onto Einar's skin. Finn was speechless at the enormity of Einar. Standing head level with most of the trees and the sheer size of his arms and legs. How could they ever hope to trap such a creature? Maybe Lorelei was right.

Anders pushed his way to the front of the group and turned to face them. "It is time. Those wards won't hold him long and when they fail, he will be upon us."

"Here, you will need this," said Erik as he handed Anders the brand he and Mick had fashioned. "It fits on the bottom of your staff like a foot.."

Anders nodded and took the rune brand and slid it onto his staff's foot. It made it awkward to use, but he hobbled towards Einar like nothing was different. The others turned and ran to the barn to get the staves. Finn and Heidi returned to the house with Lorelei as directed. Finn didn't want to leave Tallis, but she kissed him and insisted he go. As Anders got closer, he could feel the heat radiating from Einar. It was like standing in front of an oven broiler.

"I am here, son! Come no further or the wards will blast you into oblivion," he said to Einar.

"Oh, I truly doubt that, father," said Einar.

"I thought you were dead, killed by Rathgar," said Anders.

"I guess that's two things you are wrong about, father," said Einar.

"Two things?" asked Anders.

"Yes, my death and the fact that you think some whelp is my son," replied Einar.

"Whelp, what whelp?" retorted Anders.

Finn Stonefist

"The one you sent to cower in the house with the rest of the filth when you thought I wasn't looking." Einar chuckled. He threw an immense right hook through the air, colliding his fist with the invisible grid protecting Troll's Rest. The grid repelled his fist with a violent pop that surprised Einar

"Impressive father. You have been a busy little giant, haven't you?" he said. "Do you know why I am here?"

"To kill me, I suspect, on your brother's orders," said Anders.

"I am here to kill the whelp posing as my son," Einar said. "Do you know why? Because you are inciting false hope in the people by spreading lies about my son being alive. You have even stolen the King's Stone from the keep!" He punched the grid again with his other hand and got the same reaction.

"Didn't I ever tell you not to believe everything your brother says? If I had such a boy, I certainly wouldn't have told anyone of his existence. As for the King's Stone, I do not have it. Have you asked the Gods where it is?" Anders stepped closer to where the heat was so intense the sweat on his brow felt hot. "Son, you don't need to do this. Your brother has lied to you and poisoned your mind against me and anyone who may still care for you."

"Lied to me? My brother has done nothing but help me after, after . . ." Einar's voice trailed off. "What would you know about what I have been through?" Einar shouted, and this time he slammed both fists against the barrier with such force that it shook the ground and caused the grid to flicker. This time it did not repel his fists as before. Einar grinned. "Your wards are failing and soon I will be in there."

In the barn, Mick handed the newly inscribed staves and mallets to Erik, Hilde, Arna, Tallis, and Talon, keeping one for himself.

"Erik, you take your family and head west and I and my kids will go east. I marked your positions with blue ribbon twenty feet apart. Stay low and move fast, no shifting. If he sees us before we are in position, we are done for." Mick looked lovingly at the scared faces of the group and said, "Together we do this, together we win."

With that, the group left the barn and split into two smaller groups. Mick reached the back yard just as Einar struck the grid with both fists. The shock wave stopped them in their tracks.

"Come on guys, to your spots" urged Mick. They reached the first marker and Mick silently signaled Tallis to lie flat on it until she got the signal. He did the same with Talon at his mark. When Mick reached his own mark, he checked one last time to make sure the children were out of sight before lying flat on his stomach.

Just as he got settled, Einar bellowed "enough talk, I will finish this now!" Einar then began pounding on the grid with both fists. Mick could only hope that Erik and the others were in place. The grid sparked and clashed like thunder against the onslaught of blows from Einar.

Back in the house Finn, Heidi, and Lorelei were glued to the windows watching the standoff with nervous anticipation.

"I should be out there with them," said Finn through gritted teeth.

"Trust that your grandfather knows what he is doing. Gods know I'm trying to," said Lorelei as she put a hand on Finn's shoulder.

Finn shrugged her hand off. "I am the best tool we have."

"Finn, you need to calm down and control your emotions," said Heidi as she noticed Finn's arms bulging in places.

"If you shift uncontrolled, you could do actual damage to yourself or others," said Lorelei as calmly as she could.

Finn felt the familiar heat all over his body. He didn't want to shift, but he was so angry at being sidelined and so worried about Tallis and the others. He closed his eyes and tried to breathe deeply, like Heidi had taught him, in order to control the flow of power.

Einar's pounding on the grid was weakening it, and Anders knew it wouldn't be long before he broke through. Anders backed up to his position. Just then Einar roared and slammed both fists down on the grid with such force that it crackled, fizzed, and the grid lines blew apart and faded into the night.

Einar grinned and stepped forward. He lifted a foot and stomped it down only feet from Anders.

But the old giant king didn't flinch. He only stared at Einar and shouted, "You don't scare me, my son. Let me help you, please!"

Einar roared and swiped a large, powerful hand at him, knocking him back ten feet. Anders landed with a thud. Einar stood erect to let another roar out.

But a roar from Finn stopped him. The moment Finn had seen Anders get knocked down, he was out of the house and growing. Setting his sights on Einar, Finn dropped his shoulder just like in football and charged the ogre with everything he had. In two steps, Finn was across the yard and planted a shield-clad shoulder in the dead center of the ogre's chest. Einar was taken by surprise and toppled back into the woods. Finn turned and kneeled by Anders. His body looked so small and helpless from Finn's current height. Anders groaned and Finn was about to pick him up when he felt a white-hot pain as Einar's foot connected with Finn's ribs. He landed, making a dent in the ground. Einar turned back to Anders and formed a fire ball between his hands. He hefted the deadly blaze above his head, and just as he was about to send Anders to a fiery grave, he heard someone yell "NOW!" Einar looked around and saw six figures surround him and start pound staves into the ground.

"Your toothpicks are nothing to me!" Einar bellowed.

Everyone's staves were in place except Tallis. Her mallet's handle had broken, and she was furiously hammering with half a hammer. Einar saw Tallis struggling and turned his fireball towards her. He hurtled the ball towards her but was blinded by a bright light when it deflected off Finn's chest plate. Finn had got to his feet and saw the fireball careening towards Tallis. He jumped in front of it without thinking.

"You must be the whelp I have heard about," said Einar. "You're big, I'll give you that, but you are a fool to get involved in this family squabble."

"I am not a fool or a whelp, you are the fool," said Finn as he got to his feet. There was a dark scorch mark on his chest plate, and Finn winced at the pain in his ribs. He stood eye to eye with Einar and said, "Only a fool wouldn't recognize his own son when he is standing right in front of him!"

This caused Einar to pause.

"Father, it is me, your son. There must be some of the old you left. Look inside. You know it's true."

Einar stepped back and sized up the boy giant standing in front of him.

Finn focused and shifted back to his human self. "Look at me and tell me I am not your son."

Einar looked deep into the bright blue eyes of the young man at his feet and faltered. "It can't be! You're dead! My son is dead!"

Finn Stonefist

Finn turned and locked eyes with Tallis and nodded. She managed to get her staff planted while Finn had distracted Einar.

"Now!" she shouted.

Each person wrapped a hand around the runes on the staff, causing blue energy to stream from the tops and connect with Einar at his wrists. Einar looked around in surprise and roared. While Einar struggled against his new bonds, he hadn't noticed that Anders had regained his feet and was charging as fast as he could towards him. Once Anders was close enough, he hoisted the staff and threw it like a spear. It flew over Finn's head and collided with the top of Einar's foot.

Einar's skin hissed and sizzled upon contact with the brand, and he roared in pain. The brand sunk below the skin before Einar knocked the staff clear of his foot. The brand had melted into a pool of hot metal and staff burst into flame, landing across the yard still smoldering. Nothing seemed to happen at first until Einar tried to step forward and the beams of energy at his wrists split in two and seized him by the ankles, halting his progress. Einar punched the ground in an attempt to jostle the staff holders. The shock wave was enough to shake everyone nearly off their feet, but no one fell.

"Hold on!" shouted Mick. "We have to wait for the beams to turn white before we have him. Focus your minds on binding him."

The group rallied and focused on binding the angry fire ogre. The beams split again and connected with the manacle around Einar's neck, turning it bright red before it broke in two and fell to the ground with a loud clang. The beams formed a new collar of energy around his neck. The beams hummed loudly, and the ogre's knees buckled under the force. Einar was on his knees now and wasn't able to stand. He struggled against his restraints, but he was getting tired. In one last attempt to free himself, Einar got one foot under himself. He tried to stand, only to have both feet pulled from under him. He was now spread eagle on his back inside the ring of staves. Einar saw the beams turn white, and he knew he was beat. His head hurt and the world was getting dark. Just before losing consciousness, he saw Finn standing over him, his blue eyes wide with worry. "You can't be him, you . . ." said Einar weakly as he passed out.

Finn and Mick approached cautiously, ready for Einar to jump up at any moment, but as they got closer, they both realized the great ogre was out cold.

"Oh, thank the Gods," said Mick.

"He should be out for hours. He expended tons of energy and the bonds didn't allow him to recover as quickly as he would without them. They will also diminish his strength for a while, but I fear if we don't find a permanent solution, he will get free," said Anders.

"What's this? It fell off his neck when the beams of energy connected with it," said Arna.

He handed the broken restraint to Mick, who turned it over in every direction, inspecting every inch. "This is a control collar. See, its split right down the middle of the rune. When whole and applied to a subject, you need only touch this rune and it would cause great pain to the wearer."

"How barbaric," said Hilde.

"I haven't seen it used since before my time as king," said Anders.

"Well, we caught probably the most dangerous creature on Earth. Now what?" asked Talon.

Finn Stonefist

"We all need rest, but I can last a little longer. I will take the first watch while everyone gets some much-needed rest," said Erik.

"No, I will take first watch. I couldn't sleep now if I wanted," Finn insisted.

Erik knew that arguing was futile, so he herded everyone else into the house. With Anders's staff burned to a crisp, Mick helped him hobble up to the house and got him tucked into bed with Hilde's help. In the yard, Finn shifted into giant form and sat cross-legged on the ground just outside the ring of staves. He sat there staring at his would-be father and listened to his breathing. It was deep and ragged, and he looked at peace. Finn had a hundred questions running around his head, foremost being if his mother was still alive.

Chapter 9

The next morning Einar found himself still spread eagle on the ground with a headache to rival even a direct blow from Thor's hammer. He groaned and pulled himself to a sitting position. He looked around at the ring of staves surrounding him. He could hear and feel them humming. The ring had replaced the shackles Rathgar had put on him with new ones that were inscribed with blue runes. He jerked his wrists forward and felt a jolt of energy. It wasn't strong enough to hurt but was strong enough to inform him that further tries would cause pain.

"I wouldn't do that if I were you. I know little about mystical runes, but from what I am told, they don't get much stronger than these," said a man's voice.

Einar looked to his left and saw Erik's lanky figure sitting in a camp chair just outside of the ring.

"Erik? Erik Shatterfist? Boy, you got old," said Einar.

"Yeah, well, you got fat," Erik said in retort. The last time he'd seen Einar, he'd been a kid.

Einar chuckled. "Are you to be my jailer?"

"For now, yes, but it was Finn who sat here most of the night watching over you. You know your son who has waited his whole life to meet you," said Erik.

Einar was silent. Just then, Erik noticed Anders and Mick standing next to him with Hilde.

"Good, you're awake. Now, after you have had something to eat, we can talk. Unfortunately, you will need to shift to human size to enjoy this meal. No Asgardian Prairie Beast here, just plain old Midgard beef," said Anders.

"Shift?" remarked Einar. "I haven't been in human form for nearly twenty years."

"Well, you better do something about that or this meal won't even come close to filling you," said Hilde.

Einar huffed at the diminutive giantess, but he knew she was right and last night's events had left him exhausted and hungry. He closed his eyes and tried his best to remember what he looked like in human form. Suddenly, he caught a glimpse in his mind of a tall, fit, blonde-haired man. He focused on him and felt the surge of energy needed to shift. He grabbed hold of the surge with his mind, and when he opened his eyes, he was eye level with his father. Anders's face lost color as he stared at a face he had not seen in many years.

"My boy..." Anders whispered.

It was all he could do not to reach through and embrace Einar, but he signaled for Mick and Hilde to push the tray of meat and the pot of potatoes through the field surrounding the ring.

The smell of cooked roast and potatoes hit Einar like a slap in the face. He dropped to his knees beside the dishes and tore into the meat with great ferocity. He stuffed fists of potatoes as fast as he could. For a moment, he forgot about his audience. He looked up to see four different expressions, ranging from a smile on Mick's face to a disgusted look on Hilde's who looked like she might wretch. Einar timidly wiped his mouth and sat back on the grass. Swallowing hard and taking a breath, he looked at his jailers.

"Well, father, what will you do with me now?" asked Einar.

"At your son's behest we will try to help you, first by treating those burns you sustained on your hands from the ward grid," said Anders. "You will note that my binding rune has replaced the irons Rathgar fitted you with. Also, any connection he had to your mind should also be gone."

"I thought my mind seemed quieter," said Einar.

"Now, as long as you behave, and that includes no shifting, we have reluctantly agreed with Finn to let you out of the ring," Anders said. "But fair warning. We have warded the surrounding property with the same binding, so you may not try to leave this property in any form. If you do, you will receive a jolt that would rattle Thor's teeth. So do we have an agreement?"

"What you propose is madness. No one has ever come back from the dark shift, but if you want to kill yourselves, it's no skin of my nose." said Einar.

"You see right there. He has a mind of his own," said Mick to the group. "A true dark shifter would be a mindless beast, unable to control his feelings, let alone be able to speak or converse with us. That supports Heidi's claim that this whole thing is a spell and not a true dark shift."

"Wait a minute, Heidi is here?" asked Einar. "That two faced harlot is the reason I am here in the first place!"

"What do you mean?" asked Hilde.

"When Rathgar accepts the service of someone, he brands them with the same control rune you saw on my neck. So, unless you have destroyed that rune on her, she is still in contact with Rathgar and any of us he has marked," Einar explained. "He let her escape in hopes she would lead him here. Before that, all Rathgar had was a rough idea of where Troll's Rest was."

"Does she know of the mark and its abilities?" asked Erik, who had his hand on his holster.

"I don't know how she couldn't. She helped Rathgar create it. It's a mix of Huldre and dark magic. She was the first to get it."

"The kids!" said Hilde.

Mick, Erik, and Hilde ran for the house as fast as they could, with Anders hobbling after them. Hilde was first to reach the house, followed by Erik with his weapon drawn.

"KIDS!" she yelled.

There was no answer.

She yelled again and this time five bleary eyed teenagers appeared at the top of the stairs.

"YOU!" Hilde yelled as she cleared the stairs in two steps. She seized Heidi by the back of her head. Not her hair, but her head. Dragging the shrieking Huldre down the stairs and out the porch door. As Hilde and Erik got outside, they shifted into giant form, both standing about fifteen feet high. Hilde dropped Heidi in front of Einar, who glared at the sprawling girl. When she saw Einar, she attempted to run, but was stopped by the crowd that had now formed at the ring.

"What did you tell them?" she shouted at Einar.

"I told them everything," Einar said. "You see, these kind people say I didn't kill my family, and they were resourceful enough to figure how to break Rathgar's hold on me and I have to say I feel amazing."

Heidi shrieked and produced a tail from under her blue dress. It resembled a cow's tail, but she could whip it around with deadly accuracy. However, in giant form and as angry as Hilde was, Heidi's new trick was no match for the angry giant mama. Hilde used her massive hands to grab Heidi and pin her arms, legs, and tail against her body.

"Where is the mark?" asked Hilde, but Heidi was silent.

Einar spoke. "It will be hidden. Probably the hairline or the small of her back."

Erik brushed Heidi's hair to the top of her head with his hand and inspected her hair line. Sure enough, just inside her hairline on her neck was the rune. It looked like the control rune they had used, but it was twisted and resembled more of a knot than a wheel. The scar was raised but otherwise completely healed, and the hair had grown over it.

"How do we get rid of it?" asked Erik.

"What you did to me should work. Just brand your rune over that one and it should break like mine did." Einar gestured to the new brand on the top of his right foot.

Anders looked at Heidi who seemed to plead with her eyes that the old giant not do it and then he looked at Mick, who just nodded.

"Take her to the barn. I will be there shortly to prepare the brand," said Anders quietly.

Mick shifted into his troll form, making him about ten feet tall, but with a strong barrel chest and robust arms and legs. His nose got a little longer and bulbous at the end, and his ears came to a shallow point.

"Ah! That feels good," he said.

Finn had never seen Mick in troll form, and he had to say it was impressive.

"You don't understand! If you break this bond, I will lose my connection. I can provide information from inside Rathgar's keep," shouted Heidi under the weight of Mick's and Erik's massive hands.

"You can also put us in danger and be a double agent for all we know," said Hilde.

Hilde back handed Heidi, knocking the girl unconscious. She seemed shocked by her actions and quickly shifted back to human form. "Sorry, but at least she's quiet," she said with a wry grin.

No one laughed except Arna, who seem to laugh mostly out of fear of his mother.

"Let's leave Finn with his father for now," said Anders as he picked up his new crutch, it being an old aluminum crutch from when Finn had broken his leg snowboarding a few years ago, and made his way up to the barn.

In the barn, Anders could feel the heat from the forge as he walked in. The binding brand was already bright red on the fire's edge. Erik and Mick had shifted back to human form and had tied Heidi to an old chair they found in the barn's loft. She stirred and then woke with a start, struggling against her ropes. "You don't have to do this. I'm just a girl. You wouldn't hurt a defenseless girl, would you?" she begged.

Anders stood there silently, staring at her. Erik looked at Mick with a look of apprehension.

"Don't listen to her, Erik," Mick said. "She is neither defenseless nor just a girl. Huldres age very differently than us. No one truly knows how old they are but trust she is no defenseless girl."

Anders lifted the brand from the fire. It hissed in the cool air with a small stream of smoke. "If you sit still, this will be over quickly. You will be free of Rathgar, and we will be a little safer. Because you helped Finn, I am inclined to think you truly mean us no harm but, your connection to my son and his minions is too big of a risk to take."

Heidi sobbed as Mick shifted his arms to hold her head in a firm grip and Erik shakily pulled her hair to one side, revealing Rathgar's mark. Anders pressed the brand against her skin and counted one... two... three... four. Heidi screamed in pain. Just as Anders was about to say five, a blue bolt of energy shot from the brand knocking Anders to the ground. Heidi let out another scream that shook the dust from barn's old rafters.

"It is done. The binding brand has replaced Rathgar's mark; it now binds her to this property like Einar," said Mick as he helped Anders off the ground.

Anders looked at the brand. All that remained of it was a chunk of iron melted and clumped at the end of the rod. Heidi was in and out of consciousness, groaning from her ordeal.

Lorelei appeared in the barn doorway. "Is it done?"

"It is," said Anders.

"I will take her to house to rest and maybe get her to eat something," said Lorelei.

Erik helped Lorelei remove the ropes from Heidi's wrists and ankles. Lorelei hefted the girl in her arms like a babe and carried her up to the house.

Erik looked at Anders and asked, "Now what?"

"Now, we rest," Anders replied.

Out in the backyard, Einar was still confined to the ring of staves. He sat cross-legged on the grass. Finn sat in a camp chair. They watched one another.

"So, you are the boy who would be king," said Einar.

"Those are your words," Finn said. "I never asked for any of this. I didn't even think our crazy family history was true and now, everything I thought was a fairy tale is true. Giants, trolls, gods, ogres; it's all craziness, but it's real. I don't want to be king. I just want to enjoy my senior year with my friends."

"You know what I want?" Einar said. "I want nothing more than to be rid of the dark shift and get to know the son that was robbed from me."

"So, you believe I am your son?" asked Finn.

"I didn't at first but, I see it now. You have your mother's tenacity and there is a connection to you, I cannot deny," said

Einar. He rubbed his foot where the brand had struck him. There was a raised sore in the rune's shape.

"Does it hurt?" asked Finn.

"It does but, it is a small price for being free of your uncle's influence," said Einar.

"If you agree to our terms, I can turn this off and we have a salve that could help," said Finn.

Einar paused a moment and studied Finn's face like he was deciding if it was a trick. He looked at his foot, then back at Finn. "Very well, I agree," he finally replied.

With that, Finn grabbed the nearest stave and pulled it from the ground. He turned the stave, so the runes were facing the outside and jabbed it back into the ground. This action caused the energy streams at Einar's wrists and ankles to blink, then fade out.

Einar stepped cautiously from the ring and, when nothing happened, he smiled like he had expected to be hit by lightning. As soon as Finn saw his father step through the ring unharmed, he secretly hoped the other wardings were going to hold should Einar revert to his Fire Ogre state.

"Follow me and I'll take you to Tallis," said Finn.

"Ah yes, Tallis, the girlfriend. Are you two serious?" said Einar, trying to start a fatherly conversation.

Finn turned a gave Einar a look that instantly informed him it was too soon for fatherly advice.

"Don't make this weird," stated Finn as they entered the patio door into the house.

As Einar entered the house, all other conversations stopped. Everyone stared at the man that stood before them. Finn saw Tallis applying the salve to the neck of a sleeping Heidi.

"Tallis, could you apply the salve to Ei... I mean my father's foot," said Finn awkwardly.

Suddenly Lorelei pushed past Finn and came nearly nose to nose with Einar. She had to shift into elf form to meet him because even in human, Einar was still considered tall.

"If you so much as fart funny, I will end you in a second. I don't believe you can be saved; you barely look like you with your red eyes and veins and you stink of death. This is my family, not yours, and I will protect it," she threatened through gritted teeth.

"I would do the same in your place," said Einar with wide eyes.

"Mom! Stop it. If Finn trusts him, then I do too," said Tallis, looking embarrassed by her mother's display.

"Mr. Stonefist, if you will have a seat in this chair, I can take care of your foot," she said as she gestured to an armchair across from the couch.

"Please, call me Einar. Mr. Stonefist or any of my old titles don't fit me anymore," said Einar, as he sat in the chair.

The chair sagged under his weight and the frame groaned. Tallis kneeled at his feet and opened the jar of salve Thor had given her.

"Salve of the Gods?" asked Einar.

"It is," she replied.

"We all got gifts from the gods," said Arna, "Thor himself gave them to us."

Talon elbowed Arna in the ribs. "Shut your cake hole or did you forget he was working for the enemy just yesterday?" he mumbled.

Tallis applied the salve to Einar's foot. The brand healed almost immediately, creating a white raised scar in the rune's shape on the top of his foot.

"Well, that feels a lot better," said Einar. "Thank you."

"So, now what's the plan? We have taken Rathgar's two best weapons and freed them. This will not go unnoticed," said Lorelei.

"You may have freed us, but he still has her," said a groggy Heidi from the couch. She had awoken while Tallis treated Einar's foot.

"Who is her?" asked Talon.

"She means my mother," said Finn.

Einar looked like someone had punched him in the gut. "Tove, my Tove is alive? You mean I didn't kill her either?"

"No, you didn't. You were both spelled by me and Rathgar to believe you had killed Finn and each other and then never allowed to see each other in case that broke the spell," explained Heidi.

Einar's eyes flared bright red, and the fabric of the chair smoldered. He looked like he might erupt. Heidi yipped and dove behind the couch as Einar lunged for her.

"I don't need to shift to kill you!" he shouted.

Erik and Mick partially shifted and tried to restrain Einar, but his skin was too hot to touch. Anders, to the surprise of everyone, stepped between Einar and his target.

"Son, she is not worth it. Plus, she has more answers we need," he said, placing a hand on Einar's chest.

Einar paused, snarled at Heidi, then calmed himself and apologized to Hilde for burning her chair.

Anders rounded on the still cowering Heidi and said, "Can we do for Tove what we did for Einar?"

Heidi said, "You would think so, but no. We didn't know she was a Sammeloper when we cast the spell, but when we did, it caused her confluence to present when it wasn't supposed to, thus creating a creature of immense power and ability. Like Finn, it connects her to the magic of Midgard, but even more so."

"I don't know what that means," said Finn.

"Yeah, try again," Arna added.

"I'm saying the magic did something. It wiped Tove from her mind. After the spell, she didn't know who she was or what she was. She was a blank slate. Rathgar was giddy with the prospect of a weapon he could mold himself. He has spent the last seventeen years sculpting her into the perfect weapon of destruction. He has kept her secluded from everyone except himself and his most trusted advisor. I haven't even seen her in over ten years. He has her learning his hateful doctrine and training in all her forms constantly. She doesn't eat or sleep. She is the closest thing to a goddess there is on Midgard. So, to answer your question; no, it won't work," she finished.

Chapter 10

Back at the keep, Rathgar was making his way through the seemingly endless hallways and tunnels, working his way deeper into the mountain. The deeper he went, the louder the sound of clanging metal that could be heard. He finally stopped at a balcony that overlooked a great cavern as big as a football stadium and so tall the top could not be seen beyond the darkness. At the bottom was a large lake of water and next to that was an immense forge where several figures were silhouetted in the firelight furiously pounding on long rods of metal that were white hot from the heat.

A figure floated down from the top of the cavern against the hot air currents. As it got closer, Rathgar recognized it as Talax, a golden eagle who was Rathgar's captain of the guard. Talax landed on the balcony next to Rathgar. Coming nearly to Rathgar's knee, Talax bowed his head.

"My Lord," he said.

"Tell me you have good news," said Rathgar.

"My Lord, my troops have nearly finished constructing the tower on top of the mountain and the drill shaft in this cavern is about half-way complete," responded Talax.

"And what of my brother?" asked Rathgar, with a slight growl in his voice.

"Well, my Lord," said Talax, "it is as you feared. Einar and Heidi have been captured at Troll's Rest."

Rathgar's nostrils flared, and he slammed a fist on the balcony's rail, causing the balcony to tremor and the rail to crack under the blow.

"On the bright side, my Lord, Einar collapsed the magical barrier with his bare hands and in doing so, I could see all of Troll's Rest and I got a location before the rebels put a new set of wards up. The problem is the wards are so strong that when we tried to infiltrate, I lost three falcons. They were just vaporized."

"A few dead falcons are the least of my worries," Rathgar said. "Aside from the enemy capturing two of our best warriors, this is also happening." He held out his forearms. There were three tattoos on one arm in the shape of the dark binding rune and the other arm had three as well, but two of them were severely faded and had nearly vanished.

Talax couldn't believe his eyes. He cautiously looked at his own mark under his right wing. "Sire, I thought the dark rune was unbreakable!"

"Well, apparently we were wrong!" roared Rathgar.

The hammering in the forge stopped for a moment as small stones and stalactites fell from the walls of the cavern. Talax recoiled under Rathgar's rebuke, but quickly recovered his normal, stoic composure. "What are your orders, my Lord?"

"I want you and your eagles to monitor the location. They can't hide forever and when they come out, I want to know when and where they go," ordered Rathgar.

"As you wish," replied Talax and then he spread his wings and began his ascent into cavern's darkness from where he had come.

Emerging near the top of the mountain, Talax landed next to a giant metal tower. As he settled at the foot of the tower, two enormous birds swooped in and landed in front of him. The first to land with a thud was a great Bald Eagle named Tobias. His family had come from Asgard millennia ago during the great rift and had been stranded on Midgard. He looked just like a regular North American Bald Eagle, except that he, and most of his family, were about twice the size of their Midgard brethren. He was Talax's chief warrior and had the scars to show it, including a milky white eye that was blinded in the first battle against Rathgar. Despite his limited vision, he was still a force to be reckoned with in the air or on the ground. The next to land was Corvax, a great Northern Raven. She was sleek and had shiny black feathers that flowed like liquid ebony. She landed lightly, making nearly no sound. She was Talax's second lieutenant and his chief spy. She was cunning and highly intelligent. Talax didn't fully trust her because she always looked out for number one—herself—but when it came to spy craft and interrogation, no one could beat the cunningness of a raven, especially this raven.

"So, how did it go?" asked Corvax. She could tell something was bothering Talax.

"Yes, tell us what he is going to do for the falcons I lost in the assault of Troll's Rest?" interjected Tobias in a gravelly voice.

"He is going to do nothing. He wants us to finish our work. I need you, Corvax, and your ravens to monitor where we saw Troll's Rest disappear," said Talax quietly.

"What do you mean, nothing? We are just supposed to sit back and watch while the rebels have magic that can vaporize one of us?" said Tobias.

"Yes!" said Talax, becoming annoyed with this line of questioning from his underling.

"Well, I won't. I will take my best warriors and I will get vengeance!" threatened Tobias.

"YOU will do no such thing!" shouted Talax

"And who will stop me? You? The would-be king's pet bird?" retorted Tobias, as he spread his wings and scratched at the ground with his long razor-sharp talons. Suddenly there was a flash of golden feathers, and Tobias was on his back with Talax's great talons wrapped around his throat. Tobias could just feel the points of the talons on his skin beneath his feathers.

Talax met him beak to beak and hissed, "If you ever speak those words of treason again to me or anyone else and I will snap your neck like a dry twig."

"Boys, boys, calm down," said Corvax, as she tried to position herself between the two entangled raptors. "I'm sure Tobias here understands your, uh, points, perfectly. Plus, if you kill him, you would have to train a new lieutenant and you don't want to do that. Do you?"

Talax considered Corvax's council and decided Tobias was small compared to other things that needed to be dealt with. Also, he understood where Tobias was coming from. He, too, didn't like the way Rathgar had so easily dismissed the lives of their brethren.

"Tobias, get back to overseeing the construction of this tower. I see too many goblins just sitting around," said Talax.

Tobias nodded and flew off, chasing some goblins who had taken to sitting down on the job. "Back to work!" he bellowed, and goblins scattered in all directions away from the enraged eagle.

"Corvax, you will return to Troll's Rest, or at least the location we saw it at, and watch it carefully. But do not engage. If anything happens worthwhile, you let me know immediately. Take three of your best scouts. I want to know everyone that comes and goes from there. I expect regular reports. Now go!"

"Yes boss," responded Corvax, her voice cool and slick like water dripping into a pond. She cawed three times, and three other ravens joined her in flight.

As he watched his spies head south over the mountains, Talax couldn't help but wonder if he was on the right side, let alone the winning side. He ruffled his feathers and pulled himself up straight, trying to dispel any thoughts of doubt.

***

At Troll's Rest, Finn and his family had settled in for a long night of next steps. It was nearly dinnertime, and Hilde realized she needed more groceries.

"I need to go to the store in Homer. Anyone want to join and get a break?" she asked.

Lorelei stood. "Tallis and I can go with. I could use some girl time." She glimpsed Heidi sulking on the couch. "Sorry Heidi I didn't mean to offend you, it's just that . . ." She stopped.

"It's okay, as Mick pointed out I not a real girl," said Heidi.

Tallis smiled at her uncomfortably and stood to join her mother and Hilde. As she walked past Finn, she leaned in to give him a kiss, but Finn caught a look from Lorelei, and he quickly redirected it to a peck on the cheek.

Hilde opened the front door to the house and let out a shriek. Everyone else in the room jumped to their feet. Standing at the door was a great Bald Eagle.

"Hilde, watch out!" shouted Erik as he drew his weapon from its holster.

He aimed at the eagle and fired. The eagle flogged his huge wings, and the bullet sailed directly under, disappearing into the yard. Erik readied for another shot when Anders stepped between him and the bird.

"What are you doing?" Erik asked. "It was eagles just like him that attacked Finn and I at Norn's Forest!"

"That may be true," said Anders, "but he was not one of them. This is Heimdal and he is a friend."

"How can you know that?" asked Finn.

"Because he bares my crest. Show them, old friend," replied Anders.

Heimdal took a cautious step forward and stood taller to expose his right ankle. Around it was a small jade band with the Stonefist family crest on it. It glinted in the faint light of the porch.

"Well, I wish I could stick around for conversation, but I have shopping to do," said Hilde as she, Lorelei, and Tallis made their way past the giant bird.

"May I enter, King Anders?" Heimdal asked in a deep baritone voice as he bowed.

"My old friend, you do not need to bow before me. I am no longer king. I am just an old cripple, glad to see a familiar face. Please, do come in and tell us why you have come so suddenly."

Heimdal entered and stood next to the fireplace warming his tail feathers while Anders brought him up to speed on Finn, Heidi and Einar and everything else they had learned when Arna interrupted.

"Should we be telling him everything? I mean, most of us just met him and for all we know we could have another Heidi situation, and he is just the first wave to lull us into a false sense of security."

"This is nothing like before. This is Heimdal. Captain of the royal guard and one of the greatest warriors I have ever had the pleasure of knowing. He stayed loyal to me after they deposed me, and he served Finn's father with the same level of loyalty," snapped Anders.

"It's okay, Anders. The boy is wise to ask such questions. Judging by your boldness and your bearing, you are Arna Shatterfist," said Heimdal.

Arna looked shocked that Heimdal knew who he was.

"Yes, I know who you are. In fact, I already knew most of what you have told me. I have a wide network of spies and informants that are still loyal to the Stonefist family, and they have kept me apprised of your situation. When I heard eagles attacked you in the forest of the Norn, I knew I had to take a personal interest and get here as soon as I could. I would have come sooner, but I saw you had unexpected guests." Heimdal looked hard at Einar.

Einar stared back in disbelief. "I thought you were killed in the attack all those years ago. I watched you go down when the goblins swarmed the keep."

"I went down, and I was nearly killed, but my brethren pulled my lifeless body out and activated my jade ring and put me into the Jade sleep for days while I healed. I awoke the first time when Finn's mother summoned me and sent me to get Anders."

"Well, maybe you can tell us what our next step should be, since you seem to know so much," interjected Finn.

"Odin's beard, you have grown, my young king," said Heimdal, as he bowed.

"Don't do that," Finn said. "It makes me feel weird."

"You should get used to it, my King. You are the right true heir to the throne," Heimdal said. "And as for your next steps, I can only tell you that your uncle is constructing a great metal tower on top of Mount Denali. I do not know what goes on inside the mountain, but it appears to be some kind of transmitting tower. He has goblins and my brethren working on it day and night. I know this; without the King's Stone he cannot hope to activate it. In addition, I believe he is looking for the other pieces of the staff of Jotunheim."

Frustration flooded through Finn. They'd already wasted too much time. They needed to find the pieces of the staff.

Chapter 11

In the yard, Talon used the Way Finder staff to search for a piece of the Staff of Jotunheim. There were three pieces, the rod, the setting, and the Sapphire of Jotunheim. Since what they looked like was a mystery to Talon, he had to come up with his own visuals. The first clear image he came up with was a large blue gem. He said in his mind, "Show me the sapphire." With a rush of light and images, Talon felt the nausea again but fought through it. He then found himself inside an immense ice cave. Cold air blew on his skin. The room was dome-shaped and in the center was a stalagmite jutting straight up with what looked like the bluest ice Talon had ever seen.

"Hey, guys, I found it," he shouted. Then, remembering he was in his mind, he stopped himself. But where is this cave? Just then, the image rushed backwards, and Talon stared at a great glacier on the side of a mountain. A mountain he recognized.

"Okay, I have that. Now show me the setting," he thought.

Again, there was a rush of images and light, and suddenly in front of him was a gigantic figure carved from wood wearing what looked like a top hat.

"Zoom out," he thought.

The image pulled backwards, and he saw a lodge ornately decorated with totem style images of birds and whales. This was a place Talon didn't recognize, but maybe some else did. Finally, he focused on finding the rod. After the images settled, Talon found himself in a great cavern deep underground. The cavern was so tall he couldn't see the top. Extending from the darkness was a long metal rod that came nearly to the surface of the lake that covered much of the cavern floor. On a small strip of land, Talon could see a bright fire roaring inside of a large forge. He could see enormous birds lifting chunks of rock and ore into the top of a smelter. At one end, tiny figures were pouring the molten metal into forms while others pounded them straight and quenched the metal. There was a pile of metal rods that looked just like the ones extending from the ceiling. Talon saw a large figure standing near the pile. At first, he thought it was Einar or Finn in giant form, but as he zoomed in on the image, he realized it must be Rathgar. Talon noticed a rod in his hands. It looked like the others but was shorter and it had screw threads at one end, like something attached to the end. Suddenly Rathgar turned a faced Talon like he could see him except he was looking way over Talon's head. The giant roared and swiped a fist at the empty air in front of him. Talon took that as a clue that it was time to leave. He opened his eyes, and he was back in the yard alone. He was covered in sweat and felt weak. He stumbled back into the house. He heard his name being shrieked, but was too weak to react. Just before everything went dark, he could see his father running to his side.

As Talon stumbled into the house, his mother saw him first from the kitchen. "TALON!"

Mick saw his son, pale and sweaty, standing in the doorway. He leaped over the couch with surprising agility and caught Talon before he hit the ground. He scooped him up and laid his limp body on the couch. Talon was muttering but, there was one word everyone understood, Rathgar.

"If he has been using the Way Finder this whole time, he will be very drained and will need healing tea and a lot of rest," said Heidi. "The Way Finder uses a psychic connection to the host, and it can drain the unexperienced if they aren't careful."

"I'll make him a restorative tea," said Hilde.

"I'll help," said Tallis.

"Are you saying he could have died if he had been connected longer?" asked Lorelei.

"Yes," said Heidi quietly.

"Leave it to the Gods to give a child a loaded weapon and say have fun," said Lorelei.

"Now dear, I am sure Thor meant no harm when he gave Talon such a powerful gift," said Mick.

"Elves can withstand the power of great magic. His elf half is probably what saved him and allowed him to use it for so long," said Einar. "It's one reason my brother uses dark elves to do his spell work."

"Stroking my ego will not wake my son," snapped Lorelei.

Einar got quiet and sat back in his chair. Hilde returned with a cup of warm tea. She lifted Talon's head and gently tipped the cup to his lips. He unconsciously drank.

"Now let him rest now," Hilde said and shooed everyone out of the room except for Lorelei, who stayed kneeled next to her son and stroked the wet hair from his brow while holding his hand.

Hours passed as the family sat around the table, silently picking at the meatloaf Hilde had made. All thoughts were on Talon. Rathgar's name echoed in Finn's head as he fretted over what it could mean. Just then Talon sat bolt upright, causing a dozing Lorelei to jump.

"Rathgar!" he shouted.

Mick was at his side in a heartbeat. "What about Rathgar, my boy?"

"I saw him. He has the staff part of the Staff of Jotunheim. I think he is going to incorporate it into something. He is building something out of a forge. He has dozens of troops working on it." Talon felt dizzy and slumped onto the couch.

Finn Stonefist

"That's enough for tonight. We are going home, and you can rest in your own bed tonight," insisted Lorelei.

Talon resisted weakly. "No, I need to tell them while it's fresh."

He spent the next hour describing everything he had seen in his vision. When he finished, he slumped back into the couch and fell asleep. The room was quiet enough to hear a pin drop.

"What does it all mean?" asked Finn.

"That cavern is known as the Heart of the Mountain because it is right in the center of the Mountain," said Anders. "The quartz it is made of is very suitable for casting big magic. Our people hid there for a millennium until we had mastered the shift. Whatever Rathgar is planning is going to take tapping into the very core if Midgard and harnessing its magic at the source. The last time someone did that, it turned Jotunheim into a giant ice ball."

"It's simple then. We have to stop him. We have to find the other two pieces before Rathgar and get the staff piece back from him," said Tallis.

"Not tonight, you aren't. You all need rest, and this will seem clearer in the light of day." This time Lorelei was not taking no for an answer. She helped Talon to his feet and signaled Tallis to get the front door. Tallis came straight to her mother's aid.

"Yes, we will see you in the morning," said Mick, trying to sound supportive of his wife even though every bone in his body wanted to investigate what Talon had seen.

"Yes, come back in the morning, but not too early. I will have brunch ready around ten," said Hilde as she and Erik helped the Nightfeathers into their car.

Hilde shut the door and turned to face the room. "Now, as for you two," she said, pointing at Heidi and Einar. "I have no objection to you sleeping in my house as long as you promise not to kill each other or destroy what is left of my furniture. Heidi, you can have the guest room and Einar, you can have the couch."

"Since the dark shift, I don't sleep . . . ever," said Einar, looking slightly uncomfortable.

"Well, that's not creepy at all," laughed Arna. "So you're just going to stay up all night watching us sleep?"

"Well, I have a list of farm chores that have gone neglected the last few days," Ander said. "Mucking the barn and cleaning up the forge and such."

Einar actually grinned. "I would welcome the distraction. Just tell me what to do."

"And with that, boys, to your rooms, Heidi to your room," said Erik.

Everyone dispersed to their different rooms, and soon Einar was alone in the living room with a list of chores that Anders had written.

***

The quiet of Finn's room seems to ring in his ears. It felt like forever since he had been in his room and laid on his own bed. As Finn laid on his bed, exhaustion took over and his eyes got heavy. Images of the last few days filled his dreams. Everything from Thor to his father showing up. The fight he had with Einar. His heart was racing, and he felt hot. Just then, a sharp pain in his hand woke him from his nightmarish slumber. Finn woke with a start and looked at his hand, which made him jump in panic. His hand was on fire! He jumped to his feet and waved his hand around frantically, trying to extinguish the flames, but to no avail. Just then, Einar burst into the room.

"Son, calm yourself and focus on putting the fire out!" said Einar as calmly as possible.

"I'm trying, but it doesn't want to go out!" said Finn. He was in full on panic mode and could feel the shift bubbling to the surface.

"If you don't calm down, you are going to shift and since we are on the second floor, that could be really bad. Your grandpa will be less than pleased if you break his house again."

Finn took a deep breath and stared into the flames that were his hand. He focused on making them smaller and smaller. The flames reacted and slowly reduced until they were completely out. He looked up at Einar and hugged him as tight as he could.

"Thank you," he said before he realized he was hugging Einar.

The hug surprised Einar, and he didn't really know what to do, so he gently hugged his son back.

"What the hell was that? How did you know?" Finn asked quickly.

"I was in the barn doing the chores when I sensed your panic," Einar said. "At first I thought it was just a nightmare, but then it jumped in intensity, so I ran up here as fast as I could. You must have a bit of fire ogre in you."

"Is that good?" said Finn. He wasn't sure how he felt about spontaneous combustion.

"Not really," Einar said. "Your fire ogre is the dark side of an ice giant and when your negative emotions get out of control, like during a nightmare, then it can manifest in small ways."

"Would I be able to control fire?" asked Finn.

"Yes, but it's a very dangerous element. Fire comes from the most passionate part of you and can be easily corrupted to do evil. It is unpredictable, which is why most ice giants never explore that side of themselves. The ones that have, have met disaster most of the time." Einar sat on the edge of Finn's bed, which groaned under the ogre's weight. "I suggest you stick to learning how to control water and ice and stay far away from fire lest you end up like me. You broke Rathgar's hold on my mind, but I am still a darkling and I don't know what that means for my fate," sighed Einar "I am just grateful for the time the Gods have given me with you but, I fear I am still a danger to you and the others."

Finn sat next to Einar, "We've gotten you this far. I have to believe there is a way to get you all the way back," said Finn.

Einar smiled, but just then the bed buckled under the stress of the two giants sitting on it. It cracked and snapped in half, crashing to the floor, dumping its occupants. Both Finn and Einar looked at each other and laughed loudly.

Just then, the hall light came on and Finn's door opened. It was Anders. "What is all the commotion in here?"

Finn and Einar just laughed louder.

"You two are hopeless. I'm going back to bed," he said and shuffled back down the hall.

As Einar laughed, his fiery red veins blinked with shades of blue and his skin got really cool for just a second.

"What was that?" asked Finn. The laughter stopped.

Einar took a couple of deep breaths. "I don't know. I felt cold suddenly."

"Maybe you need more clothes. You have been wearing the same tattered shorts since you, uh, arrived," said Finn.

"I guess I have," said Einar. "But I doubt you have anything that will fit me, let alone stand up to my hot nature."

"I don't, but I think I know how we can get some," said Finn.

They got off the floor as quietly and two large bodies can get off a crushed bed. They tiptoed down the stairs to the hall closet, where Finn retrieved Anders's box made of Asgardian wood.

"Dad still has his box from the Gods. How did he get it from the keep?" asked Einar.

"I don't know, but I know this box is where I got the clothes I have on now, and they can hold up to shifting so I imagine they can withstand a stone giant fire ogre or whatever you are," said Finn.

Finn removed the box from its resting place on the top shelf next to old photo albums. When he wiped the dust from the top, he touched the rune and the box hummed. The rune glowed blue faintly.

"I don't know if anyone is listening at the other end of this thing, but I need a set of clothes for my father, Einar Stonefist."

At first, nothing happened. The box remained empty. Then suddenly the box got considerably heavier. Finn slid the top of the box open. He reached inside and retrieved a T-shirt, jeans, socks, underwear, and a pair of work boots and a belt with a buckle in the shape of the Stonefist family crest. He handed the pile to Einar, who took them straight into the bathroom to change. A few minutes later, he emerged fully dressed.

"How do they fit?" asked Finn.

"They fit perfectly. Like something tailored them just for me," said Einar. "Hey, does your grandpa still keep a tub of Rocky Road in the freezer?"

Finn leaned close. "Don't tell Hilde, but yes. He has to hide it from her, or she throws it out."

***

The next morning, Hilde came down to start her famous brunch. Soon the house smelled of fresh coffee and bacon, eggs, pancakes, and fried hash browns. The smell had a stirring effect, and soon bleary-eyed people emerged from their respective rooms and gravitated towards the food. Hilde had to hold Arna and Finn off with a kitchen knife.

"Wait until the Nightfeathers arrive," she ordered.

Sullenly, they complied and consoled their hunger with glasses of orange juice. Just then, the doorbell rang. Finn and Arna nearly bowled each other over, trying to get there first. Finn shifted one arm and held his cousin at bay while he opened the door.

"Hey, no fair!" said Arna

Finn just smiled and then saw who was at the door. It was Heimdal, not Tallis.

"My king," said Heimdal as he bowed low.

Finn rolled his eyes and hollered, "Grandpa, it's for you"

Anders appeared by the door, still in his pajamas.

"Come in, Heimdal. Have you eaten?" he asked.

"Yes, my K... Anders, I had a salmon before I came, but that is beside the point. I have dangerous news."

"Well, don't just stand there. Spit it out, friend," said Anders.

"My scouts tell me that ravens have surrounded the property and are watching from every angle. While the warding prevents them from actually seeing you, they seem to have pinpointed this location. Probably during Einar's attack. If you leave, they will spot you," said Heimdal.

"Some of us left last night to go grocery shopping and nothing happened. Why didn't they attack us?" asked Hilde.

"They are probably under orders to observe and report only. At least that's what I would do, and I taught their current general, Talax," said Heimdal.

"We are waiting on the Nightfeather family and once they are here, we can eat and plan our next step. Until then, come in and make yourself comfortable will you, old friend," said Anders.

With that, Heimdal entered the house and perched on what was left of an armchair. Just as he got settled, the front door burst open with Mick stumbling through with an armful of books. Tripping on the carpet, he nearly dropped the books on Heimdal but steadied himself just in time. Mick's hair was pushed to one side, and he had a wild look in his eyes. Behind him Tallis made her way to Finn's side, and Talon came in looking more rested but still pale from the events of last night. Lorelei made her way past her husband and went straight to the kitchen with her famous scalloped potatoes and fruit salad dishes to add to the already large spread Hilde had made.

"Anders, Finn! You won't believe what I have found!" Mick dumped the books onto the couch in front of him.

"Did you sleep last night?" asked Finn.

"No, he didn't. The old fool was up all night ransacking our family library," said Lorelei.

"First, we eat, then we talk. Besides, I have a feeling this maybe the last family meal we have for a long time," said Hilde as she shot a worried look Erik's way.

"Yes, yes, let us eat together one more time without talking of monsters and evil plans," agreed Anders.

Quin Folkestad

The group surrounded the large family table and enjoyed the enormous meal prepared by loving hands. There were jokes told and sounds of laughter filled the room. Finn noticed that for just a minute everything felt normal. Even Einar didn't seem out of place to him anymore.

"Is this what an intact family feels like?" he wondered, but he knew one piece was missing and he had to find her. He knew in the back of his mind that the staff was important but, saving his mother was something he would do. Alone if he had to.

After brunch, everyone sat in the living room as Hilde and Lorelei served coffee and hot cocoa to everyone.

"Dear, I think now would be a good time to tell everyone what you found last night during your research," said Lorelei to Mick.

"Oh, yes dear," said Mick, as he took a sip of his cocoa and put it down. He stood and gathered the books. "Now, everyone involved with the staff all those years ago had their memories of it wiped, including the king, Anders. That way no one would know where any of the pieces were hidden and thus preventing anyone from reconstructing it."

"We know this already," said Finn impatiently

"That is true, my boy, but what we forgot to wipe all those years ago was the history books. In our family history, I found a clue. Anders, do you remember who your chief of magic was?" asked Mick.

Anders paused for a moment. "Well, now that was a long time ago but, now that you mention it, I can't recall who it was."

"Correct!" said Mick. "Because you had him wiped from yours and everyone's memories. Now remember, my wife, being an elf, has all of her family history and in it she has records of all the deeds of her people and that includes her parents."

"Grandma and Grandpa?" asked Tallis and Talon at the same time.

"Your grandpa was the Chief of Magic for the then King Anders and was so for many years, and he would have known where Anders had the pieces hidden. But when it came time to wipe it from his memory, something went wrong. We don't know if it was because of his Elven mind or if something went wrong with the spell. Whatever the reason, it didn't work. It only made him mad as a hatter. He had to go into hiding for fear he would give the locations away unintentionally. The minds of his direct family members were altered to think he had developed Elven Alzheimer's, and he was put into the senior citizen home under Elven care in Homer."

"If this was never to be known, how do you know it?" asked Finn.

"Well, that my boy was a bit a luck or the will of the Gods or who knows, but during my, uh, research, I knocked my drink over, and the tea spilled onto an old journal of Lorelei's mother. I had read it looking for clues but found nothing until the tea spilled on it and in between the lines was a set of Elven characters that appeared." Mick looked around the room at blank stares. "Before her mind was wiped and her husband taken from her, Lorelei's mother had written what had happened to her husband, probably in hopes of this very moment. That we would find the truth and help him."

"I still don't see how this is going to help us," said Finn.

"Each part of the staff on its own is a powerful object, and so they won't just be thrown anywhere. They would be very well protected. Lorelei's father might hold a clue on how to retrieve the objects safely."

"I want to talk to him," Finn said.

"Agreed," Mick said. "Lorelei will go with you. And after you two return with any information you can glean from his ramblings, we will go retrieve the Sapphire of Jotunheim."

"How do we avoid Rathgar's spies?" Lorelei asked.

"Before anyone leaves or does anything else, Heimdal, I need you to take care of our raven problem," said Anders.

"I'm on it," Heimdal said, and he made his way to the back-patio door. In one motion, he was airborne and headed south towards the river.

He saw his first target from the corner of his eye, a small raven sitting just outside the barrier, high in an old spruce tree. Heimdal soared high but still inside the barrier, so he was invisible to the unsuspecting raven. In a quick flash, he reached out with his talons and snatched the onlooker by the head and snapped his neck like a dry twig in one swift motion. The next two were just as easy since they positioned themselves as close to the barrier as they could without being vaporized. Now all that was left was Corvax.

Heimdal circled the property looking for her, but she was no novice, unlike her three cohorts. Then, just to the south of the property, he spotted her in a birch tree, hiding amongst the leaves stiff as a statue. The tree was about a hundred yards outside of the barrier. That was smart. She could see him coming. Heimdal flew straight up. As he approached the barrier, his jade ring glowed bright green and allowed him to pass fully unharmed. Once through the barrier, he flipped into a straight dive at his target, but she saw him coming. She didn't flinch until the last second when she dropped from her branch, spread her wings, and soared along the forest floor. Heimdal clipped a wing on the tree's trunk but recovered quickly enough to stay on Corvax with deadly precision.

Corvax looked over her shoulder and cawed with laughter as she banked straight up, but not before Heimdal swiped at her with his great beak snagging some tail feathers. Heimdal could see Corvax's flight was erratic because of the missing feathers, so he put some speed on. He got nearly close enough to grab her with his talons, but he banked right and clipped her with a wing, knocking her into a nearby tree. Corvax fell lifelessly to the ground and rolled to a stop.

Heimdal landed cautiously nearby and stepped closer. He kicked her onto her back. She lashed back with her talons, which, being much smaller than Heimdal's own talons, easily deflected him. He put a foot on one of Corvax's outstretched wings and stepped down. He could feel the fragile bone crunch like bubble wrap under his weight. Corvax cawed in pain, but she knew she was going nowhere.

"Just kill me," said Corvax.

"Oh, I need you alive. We seem to be collecting chief lieutenants, and you will be a very informative addition. Plus, your wing will never heal right without proper care and Rathgar doesn't strike me as the kind that has healthcare for is employees." Then Heimdal punched Corvax with his foot. rendering her unconscious.

...

Chapter 12

As Lorelei and Finn drove the fifteen miles from Troll's Rest into Homer, it was quiet. Finn had known Lorelei most of his life but to be alone in the car with her without Tallis to play go-between. He felt nervous and very much on the spot.

Lorelei, sensing Finn's discomfort, broke the tension. "Have you ever met my father?"

"No, Tallis has never spoken of him," Finn responded.

"I can see why. She only sees him on holidays, and in his state he is hard to get to know. I think it always scared her a bit to see him. He can be very unsettling," said Lorelei.

"What do you mean 'unsettling?'"

"Well, he doesn't seem to make a lot of sense, and he gets agitated easily. It's like he is trying to say something important, but something stops him. He..." she paused. "You'll see."

The blue gray building of the senior center looked cheerful with its hanging baskets of flowers and the small courtyard that was well taken care of. It certainly didn't look like a place housing a deranged elder elf. As they entered the building, an older lady with white hair and bright red lipstick sitting behind a large reception desk greeted them.

"Lorelei!" said the woman.

"Hello, Gay, how are you today?"

"I am well," said Gay. "I see you have company today."

"Yes. This is Tallis's boyfriend, Finn, Finn Stonefist. He heard I was coming to visit, and he wanted to meet the famous Aaron Edon that we talk so much about," said Lorelei.

It wasn't until Lorelei told Gay Finn's name that something changed. Finn hadn't noticed at first, but he could sense Gay's aura. Then he saw it.

"You're an elf!" Finn blurted out, then realized it was louder than he intended. He shrunk back at the sound of his own voice and looked around to see if anyone heard him, but the lobby seemed empty except for the three of them.

Gay laughed out loud. Her laugh sounded like a witch's cackle.

"Yes, I am, young giant, and I know exactly who you are. Your grandfather and I have known each other for a very long time. And don't worry about humans hearing you. There are none on staff, and the patients barely know what day it is let alone what they hear, if they can hear." Gay handed Lorelei a clipboard. "I'll need you to sign a consent for young mister Stonefist."

As the three of them walked through the corridors, Finn looked at all the different patients and he could sense their auras. "Is everyone here like us?"

Lorelei said, "Many are, but not all. This place was taken over by the Elven high council to provide a place for us to house our kind when they need more help than their families can provide."

"This is also a place that is safe for them to shift should that happen unintentionally," said Gay.

"How do you keep the human patients and guests from seeing?" asked Finn.

"The property is protected so that instead of a rampaging giant or rambling gnome or an enraged dwarf they just see a human throwing a fit," said Gay.

As they reached the end of the corridor, they came to a set of double doors with large windows in each one. Outside was a green lawn with a pond in the middle and a bench just to the right of it. On the far side of the lawn, there was an area with tables and chairs shaded by a large cloth canopy. As they stepped outside, the air in the courtyard was warm and fragrant with the smell of flowers. It was encircled by large flower beds that seemed to burst with blossoms. There was a large cherry tree in the center of one bed that still had blossoms on them. Finn was amazed that there were so many flowers for the time of year. Most flowers wouldn't have even bloomed yet.

"How do you keep up such a garden?" Finn asked.

"It's not us, it's all him," said Gay as she gestured to a man kneeling at the side of the pond feeding the few ducks that called it home.

At first Finn had dismissed the man as one of the staff, but then realized the man was the only other person in the garden.

"He can somehow keep it like this all year. Only our kind can see it for what it truly is, a veritable oasis in the middle of a bustling city," said Lorelei.

They approached the man, who didn't seem to notice them at first.

"Hi papa," said Lorelei.

The man looked up and an enormous smile erupted across his face.

"Little Lori, you're here!" he said as he embraced her. Over her shoulder, he glimpsed Finn and jumped back.

"Who is this imposter?!" yelled the man.

"Papa, let me explain," said Lorelei quickly. "This is Finn, Finn Stonefist. Anders's grandson. Finn, this is Aaron, my dad."

Aaron looked down and grabbed the nearby garden hoe and raised it over his head.

"That is not possible! He is dead and they can fake appearances," he said.

"He is not an imposter, Papa," insisted Lorelei.

"You could be a fake sent by Him to trick me into giving secrets about the shiny."

Lorelei turned to Finn. "Don't be afraid, just show him you are not a fake. Show him who you really are."

At first, Finn was confused, but judged that showing his true self was better than getting brained with a garden hoe. He reached into his coat pocket and produced the King's Stone.

At the sight of it, Aaron stumbled backward a couple of steps and yelled, "FAKE!"

"Finn, show him now," yelled Lorelei.

Finn focused his mind and just as Aaron was about to swing his impromptu weapon, Finn shifted into his full thirty-foot form. He then allowed the King's Stone to climb his limbs and chest. There was a flash and the Guardian's armor appeared on Finn with the Stonefist crest etched into the breastplate, just as before. Finn looked down and saw a dumbstruck Aaron, who had dropped his hoe and fallen to his knees. Lorelei was at his side, and Gay was standing with her mouth wide open in a silent scream. Finn shifted back to human form and approached Aaron, who was trembling on his knees. Aaron leaned forward and grabbed Finn by the ankles and said, "My king!"

Finn kneeled before Aaron. "I am not king yet. Rathgar is not defeated yet, and that is why we are here. He has a terrible plan to use the Staff of Jotunheim on Midgard's magic. And we need your help. I need to know everything you can tell me about the Sapphire of Jotunheim."

Aaron became pale and shook.

"Mr. Edon, are you okay?" asked Finn, giving a worried look to Lorelei.

Lorelei kneeled next to her trembling father and put a hand on his shoulder. "Papa, the Gods have taken their favor from Rathgar and given Finn the King's Stone. They want him to stop Rathgar."

Lorelei's words seem to calm Aaron some, but not much.

"But shiny squish, squish. Never go, never see, NEVER TOUCH!" Aaron stammered.

"What does that mean?" asked Finn.

"I don't know," said Lorelei. "This happens when he tries to remember the old days. He just rambles and makes no sense.

Finn looked Aaron in the eyes and pleaded with him. "Sir, you are the only one who knows if there is anything guarding the jewel. You alone can give us the clues we need to retrieve the jewel safely."

"Indiana Jones had it right! No touchy!" said Aaron and then returned to repeatedly muttering, "shiny squish, squish..." quietly while he trembled in Lorelei's arms.

"I think that is quite enough!" said a voice from behind them. Finn turned to see a slim, well-dressed older woman standing directly behind Gay. Her sudden appearance startled the old nurse, such that a small yip escaped her lips.

"Madame Edon!" said Gay.

"Gay, please take Aaron to his room to rest. I think he has had enough excitement for one day," said Madame Edon.

Lorelei, who helped get her father to his feet.

"Is that your...?" Finn asked.

"Mother? Yes," said Lorelei.

"Hello, Lorelei" said Madame Edon shortly.

"How long have you been there?" asked Lorelei.

"Long enough. Finn, it is a pleasure to make the acquaintance of the one true king. Please call me Edna." She took Finn by the hand.

"Mother, you have to know we wouldn't bother him with this if it wasn't important, but we found your old diary that you hid an entry in, and we had to talk to Papa."

"I understand, child. I left that entry in hopes someone someday would find it and that we could restore your father to his regal self. While I don't remember those days, I remember that entry. It has been the only thing keeping me going all these years. It killed me, but I had to lie to you and your brothers," said Edna.

"I know you did it to protect us," said Lorelei.

"Unfortunately, we got little from him on the subject. Could you enlighten us? What protections guard the gem?" asked Finn.

"Like everyone else, my knowledge of those things was taken from me," said Edna. "But I can tell you that if my Aaron set up the wards, and they will not be easily bested and there will be a cost. He was always big into the Christian saying an eye for an eye,"

"I am sorry, but we must tell the others what we have learned, mother," said Lorelei.

As they left the garden, Finn couldn't help but notice how dark it had gotten.

"Is it evening already?" he asked.

"It's the magic of the garden," said Lorelei. "Time moves slower in there. So, while we were only in there an hour, most of the day passed on out here. You'll get used to it."

The car ride was quiet. Both were deep in thought. Finn wondered what Aaron's ramblings meant and what the cost could be that Edna spoke of. As they pulled into the driveway, their families met them on the front porch.

"You were gone for hours," said Tallis as she hugged and kissed Finn.

In the living room, Finn could feel the group's anticipation of knowing what he and Lorelei had learned from Aaron. So

Finn told them about the garden and the amazing magic surrounding it.

"The only bad thing is when I asked Aaron about the jewel, he started talking in gibberish. He kept talking about a shiny which I think is the jewel and that it should never be searched for or seen or even touched, and something that goes squish, squish and then Edna said that if Aaron protected the jewel, there will be a cost in retrieving it. Although, she didn't know what it could be."

"The babbling results from Aaron's mind struggling to tell you the truth but the mind spell trying to stop him, but he may have given you some helpful info that we can't decipher until we get there," said Mick.

"So, you think you're going as well, do you?" said Lorelei.

"I do. Someone has to watch over them," Mick responded.

"I'm going too!" said Erik and Einar at the same time, then gave each other a strange look.

"The least I can do I protect my son. If you will have me," said Einar.

"Easy now, not everyone can go," said Anders. "Some of you will have to stay here and protect Troll's Rest. The capturing of Rathgar's chief spy will not go unnoticed. So, I propose That Finn, Arna, Mick, Tallis, and Einar go and the rest of you stay here and prepare for their return."

"I didn't think my father could leave the property because of the binding rune," said Finn.

"I have something that might help that." Anders stood and disappeared into his bedroom. A few moments later, he returned with a small wooden box. Inside were several small silver rings bearing the Stonefist insignia. "I took these with me when I left the keep. Mostly as mementos, but I had a feeling I would need them again someday"

Finn Stonefist

"What are they, grandpa?" asked Finn.

"Well, after your uncle's first attack, I was injured and weak. I couldn't rule so; the elders decided your father should take my place as king because the people needed a strong and healthy ruler."

"That was never my wish, father....." interrupted Einar.

"Oh, never mind that. It was a smart move. A move I would have made. Anyway, after the attack and after I had recovered, I went looking for the Norn that took your grandmother and who left me broken and stuck in human form but, before I left I took these rings. They were given to my most trusted guards. Sadly, they were all killed in the attempted coup."

"Father, that would mean those are the rings of fealty! I thought we lost them after the attack," said Einar.

Anders got a sheepish look on his face. "I know I shouldn't have taken them, but I had lost so much already. I just wanted to keep the memory of my men alive somehow. You see, each ring is bound to the King's Ring." Anders produced from his pocket a silver ring with a large blue stone in the middle surrounded by twelve smaller stones each of a different color. "The center stone is Asgardian sapphire surrounded by a birthstone for each month of the year. There are twelve stones and twelve rings. The rings are dwarven made all hewn from Asgardian silver and will fit whoever wears the ring. Now since I am the last coronated king of Midgard who isn't a dark shifter, the master ring will only work for me." Ander slipped the ring over his right middle finger and stared at it with a puzzled look.

"What is it grandpa?" asked Finn.

"Well, when I put the ring on, the stone should have glowed as a sign it recognized the king but, nothing happened," said Anders.

"No disrespect old man, but you're not king anymore. The Gods have given their favor to Finn," said Heidi from the back of the group.

Everyone looked shocked at her boldness and Hilde looked like she might smack the smart mouth little girl.

Anders put his hand up. "It's alright. She is correct. I hadn't thought of it, but like the King's Stone, the King's ring works on the same principles. It says on the inside of the ring, 'He who wears the ring walks with the Gods.' I had never thought much about it, but it must mean that if you wear the ring, you have some favor with the Gods. Here Finn, you try it on." Anders handed the ring to Finn.

Finn shrunk back. "The last time I used something from the Gods I shredded Aunt Hilde's living room. The king's ring seems a little too official for me. I mean, this would make my claim to the throne official. I don't know if I am ready to take that step. I don't even know how to be a king."

"Finn, if this ring works for you, then not even Rathgar can challenge your claim to the throne," said Mick, trying to reassure him.

"My boy," said Einar, "Do you love Midgard? Do you love your family? Do you want to stop Rathgar?"

Finn nodded yes to all of his father's questions.

"Then know that you have the support and love of the Gods and your family. We will not let you fail. This ring is merely a symbol of the king I know you are inside, and I know this because you are my son and you come from a long line of great kings and queens and you will do extraordinary things, but right now we need you to put on the damn ring so we can stop my psychotic brother."

Finn took a deep breath and accepted the ring from his grandfather's outstretched hand. It was larger than Finn's finger and felt cool and heavy as he slipped it over his right middle finger. Just then, the ring hummed, and it shrank down to fit snugly around his finger. The blue stone in the middle glowed bright causing the surrounding stones to sparkle in its light. The ring had accepted Finn as the rightful king.

"So now what do we kneel and kiss the ring or something?" said Arna jokingly.

"Not quite, but you have to swear an oath," said Anders, and he reached into the box of smaller rings and retrieved one with an orange stone. The stone was about half the size of the King's ring and looked like an orange berry surrounded by silver leaves.

Tallis looked in wonder. "That is the most beautiful Topaz I have ever seen. They are normally so dull and brown."

"This is an Asgardian stone mined in Asgard and gifted to the first queen of Midgard," said Anders as he handed it to Finn. "Take this ring and present it to Tallis and repeat after me."

Finn looked like someone had just told him to propose. He was pale, and he looked like he might throw up and burst out laughing at the same time. Sweat covered his brow and his stomach was in knots. He took the ring from his grandfather and immediately started to shake like a leaf. He was certain he was going to drop it. He held the ring up to Tallis, and she gave him a wry smile, which only made his nerves worse.

"Now, say these words. 'Do you Tallis Nightfeather swear your allegiance to the realm of Midgard and to me Finn

Stonefist as King of Midgard and king of all Asgardian citizens?"

As Finn repeated the words, he was sure he was going to shake to death. When he finished, Tallis stared into his eyes, making him even more uncomfortable.

"Why Finn Stonefist, I do," said Tallis laughingly, as she gave him her right hand.

Finn took it and with a heavy sigh, he slid the little ring onto her right ring finger. The stone glowed brightly, and the ring assumed the correct size.

"Each of you will have to take the same oath to receive your rings. With them, you will be duty and honor bound to serve Finn and the realm. With his one ring, he can find you anywhere in the nine realms and he can feel when you are in danger or in need of him. Should you be in dire straits, simply touch the stone on your ring and it will cause the corresponding stone on the Finn's ring to glow. He can then touch it and a portal will open to take you to wherever he is. Also, if he should need your presence, he will signal you by touching your corresponding stone, then pressing his sapphire. Your rings will instantly bring you to his aid. The first few times that you portal it is rough, so I suggest practicing in the yard over short distances. These are powerful tools meant only for the king and his most trusted guards. In the wrong hands, someone can cause actual harm."

With that, Anders continued to pull out rings and hand them to Finn. Talon's ring was also a Topaz since he was Tallis' twin, but he had a wolf's head for a setting with the gem held in its mouth. Anders explained the wolf was Fenrir and a symbol of strength. The next was Arna/ Being born in July, his was a bright red ruby and when he said his oath it glowed like a small flame. The stone sat in the middle of a silver sun that glinted orange when the stone glowed. Heidi wasn't so keen on swearing another oath to another supposed king, but she needed protection and she could use whatever favor with the Gods, it would get her.

"What month were you born?" asked Finn, trying to sound official and hide his nervousness about offering another girl a ring.

"Well, Finny, when I was born, we didn't have months. We just had the seasons to measure time, but I have always been partial to Emeralds," she said as she batted her long dark eyelashes over her bright green eyes.

"Right," said Finn with a catch in his throat.

"Emerald it is!" said Anders.

Finn repeated the oath and Heidi accepted the terms. The blue topaz glowed brightly in its tree-shaped setting.

"A tree, very fitting.?" said Heidi

Hilde stepped forward. "I'll take the oath. Mine is April."

"I know Auntie, and thank you," said Finn and repeated the oath and handed her the ring. It had a bright clear diamond that sat in a setting of two cupping hands.

Erik was next. Anders pulled the February ring from the box. It had a deep purple amethyst in the shape of a heart. The stone sat in the middle of the head of a silver dragon.

"That is Jormungandr, the world serpent who lives in the sea near the heart of Midgard," said Mick.

"Well, that's pretty cool," Erik said. He took the oath and received his ring.

Mick and Lorelei stepped forward.

"You two wish to take the oath?" asked Finn.

"Actually, my boy, we did already many years ago, but when we had children, our rings were passed to new guards, but we were on the original guard for your grandfather," said Mick.

"Wait, what?" Tallis said. "You guys were elite trained soldiers?" Talon looked equally surprised.

Lorelei looked at the gaping mouths of the children and said, "We were cool once too, you know!"

"As having already sworn the oath, your oath will transfer to Finn if you but accept the rings back," said Anders.

Mick looked at Lorelei. "One more adventure, my love?"

"Once more for old times and old friends in the past and present," responded Lorelei. They accepted their rings and put them on.

"Fits like a glove and feels like an old friend," said Mick. Mick's ring was an alexandrite for May and was in a setting of silver feathers. Lorelei's was a Forget-me-not with each of the five petals made of blue sapphire. It was the only gold ring in the bunch.

Finally, it was Einar's turn. He stepped forward and asked, "May I take the oath and help my son?"

"If you do this, you will be effectively giving up the throne to your son and you will no longer have a claim to it unless he dies with no heir," said Anders.

"Whoa, heavy," said Arna

"I had my time and now it is his time," Einar said. "The Gods have made that clear. I only hope to help him be a better king than we were."

Anders agreed and gave the ring to Finn. It was a large ring with a silver fist in the middle, studded with garnets on the fingers. Finn took the ring and faced his father.

"Einar Stonefist, do you swear your allegiance to the realm of Midgard and to me Finn Stonefist as King of Midgard and king of all Asgardian citizens?"

"I do," said Einar. He raises his hand to accept his ring.

Finn hesitated and asked, "Do you also swear to do everything possible and impossible to save my mother?"

This shocked Einar, but he knew the answer. He put a heavy hand on Finn's shoulder and looked him in the eyes. "I will scour the nine realms until I can find a way to save her, this I swear to the Gods, this family, and most of all to you, my king and my son." A tear filled the corner of his eye.

Finn could feel the emotions welling up and quickly handed Einar the ring. He wiped the tears that threatened to escape.

There were still two rings left.

"What do we do with the other two?" he asked.

"The one that has an emerald alexandrite is your mother's and the other one with Tourmaline is for your grandmother, should she ever return to us," said Anders quietly.

Anders snapped the box shut, thus breaking the solemn silence that had followed. The rest of the evening was spent in the backyard playing a kind of hide and seek. The others would hide, and Finn would use the King's Ring to find them. It wasn't very fair game since Finn could portal them to him or just portal in right next to them. After a while, everyone felt comfortable with the rings and only Arna and Erik threw up on their first portals. Tallis and Talon handled it like old pros. Mick explained it was their elf half side. Elves were hardier towards the effects of magic. Finn also seemed to portal easily. He figured it had to do with the fact that he was a Sammeloper.

Later that night, sitting around the fire in the living room, Finn asked, "Can we leave first thing in the morning?" He didn't want to wait another minute to go after the Sapphire of Jotunheim.

Erik seemed to think about this. "We need to charter a boat or plane to get us to China Poot Bay and then there is the matter of going and coming back with a huge gemstone without being noticed by Rathgar's spies."

"There's also the matter of what is guarding the sapphire," said Mick.

"You guys are so human in your thinking," Heidi said. "So limited."

"What's your suggestion?" asked Erik.

"Talon can take us undetected, or at least most of the way," she said.

Everyone stared at her with confusion. Especially Talon.

"The Way Finder can do more than show you the way. It can take you there as well," said Heidi.

"You just thought to tell us this now?" asked Mick.

"Well, the catch is that the easiest way to get back is through the same portal you walked through," Heidi said. "So the portal caster, in this case Talon, will have to hold it open the whole time you are there and since last time nearly killed him, this will most certainly kill him."

"Can we fortify him?" asked Hilde.

"A rune of strength would fortify his body," said Mick.

"And I know a tea that can strengthen his mind and spirit for a short time. Maybe an hour or two," said Hilde.

"How do we give him the rune?" asked Lorelei, glancing nervously at her son.

"There is really only one way to do it, so we are sure it will connect with him. We will need to brand it over his heart," said Mick.

"Does Talon get choice in the branding decisions in his life?" asked Talon.

Finn Stonefist

"You get a choice," Mick said. "But this is the only sure way. Even the strongest amulets can break under this kind of magic. In order to make sure the strength comes from your very soul, we must bind it in flesh and fire."

Talon thought for a moment. "I guess this is the first test of my oath. I made an oath to serve the king, and that is Finn so, if Finn asks this of me then I will do it." He looked at Finn. "Do you ask me as king to do this?"

Finn hesitated for a moment. "I do, Talon, but not only as king but as your friend. I will get the rune as well. I think a good king should only ask of that which he will do himself."

"You boys prepare yourselves," Mick said. "Your first rune is no joke. It will hurt and it will be with you your entire lives."

With that, Mick, Erik, and Anders went to the barn to prepare the brand, and Hilde and Lorelei went to the kitchen to prepare the tea. Tallis threw her arms around her brother and Finn.

"I know why you are doing it, but you are fools none the less," she said.

"True," Talon said. "Just hope it doesn't run in the family."

About an hour later, Erik appeared in the backdoor. "Finn, Talon, it's time."

The boys stood and walked towards the door. Tallis stood to follow, but Erik stopped her. "It's best if you stay here with your mom," he said.

Tallis thought paused, then kissed each of them on the cheek and took her place next to her mom. Lorelei was on the verge of tears when she hugged them. "I am so proud of both of you. We will see you shortly."

Finn and Talon followed Erik out to the barn in silence. As they entered the barn, Anders and Mick greeted them.

"Normally when a soldier receives their first rune there is a lot of ceremony, but given the times, a drafty old barn and us are all ceremony you can expect," said Anders.

"Now remove your shirts and Talon take a seat on the stool. It is important that you hold as still as possible until I am done. If the rune is not completely seared in, it could fail, and that could be disastrous," said Mick.

"How bad is disastrous?" asked Talon.

"You could explode, but I won't let that happen!" said Mick upon seeing the color drain from Talon's face.

Just then Arna busted into the barn. "Wait!" he yelled.

"Arna, what are you doing here?" asked Erik.

"I want the rune too."

"Why?" Anders asked.

"Well, Talon, Finn and I have done everything together for as long as I can remember so I figured why should I miss out on this. I took the same oath, and I think we are going to need all the help we can get tomorrow," said Arna.

Just then, Einar appeared in the barn's doorway. "Father! It occurs to me that tradition dictates that a soldier's first rune be given by the father. I would like to do this for my son if it is okay with him."

Finn's heart warmed. "I would love that," he said.

"I want the rune as well! Why should only the boys get it. I took the same oath and I am going on the same journey and will be in the same amount of danger," said Tallis, appearing from behind Einar.

"Very well, and bolt the door before anybody else joins us," grumbled Anders.

"Okay Talon, you will go first, remove your shirt and sit. Did you understand the process?" asked Mick.

Finn stepped forward. "As king, shouldn't I go first to set the example for my men?"

"We thought about that but as a Sammeloper we don't really know how the rune will react to you," said Mick. "You see, it enhances the active abilities in someone and since the others haven't gone through the shift, yet it will only enhance their human form."

"It's okay we got this," said Talon

Talon took a deep breath and sat on the stool. Mick stood in front of Talon with a brand at the end of a short rod. The rune was three lines in the shape of an arch. He applied the white fiery brand to Talon's skin just above his heart. Talon didn't cry out, instead he gritted his teeth and gripped hard on the stool. The branded flashed green and Mick pulled it away. Talon slumped forward, catching his breath. Covered in sweat, he hugged his father and stood to near the fire to inspect his new rune. Tallis removed her t-shirt, making Finn blush and Talon look like he was going to wretch. Mick repeated the process to Tallis. And like her brother, she did not make a sound. She just gritted her teeth until the brand flashed green. She stood from the stool with no help and hug her father. At the fire, she replaced her shirt mainly for her brother's comfort.

Next was Arna, who whipped his shirt off and took a moment to flex in the dim light of the barn.

"Let's do this!" he said like he was pumping up for a playoff game.

"Do you remember the explanation?" asked Mick.

"Yes, hold still and no exploding, and if I wiggle, I go boom. Got it. Let's do it before I lose my nerve," replied Arna.

Erik appeared in front of him. "You're an idiot, but I am very proud of you. Oh, did you ask your mother?"

Arna shrugged and said, "Kind of."

"Works for me," said Erik. He was holding a short rod with a white-fiery brand at the end. Erik held it above the Arna's chest. Arna could feel the heat pulsing from it.

"Now Erik, press it firmly into his skin just over his heart. Hold it there until it turns green. It should only take a few seconds," instructed Mick.

Erik gripped the rod firmly with both hands and pressed the brand against his son's chest. Arna screamed at the top of his lungs.

"Don't move Arna!" said Anders.

Arna gripped the edge of the stool and focused on his dad. Suddenly he fell quiet, and the brand went from white-hot to bright green.

"That's it, Erik, pull up!" said Mick.

Erik stepped back, pulling the brand off Arna's chest. The fresh brand on his chest turned bright green, then healed almost instantly. The rune left behind remained green, but did not glow anymore. Erik quickly replaced the brand on the fire and helped Arna to his feet.

"How do you feel, son?" Erik asked.

Arna looked up and his eyes flashed with a green light for just a second. "What a rush."

"Do you have any lingering pain?" asked Mick.

"None. I feel no pain. In fact, I feel fantastic," said Arna.

"That is a combination of adrenaline and the rune connecting with your essence. It will pass," explained Mick.

Arna looked slightly disappointed but enjoyed the euphoria for now.

"Okay Finn, it's your turn," said Anders.

Finn Stonefist

The barn fell quiet as everyone looked at him. Finn suddenly realized the gravity of what he was doing and he had to be honest with himself; he was scared.

Finn took his place on the stool and looked at Einar. "Thank you for being here."

"I can't think of anywhere else I would rather be. Honestly, I never thought this day would happen. My son a king and me getting to give him his first rune. I thank you for saving me."

Einar gripped the brand by the rod and, with a single arm, pressed it against Finn's chest. Finn felt the hot searing pain and gripped the stool with everything he had, but he couldn't hold back the roar that erupted from within him. Suddenly, he felt the shift building up in him. He tried to suppress it, but heard his grandpa yelling over his roar to let the shift happen.

Finn closed his eyes and allowed the shift to flow over him. He could see the ground shrinking away as he grew to full height. Just as he reached full height, his head struck something. Finn felt dizzy and nauseous. Just then, the world went black, and Finn saw his loved ones scatter from beneath him. And like a great lead weight, Finn came crashing into the barn's floor out cold, but not before his head collided with an old rafter, shattering it, and raining debris down on the scattering group.

Once the dust had settled, Arna was the first to emerge from a pile of rubble and rafter pieces.

"Now what do we do?" asked Arna.

"We cover him and wait for him to come around," said Anders.

Just then, Finn stirred.

"Wow, that was fast!" said Erik.

As Finn opened his eyes, he could see the sky through a hole in the barn roof.

"What happened?" he asked, trying to sit up, but his body was still in giant form, and he was buried under debris from the roof.

"Take it easy. The rune reacted, and you nearly exploded," said Mick.

"Exploded?" said Finn and Einar at the same time.

"I think, but your grandpa's instinct to have you shift allowed the magic more room, so to speak, and you didn't explode," explained Mick.

Finn tried to let that sink in, but came up sort. He'd almost exploded?

"You should return to human form and we can all go in the house and get cleaned up," said Anders.

"That's just it. I have tried twice while we were talking, and I can't seem to shift back! I think I'm stuck." Finn tried again and again, wound up still in giant form.

"Now don't panic. I am sure we can find a solution to this," said Mick. "Now let me see your rune." Mick shifted into troll form, so he was tall enough to see the rune. He looked it over closely and mumbled to himself.

"Yes, yes, not to worry. The rune is active and working, but it is still trying to regulate the power with Finn's essence. As a Sammeloper, your essence is near god like, so it may take a minute for the rune to get used to that much power. The odd thing is I have only ever seen this reaction one other time."

"When was that?" asked Finn

Mick looked wearily at Anders. "Your uncle, Rathgar, received the same rune, but it failed, and instead of blowing him up, it left him in a partially shifted state. He can't return to human form. That's why he stays in giant form," said Mick

"Must be a family trait," said Anders.

"Am I stuck like this forever?" asked Finn.

"I don't think so. The rune is intact. It's just taking its sweet time settling. Try to shift again, but really focus. You must take control of your own power," said Anders.

Finn sat up fully and focused with everything he had on being in his human form again. At first, it felt like starting an old car. Almost like the magic was fighting him. Then suddenly something clicked, and he could feel himself rush to the ground. When he opened his eyes, he was human sized again and standing next to Mick, who had also resumed his own human form. Finn looked down at his chest and stared at the green rune glowing just above his heart.

"What a rush," Finn said.

They extinguished the fire and returned to the main house. Finn, Tallis, Talon, and Arna came into the house without their shirts on to show off their new runes to their mothers.

"We heard screams and a terrible crashing sound. Are you all okay?" asked Hilde.

"We are fine, but the barn did not fare so good," said Erik.

"That is a worry for another day," Mick said. "For now, I suggest we all get some sleep because tomorrow we go on an adventure!"

Chapter 13

The morning came fast and after a quiet and quick meal of grits and bacon, Finn, Arna, Tallis, Mick and Einar prepared for the journey. Erik offered a firearm to each Mick and Einar, but they declined, stating that human weapons would not help with anything they might encounter in the cave.

"I wish I could come with you," said Erik.

"I know, my friend, but we need you here to watch over everyone," said Mick.

"Alright, little miss knows-it-all, how do I do this?" Talon asked Heidi.

"You will need to picture a doorway in your mind's eye and focus where you want that door to take you," Heidi said.

Talon gripped the Way Finder, closed his eyes, and formed a doorway in his mind. The Way Finder hummed in his hand then . . . nothing.

"I had it, but I couldn't get it open in my mind, like it was locked," said Talon.

"Hm, try focusing on an actual door you have used before," said Heidi.

Talon looked around the room and chose the back-patio door. He stood in front of it. He closed his eyes and focused on opening it in his mind. It worked! He saw the door open in his mind and a green forest with a river running through it on the other side.

"I did it! It's difficult though," said Talon.

"This should help," said Hilde as she handed him a mug with a hot gray-green liquid in it.

Talon sniffed the hot contents. "It smells awful!"

"Well, it will probably taste worse, so don't sip it," said Lorelei.

Talon nodded, held his breath and gulped the liquid as fast as he could. He felt the effects almost immediately. Awake. Alert. Near invincible. "Okay, let's do this," he said.

Talon stood in front of the door again and closed his eyes. This time, he opened the door in his mind with ease. He turned his head and faced the group. His eyes were milky white and glowed faintly. In an echoed voice he said, "Go through the door, I got you as close as I could."

The group moved toward the door, which to them seemed unchanged.

"The tea will only work for about an hour, then it will all be on Talon, so don't dink around out there," said Hilde.

They nodded and Finn opened the door and where he expected to see the backyard, there was a pine forest with birch trees scattered in between large rocks along the bank of a rushing river.

"Pretty cool huh?" said Talon.

"Very cool!" said Arna.

"You had better go. I can already feel the strain." said Talon.

"How far are we from the cave?" asked Finn.

"If you hike about two miles east, you should find the cave. Finn, you should be able to sense the warding around the cave," said Talon.

"How do you know?" Finn asked.

"I just do. It's like the staff is talking to me. Now, go!" urged Talon.

One at a time, they stepped through the door and in an instant, they were standing in the middle of the forest along a river. Finn turned to look back from where they came, and he could see the porch door and the rest of his family standing in the house.

Once everyone was through, Arna pulled out his trusty scout compass and found east. "This way," he said, pointing to the right.

"Actually, cousin, it's this way," said Finn, pointing upriver. "I can feel it."

Arna shook his compass and held it to his ear like it would help. There was no trail, and the terrain was rough and uneven and mostly uphill. The roar of the river pounded in their ears, and there was just enough rain to keep everyone soaked. Despite that, the group was in high spirits and making good time. Finn could feel the warding getting stronger. After about thirty minutes, Finn stopped in his tracks.

Arna walked into him. "Hey what's the deal, boy king?"

"We're here," said Finn. There, between the trees, they could just make out an opening in an outcropping of rocks.

"Doesn't look like much, does it?" said Arna.

"I think that is the idea," replied Mick.

"Look at the top of the opening. There are three runes," said Einar.

Sure enough, there were three runes carved in the stone. They were small but distinct.

"What do they mean?" asked Tallis.

Finn narrowed his brow. "Destruction, danger, and death."

"When did you learn to read ancient runes in Futhark?" asked Einar, surprised at Finn's translation.

"No idea," said Finn.

"My guess is it is a combination of your inherent abilities, coupled with the rune on your chest," said Mick.

But it wasn't the time for explanations. They needed to get moving. Finn insisted they search the area to make sure they were the only one there. He couldn't shake the feeling that he was being watched.

"Let's hurry. It's already been an hour. I don't think Talon can hold much longer," said Finn.

As they each entered the cave, the runes glowed blue. As Einar walked through the opening, he got dizzy and braced against the wall.

"Are you okay?" asked Finn.

"Fine," said Einar.

The cave extended another quarter mile and opened into a large room. Ice and stalactites covered the walls and ceiling.

"Wow, we must be under the glacier!" said Tallis

Two enormous stones carved into the shape of fists flanked them, one on each side of the room. Just behind them was a pedestal where the large blue gem rested. A single shaft of light bled through the overgrown ceiling and struck the gem to make it sparkle in the sunlight. This gave the cave a dim glow.

Suddenly, something struck Einar from behind, knocking him to the ground. The group spun around to see an old woman with a large, gnarled diamond willow staff standing there.

"You!" shouted Finn, and he quickly shifted into giant form.

"Finn, who is this woman?" asked Tallis.

"She is the woman from the woods, The Norn. She attacked me and she has my grandmother somewhere." Finn roared.

"Pleased to meet you again, young king." said the Norn.

"Why are you here?" demanded Mick, now in full troll form.

The Norn chuckled. "You trolls are so dense. I'm here for the same thing you are. The Sapphire of Jotunheim. My friend Rathgar wants it, but not just anybody can take it. Only the king can remove it from the pedestal. If anyone so much as touches the stand or the gem . . . Poof, instant death. The problem was Rathgar couldn't find it before the Gods took their favor from him so now that he isn't king. So until he kills you, he needs you to remove it. Once it's off the stand, it's fair game. So, he sent me to persuade you to give it to me. And thank you for giving me the best bargaining chip." She bent down and touched Einar's forehead. A rune appeared on his skin.

"The rune for fire ought to spark things off nicely," she cackled.

"What will that do to him?" demanded Finn.

"When he wakes, the fire ogre will come crashing to the surface and all that anger and pain will blast through in a tidal wave of death," explained the Norn.

Just then, Einar stirred. He opened his eyes and looked around. Remembering that he was attacked, he jumped to his feet but was quickly brought to his knees by a searing pain in his head. Einar roared out in pain just as he noticed the Norn standing near him.

"What have you done? I will kill you," he roared at her.

"Can you undo it? Can you help him?" begged Finn.

"I can for the stone," the Norn replied.

"Don't listen to her. Everything she says has a double meaning," said Mick.

"He's right, son, don't do it," pleaded Einar.

"If I don't, you will become a fire ogre again, and I can't let you go. I just got you back in my life. You can't ask me to do that," said Finn.

"This is the time you must think like a king and not like my son. You must think of everyone who will suffer if Rathgar gets that stone," insisted Einar.

Mick rushed forward and swung an enormous fist at the Norn, but she was ready for an attack. She easily deflected the blow and knocked Mick across into the room without so much as touching him. Einar's skin steamed, and his eyes returned to their red color. He roared out and began shifting into his ogre size, which was almost as large as Finn. The Norn waved her hand and Einar froze in place. "Now, are we done trying to do this the hard way, or are you going to get me my stone?"

"Alright, I'll do it!" said Finn.

Einar struggled against the invisible force holding him. Finn made his way toward the stone fists. As he passed between them, he got the distinct feeling that the fists were judging him. In full form, Finn barely fit between the two stone fists. As he approached the stand with the jewel, he could tell it was about the size of a large football. A shape he was familiar with. He hefted the gem from its setting. It fit nicely in his palm, but he knew it would be much more of a challenge for the old crone to handle. He walked back to the Norn and stretched out his hand with the jewel in center of his palm. The Norn became entranced by the sapphire and dropped her staff to use both hands to retrieve the stone. Immediately, her hold on Einar was broken.

Just as the Norn was about to wrap her bony finger around the stone, Finn clasped his hand closed and yelled to Einar. "Now!"

The Norn spun and reached for her staff, but not before Einar had snatched it. He struck her with such force that it knocked her back onto the pedestal that held the stone. Einar went in for a second blow, but was stopped by Finn.

"Don't! Look!" said Finn. Einar looked and saw what Finn did: the Norn was touching the pedestal.

She jumped away from the pedestal as a gray film started at her hand and spread up her arm. She shrieked and wiped frantically at it in vain. The grayness continued to cover her at an alarming speed as she tried to run, but it hardened into a stone identical to that of the pedestal. Suddenly, the entire room shook and trembled. Then, with a great roar of grinding stone, the two fists propelled themselves forward, crushing the now stone Norn in between them. When they retracted, all that was left of the Norn was dust and rubble. Einar collapsed into Finn's arms.

"We have to get him to Aunt Hilde," said Finn. He slipped the stone into his backpack and hefted an unconscious Einar into his arms. The cave trembled and shook violently.

"We need to leave," said Arna as he dodged falling rock and ice.

In silent agreement, the group ran for the entrance. As Finn tried to cross the entrance, something invisible wouldn't allow him to cross.

Einar opened his eyes and said weakly, "Finn, I have to stay. You must pay a cost of something you love. I must stay until the stone is returned. At least here I can't hurt anyone."

"Wrong! There has to be something else. Why is everything trying to keep my family apart? Hilde can fix you," said Finn.

"Son, do this for me. I don't want to become an ogre again. I don't want to hurt you. You can feel this is the right thing," said Einar through gritted teeth as he fought the dark shift.

Finn looked back at Mick. "Isn't there anything we can do?"

"The magic here is strong enough to hold back the dark shift and protect him until we can return," said Mick.

"Now, I need you to help me back to the main chamber," said Einar.

Finn gave his backpack to Tallis. "Get home. I will be right behind you."

Tallis took the bag and ran back towards the portal with Mick and Arna. Finn helped Einar to his feet and guided him back to the main chamber. As they entered, the trembling ceased and where the pedestal once stood, a stone throne was in its place.

"Take me there," said Einar.

Finn helped him into the chair. Einar sat back and almost at once, the gray film began to cover his body.

"Son, I love you and I will be waiting for you to return. I will be just fine." said Einar, allowing a single tear to fall down his cheek as the stone film covered his face until he fell silent and still.

Finn sobbed into the now stone shoulder of his father and then let out a roar that shook the cavern. Then he gathered his emotions and turned to leave. He took one more look at his father, peaceful and regal, sitting on his stone throne. As he exited the cavern, he noticed the Norn's staff laying on the floor of the cave. Finn grabbed it, thinking it might come in handy. Staying in giant form, Finn quickly caught up to the others at the portal. As he slowed, he shifted into human size.

Tallis hugged him. "Are you okay?"

"I will be when we end Rathgar and get the stone back to where it belongs. Then my father will be free." Finn's expression was cold and angry. He was the last one to cross the portal back into the main house. As the portal closed, he watched the image of forest swirl out of view.

Talon collapsed onto the floor. Lorelei and Heidi helped him to the couch, where he promptly fell asleep.

"Well, not bad. You didn't die," said Heidi to a snoring Talon.

"What happened? Where's Einar?" asked Anders.

"We will explain everything, won't we Finn?" said Mick, turning to Finn only to see him going out to the backyard. "Correction, I will explain everything. I think it is best Finn have some alone time. He had to make the hardest choice of his life so far." Then he told them about the cave. The Norn. And the cost that came with retrieving the stone.

"I just wish I knew how to help him," said Tallis.

"Just be there for him. He will need you more than ever now," said Lorelei.

With that, Tallis stood and silently went to Finn's side. The two sat there for hours in silence.

Finally, in the failing light of day Finn said, "Tomorrow we go for the setting then, we go after my would-be uncle."

Chapter 14

Finn covered a sleeping Tallis in a blanket and walked up to the barn. Shifting into giant form, he investigated the hole he made in the roof the last time he was there. The King's Stone hummed inside his backpack.

Finn pulled it out and stared at it. "What am I supposed to do with you? Great, now I'm talking to rocks." Just then, the stone dissolved and climbed up his arm and took the form of his Guardian Armor.

"What are you doing? I don't want to train right now," said Finn, sure he looked crazy.

The armor hummed and a large double-bladed axe materialized in his hand. Finn looked at the weapon in awe.

"What exactly am I supposed to do with this?" he asked.

His arm twitched, then it made a sideway sweeping motion. "I said I don't feel like training!" Finn shouted and threw the axe as hard as he could.

It flew across the barn, circled around, and landed back in Finn's hand. He threw it again, and again the axe returned. This time, he threw it with all his strength as a giant. Satisfied, he turned to leave when something struck him hard in the head. When he spun around, the axe was floating at his eye level. It swung again and in reflex Finn put his arm up to absorb the blow, but instead of the pain he expected to feel that comes with a severed arm; he heard a clang and when he opened his eyes; he saw a large round shield covering his arm.

"Ha! You can't hurt..." Thunk! The axe handle caught Finn in the face.

"Cheap shot, eh? Try it again," Finn taunted the disembodied weapon.

The axe seemed to understand and volleyed another blow towards Finn's head, but he was ready this time and easily deflected it. The process of parry and thrust continued until Finn was exhausted. He collapsed on the ground sweaty and too tired to be angry.

The stone dissolved once more and resumed its normal brick shape. He looked down at the stone brick in his hand and said, "Thank you."

The brick ceased its humming, and Finn returned to the main house feeling full of purpose and hope. "Like in football, sometimes you just have to hit something," he thought as he entered the house.

"The time has come that we plan to go after the setting for the jewel. With that, we will have two out of three pieces to the Staff of Jotunheim. With those, we can take the fight to Rathgar and stand a chance at winning," said Anders.

"That's great and all but why don't we just destroy the pieces or give them to the Gods to protect." asked Talon.

"We need the jewel to free my father," said Finn

"Plus, don't you think if they could be destroyed, I would have done that years ago? As for the Gods they rarely meddle in Midgardian affairs except for Thor, who has a soft spot for the human world," snapped Anders. "I am frustrated that at for hundreds of years this staff has been here, and I am the one king to lose it not once but twice. Now because of my hubris the world is in danger from one of my sons while the other is a stone statue in the wilderness and my seventeen-year-old grandson has had to endure more in his short years than anyone should have to and I am nothing more than an old broken giant stuck in human form!"

Finn stood and put his hand on Anders' shoulder. "Grandpa, no one blames you for any of this. This is Rathgar's fault and the Gods wouldn't have given Midgard the staff if it wasn't the safest place for it. As for your physical state, I might have something to help you more than that old metal crutch," he said and went to the front closet and came back holding the Norn's staff.

"I brought this back from the cave after we killed the Norn. I noticed when she dropped it, she had a limp a lot like yours, but with it she seemed fine. Try it out," said Finn, handing the staff to Anders.

The presentation of this gift stunned Anders. "The Norn's staff is a powerful relic made from a willow tree that grows directly from Yggdrasil, the World Tree. Its complete abilities are unknown." Anders cautiously took the staff in hand, closed his eyes, and waited for worst.

"How do you feel?" asked Mick.

Anders opened his eyes. "I feel noth..." Suddenly Anders was cut off with a sharp pain in his bum leg. The twisted limb shook and felt hot. Anders was afraid he was going to catch fire then. It cooled and quit shaking. He collapsed into his armchair.

"Anders!" cried Hilde.

"I'm fine, leave me be," he said.

Pulling his pant leg up and where there was once a twisted atrophied limb, there was a strong-looking leg just like his other. "Finn, I am forever in your debt! Thank you." Anders hugged Finn in a powerful bear hug. "One great gift deserves another. My gift come as an apology. I should have been totally honest with you children from the start but, now, I have to tell you children a truth about our people and this situation that you need to know. You have to know that our struggle isn't new."

"We know you and mom and dad were there like a hundred years ago when Rathgar attempted a coup," said Arna jokingly.

"More like two hundred years ago," said Erik.

"WHAT!?" said Arna, Finn, Tallis and Talon in unison.

"It's true children," said Lorelei.

"I was a baby though, so am I two hundred years old too?" asked a very confused Finn.

"No, my boy, Rathgar's successful coup was only seventeen years ago, but his first attempt where I was crippled, and your grandmother taken by the Norn, was nearly two hundred years ago. When we go through the shift for the first time, we become connected to the magic of Midgard and it extends our lives a great deal."

"So, how old are you?" asked Finn.

"Let's just say this year I won't be turning seventy-seven. I will turn five hundred and eighty-two years old," said Anders.

"That's a lot of candles," said Arna.

"No disrespect, grandpa, but what does this have to do with finding the next piece?" asked Finn.

"Well, based on the images Talon showed us of Saxman Village, I can only think I did one thing before the mind spell. I always had a good relationship with the indigenous people of Alaska, and I must have entrusted the piece to them to guard. The Tlingit shaman are human, but they have a strange ability. They can see us for what we really are, they can see our auras, which made them quite dangerous during the great war and even more powerful allies. They would have been able to tell if anyone of us were there to take it. What I don't know is what I charged them with regarding giving up the item."

"What does it look like?" asked Tallis.

"That's just it, I don't remember, and neither does anyone from those days," said Anders.

Finn Stonefist

"Let me try the Way Finder. Maybe I missed something," suggested Talon. He retrieved the staff and closed his eyes. Images appeared on the wall in front of him. Garbled at first, but they cleared after a moment. Talon focused on what the setting could be. The images settled on a tall, old looking totem pole with a raven on top.

The image cleared and Talon opened his eyes. "Sorry, that's all I could get. Seems not even the Gods know exactly where it is."

"We will just need to go there and look around ourselves," said Finn.

"If we leave now, it is still early enough that we can portal in without being seen," said Anders.

"You can't go," said Finn. This was way too dangerous a mission for his grandpa.

"The hell I can't! For the first time in two hundred years, I feel like my old self and I have already lost my son. I will lose no one else. I am going and that's final!"

There was no arguing with that.

Erik asked, "There is something that has been bothering me. How did the Norn know where we would be? No one outside this group knew of our plans except Aaron, but he couldn't tell anyone, could he?"

Lorelei immediately got a worried look on her face and pulled out her phone, making a call. Someone answered, and Lorelei left the room. When she came back, she was white as a sheet as she slumped onto the couch.

"Mom, what is it?" asked Talon.

"Is grandpa okay?" asked Tallis.

"He's okay, but security caught an old woman in his room shortly after we left. She was standing over him, but when they confronted her, she just vanished. Dad has been in an agitated state ever since."

"It must have been the Norn probing his mind for whatever she could glean, and she must have gotten just enough to find us," said Finn.

"We must assume that Rathgar has sent spies out everywhere to find the two pieces, and he nearly got one," said Anders.

"Rathgar has access to all the royal records. He could have discovered the hiding places, or at least enough clues to find them as we did. We should leave now and hope we are not too late."

With that, everyone prepared to leave. Heidi took some time to show Talon how to use the Way Finder to create a more stable portal, since the first time didn't kill him. He could now pass through with the group and close it on the other side. It would make a quick exit near impossible since he would have to open a new portal, but at least he could go on the trip and opening a portal should be less taxing than holding one open.

"Heidi, I am trusting you to help Heimdal and watch the place while we are away," said Anders with a very serious look.

"I understand," said Heidi.

Talon opened a portal through the same door as before. The group emerged in a parking lot in front of a large native lodge with carvings decorating the outside and totem poles of different sizes and shapes dotted the surrounding property. Talon closed the portal just as Heidi had shown him and joined the group.

They walked up to the lodge door. Finn gave it a tug, but it was locked.

"Now what?" asked Arna.

Finn Stonefist

"I'll shift a little and pull it open, no problem," said Finn. He shifted his arms and was about to pull the doors open when a man behind the group and started speaking.

"I wouldn't do that if I were you, young giant; you wouldn't like the result at all," said the man.

The group spun around to see a tall, slender man wrapped in an ornate blanket. He had a traditional Tlingit hat on his head. Finn shifted into full giant form and let out a roar directly into the man's face, blowing his hat clean off. The man didn't even flinch.

"That's impressive, young one, but you do not scare me. I know of your kind and I know why you are here."

"So, are you friend or foe?" asked Erik.

"That depends if you are friend or foe," said the man.

"Enough of this, Jimmy, of course we are friends," said Anders, using his newly acquired staff to push his way to the front of the group.

"You came back just like you said all those years ago," said the man.

"Everyone, this is Jimmy, the local shaman and an old friend," said Anders. "Do you remember why this place is connected to the Staff of Jotunheim?"

"Do you not remember, giant king?" asked Jimmy.

"I really don't," responded Anders. "And I'm not the king anymore." He nodded to Finn, who frowned in reply.

"Many generations ago, you gave my people a magnificent gift and told us to guard it until the day you would come back for it, but that was a very long time ago. It has been passed from shaman to shaman over the years and we have guarded it with our lives. Now you have returned, but I am only to give it to the one bearing the King's Stone," said Jimmy.

Finn shifted back and retrieved the stone from his backpack.

"That is a nice rock, but I want to see what it can do," said Jimmy.

Finn sighed and stepped away from the group. He gripped the stone and shifted into the Guardian armor. Standing at full height, the sun glinted off his chest plate.

"Very nice!" said Jimmy.

"I showed you mine. Now show me yours," said Finn in a deep voice.

Jimmy pointed at a totem pole with a raven on it. "That which you seek is there."

Right there in front of them? That was too easy. Finn walked over to it. He was eye level with the raven on top. At first, he saw nothing out of the ordinary, then the morning sunlight caught something on the wooden bird. It glinted near the ankle of the raven.

Using one of his oversized thumbs, Finn tried to rub the paint off. Instead, he snapped the raven clean off the top of the pole. He glanced over at Jimmy, who seemed unbothered by this result. Finn examined the wooden figure and saw that one foot wasn't wood but metal that had been painted over to make it look like the rest of the totem.

Finn looked down at Jimmy and said, "Sorry," and crushed the wooden bird in his massive hand. He cleared the debris from his palm and found a small metal object in the shape of a raven's foot. He shifted down to human size and realized the foot was much larger than he thought. The talons were outstretched, and it covered the whole thing in a silvery metal that glinted with the slightest light.

"What is it?" asked Talon.

Finn Stonefist

An awe-struck Mick approached and hefted the raven's foot into his hands. "This is the foot of Munnin cast in Asgardian silver." Seeing that no one knew what he was talking about, Mick continued. "There is an old legend that after the fall of Jotunheim and the great war here on Midgard, one of Odin's ravens, Munnin, the raven of the mind, was injured in a battle protecting humans. As a symbol of protection by the gods, Odin had the foot dipped in Asgardian silver and it was presented to humanity as a gift. Over the millenniums it was lost but it must have been found and given to Rathgar two hundred years ago because here it is safe and sound."

"Jimmy, you kept this right out in the open for all these years?" said Anders shocked at how careless his friend seemed to be with such a powerful relic.

"I asked my mentor the same thing, and he told me that sometimes the best place to hide is where the seeker is looking," replied Jimmy.

"What does that mean?" asked Anders.

"It means sometimes in plain sight is the best place to hide. I think the human Sherlock said something similar," explained Mick.

Anders did not look convinced.

"How does this hold the jewel? The talons are splayed out flat," asked Erik.

Finn pulled the football-sized jewel from his pack and stepped towards Mick, who was holding the raven's foot. Suddenly, the jewel glowed brightly, and the foot hummed loudly. Then, like it was still attached to a raven, the foot wrenched itself from Mick's grasp and latched onto the jewel. There was a clang, and a pulse of light emanated from the now joined objects in all directions.

Finn stumbled backwards, holding the newly formed scepter. "Is that supposed to happen?"

Fear filled Jimmy's eyes. "For nearly two hundred years, the great staff has been separated from itself. That pulse was the two pieces calling to its brother the shaft. The enemy will know where you are now, no matter where you go. Whoever holds the staff will be drawn to the now joined scepter."

Suddenly, Jimmy arched backward, and a shiny metallic point protruded through his chest. It retracted and Jimmy fell to the ground, gasping for air. Where Jimmy had been standing, a woman now stood. She was tall, with dark brown hair and slight features. Her eyes flashed blue as she wiped the bloody dagger on her sleeve.

"He was right," she said, "we just had to wait for you to find the setting and it would show us where you were."

"Who are you?" roared Finn, already in giant form.

Erik, Hilde, and Mick had also shifted and stood in front of Jimmy's now lifeless body.

"I am the here to collect the pieces, and I am the one who decides if you live through the exchange," said the woman in a cool tone.

Her face was devoid of emotion, almost like she was bored with this task.

"Well, finders, keepers!" yelled Arna from behind his father.

"I was hoping you would say that," replied the woman. She jumped high into the air, landing a combat boot squarely in Finn's chest, knocking him to his back and causing a massive crater in the parking lot. Mick and Erik jumped into action and swung two enormous fists in the woman's direction, but they were both brought to their knees in a flurry of fists and feet colliding with their faces.

Finn Stonefist

Finn got to his feet and pulled the king's stone from his pocket. He looked at it and said, "I could use you right now." In a flash, Finn was clad in the Guardian's Armor, complete with his new double-bladed battle axe.

"So you're the imposter king that the gods have chosen over Rathgar," said the woman.

Finn grabbed the woman with one hand and slammed her onto the pavement as hard as he could. He held her there and put the axe to her throat. He bent close to her face and growled, "Who are you?"

From beneath the weight of Finn's massive hand, she groaned, "I'm your mother."

Finn stumbled backwards, releasing his grip on the woman. "My mother?"

"If you believe the lies, then it is true. You are my son and Einar, my husband, your father and my one true love is alive, and I didn't slaughter my family all those years ago," said the woman as she picked herself up off the ground. "But, I don't believe the lies." And she charged Finn again.

Finn dropped his axe and held up both of his hands and said as quick as he could, "You are Tove Woodsplitter Stonefist, you are my mother, you are a Sammeloper like me, and Einar is alive!"

Tove stopped dead in her tracks. "Einar's alive? Lies!"

"Well, mostly, he's encased in stone, but I can fix him and yes, he is alive and not a dark shifter any longer," explained Finn.

Tove thought about what she was hearing, and flashes of memory rushed back. She stumbled, but not before Anders entangled his staff between her feet, causing her to stumble even more. As she turned to strike him, Mick punted her like football, sending her flying into the trees end over end for more than a hundred yards.

"Talon now would be a great time for a portal," urged Anders.

"We should capture her! This could be our chance to help her!" said Finn.

"She is too dangerous right now. We will find a way, I promise," said Anders.

Talon opened the portal quickly, despite his nerves. Finn shifted back to human form and hefted the scepter. Grabbing his backpack, he rushed through the portal just as Talon closed it behind them.

As Finn walked into the room, he could see everyone gathered in the center of the room. On floor laid Jimmy. He was pale and lifeless. Tallis was at his side with her salve and the book of instructions.

"Tallis, you can't use that on a human. We do not know what that kind of magic will do to him," said Mick.

"We have to try something! We can't just let him die," Tallis insisted. "It says I have to pack the wound with cloth soaked in the salve. Hilde, do you have clean rags we can use?"

"I do," said Hilde, and she went to get them.

Hilde returned with a modest stack of clean white linens. Tallis took them in her hands and soaked a few in the salve. Her hands were shaking as she shoved the cloth into the gaping hole in Jimmy's chest. Almost at once, she could see the flesh knit together from the inside out. Jimmy's breathing became less ragged, and the color returned to his face, and he started to groan and stir.

Everyone stood in amazement as Jimmy opened his eyes. "Was I just dead?"

"Just a little, but now you're not," said Arna, helping Jimmy to a sitting position.

"And now we need to get you to safety. Talon can get you anywhere you want," said Anders.

Jimmy described the place to Talon, who was able to open a portal to what looked like a mountaintop in the middle of nowhere.

"Finn, can I have a word with you before I go?" asked Jimmy.

"Talon, close the portal behind us and I will signal with my ring when I am ready to come back," said Finn

The two of them stepped through the portal onto a great meadow high in the mountains.

"A long time ago, my people used to complete a pilgrimage to this place just before being excepted as adults among our people," explained Jimmy.

"What would they do here?" asked Finn.

"They would spend many days fasting and communing with the Great Spirit. They would ask questions that weighed heavy on their hearts and sometimes they would get answers and sometimes they would get guidance on how to find the answers, and sometimes they would get nothing and have to figure things out on their own. I have a feeling you have a few heavy things that weigh on you, my young friend. Am I right?"

It was like the old shaman had been reading his mind.

"I can't sleep or eat or enjoy anything. I don't even know if we can beat Rathgar. He has an army of soldiers and dark... everything! How are we supposed to stop him and keep the world safe? You know what I expected to do this summer? Nothing but hang out with Tallis and Talon and Arna. I am supposed to go to parties and turn eighteen and start my senior year! Instead, I found out that my crazy family history isn't that crazy and that I am some kind of savior king oh, and both my parents were turned evil by my uncle and my grandmother is a kidnap victim and I just killed the one person who could tell us where she is. So yeah, things are a little heavy right now!" Finn collapsed to a sitting position on the ground with a huff.

    Jimmy smiled and joined him on the ground. "While I know little about your world, I know more than you think. As for your family, you're right; they are crazy, but they are also one of the most noble people I or my people have ever known human or otherwise. As for being a savior king, I would say don't worry about that. Worry about helping your family the best way you know how. The king stuff will come later. If it was me, I would take all the tools given to me and plan and yes, Rathgar has an army, but you do too. You just need to find them. And the army you have now fights with love, not fear and if movies have ever taught us anything, love always wins. You have an amazing group of people just waiting to follow you to the ends of the worlds and beyond. All that other stuff will sort itself out, I promise, but you should know that Rathgar's plan is not what we think. When I was almost dead, I saw everything in the world all at once and there is a terrible darkness surrounding Rathgar. Be aware of everything because nothing is as it appears."

    Finn considered his words. "Thank you . . . for the advice and for everything. What will you do now?"

    "I think I will stay here a while and commune with the Great Spirit and do a little soul searching myself," said Jimmy.

    "Well, thank you for being my Great Spirit and giving me some direction," said Finn as he hugged Jimmy. Finn touched the center stone on his ring and the Talon's corresponding stone and a portal appeared where he and Jimmy had come through earlier.

Finn Stonefist

Chapter 15

Finn walked through the portal, returning. "I know what we need to do to defeat Rathgar."

"Don't you want to talk about the fact that your mother showed up at the village and tried to kill us?" asked Arna.

The room was quiet. Finn looked at all the caring faces staring back at him and thought about what Jimmy had told him.

"I want to do for my mother what we did for my father, but we can't right now. Right now, we have the tools to deal with Rathgar and that is what we should focus on. We need to focus on what we do and don't know and what we do and don't have. What we have is easy; we have the gifts from Thor and most of all we have each other."

"What we don't have is any clue what the machine Rathgar is building is for and what his end game is," same Talon.

"Jimmy warned me that not everything is as it seems and that we have it wrong regarding what Rathgar is up to," said Finn.

"He's right," said a voice coming from the front door. Everyone turned to see Edna Edon standing in the doorway.

"Mom, what are you doing here?" said Lorelei.

"Well, after your visit and the subsequent visit of that witch, I thought it best to come and find out what was going on and see if we could help," said Edna.

"We?" asked Lorelei.

"Yes, we," said Aaron.

"Papa! What are you doing here?" said Lorelei, and she ran and hugged him tight. She pulled back and looked at him hard. "You seem different."

"I am different," said Aaron. "When the Norn probed my memories, I too saw everything she saw and somewhere in there the memory spell broke, and it restored my full capacity. No more was anything stopping me from remembering."

"Are you saying you remember everything?" asked Anders

"That is exactly what I am saying, my old friend. I remember everything from that time, and I know what Rathgar is up to, but I need for Finn to meet his army and there I will explain everything."

"My army?" asked Finn.

"They will meet us at the Thing," said Aaron.

"The Thing?" asked Finn.

"It's what the old Vikings would call a great meeting of all the clans a Thing," Talon said. "I read about it. They used it as a time to celebrate and to council with one another."

The room was quiet as slack jaws stared back at Talon.

"What, I know stuff too," he snorted.

"This one will be held in a place you are already familiar with, Gun Sight Mountain," said Aaron.

"Speaking of which, we should go. It's a long drive and we don't want to keep the families waiting," said Edna.

"And we must do it before the summer solstice,"

"I can get us there in a blink of an eye," said Talon.

She narrowed her eyes at him. "How do you propose to do that?"

"With the Way Finder," said Talon, and he produced the drumstick-sized rod from his back pocket. He touched the rune and almost instantly it grew to full length.

"I can't believe my grandson bears the Vei Visner!" said Aaron. Both he and Edna stared in amazement.

"I can open a portal directly to the spot," said Talon. He closed his eyes and imagined the front door growing wider than it was, and he pictured the scene on the mountain top from the last time they were up there. The others could hear a faint hum coming from the front door and a dim light shone from the other side. Talon's eyes opened, and they were milky white. "It's open, let's go while we can," said Talon in an echoed voice.

Finn led the group. As he opened the door and stepped through, he didn't wind up on the barren rock platform he expected. Instead, the whole mountain top had been transformed into a lush garden. The boulders from their wrestling match with Thor were gone and replaced by thick grass that smelled sweet with clover blossoms. To his right, he could see a tented area with a large table and chairs. The table was set for a feast and laden with every kind of food he could think of. He could smell it from where he stood, and he realized how hungry he was. As Finn scanned the garden, he could see fruit trees of all kinds and some kinds he didn't recognize. The air buzzed with bird song and bees busily going about their work, as if they didn't notice they were high on a mountaintop. Finn was baffled that someone or something could change such a barren rock face into such a place of beauty, but there was something else. Finn felt at peace here. As if all of his worries didn't seem so worrisome anymore. His mind felt clear and he could order his thoughts. He turned and found Talon.

"Talon, did you take us to right place?" Finn asked.

"As far as I know, this is Gunsight Mountain," replied Talon.

"This is the right place alright," said Anders.

"It's fairy magic," said Mick.

"Fairy magic?" asked Finn.

Finn Stonefist

"You see, Finn," said Aaron, "The Thing is more than just a meeting of the clans; it is a place as well. It is what is left of the old world from when our ancestors first came to Midgard thousands of years ago. It is the first and last veritable garden of Midgard. It is heavily protected by the strongest and oldest of magics. From the human perspective, this place hasn't changed a bit. I would reckon not even Rathgar could find us here. The Thing exists out of space and time. And time stands still here while it moves normally outside. Some say a couple of humans found this place on accident once and that is where their myth of the Garden of Eden came from. It was never proven. The Thing hasn't been called upon since the great war when the humans rose against their oppressors. It takes a great deal of magic to bring it into alinement with Midgard so that we may enter it. I am actually very impressed Talon could access it directly without help," he finished.

"He didn't. I sensed him making the portal and gave him a little nudge, but he did most of the heavy lifting. Not bad for a novice Way Finder," said a woman as she approached Finn and the others. She was short with round hips and stern but pleasant face. Her hair was brown as chestnut and came to her waist in a long braid with clovers and flowers interlaced throughout it.

"Finn, may I introduce you to Lady Lily Swansong, Queen of the Fae," said Anders.

"How are you, you old rock pile?" said Lady Lily as she hugged Anders and then turned to Finn and looked him over carefully. "You are young."

"I'm sorry?" replied Finn, not entirely sure what he should say to that.

"That's a good and a bad thing," said Lady Lily. "It means you can be molded. It just depends on who does the molding."

"The question is, will you be molded, or will you do the molding?" said a gruff voice from a muscular man with a bushy black beard long enough that he almost was walking on it. He was not very tall, only coming to Finn's bicep. Next to him, holding his arm, was a round little woman of similar build and height, but no beard. She had bright red hair and a smile on her lips that Finn suspected was there all the time. She had a kind face and bright green eyes.

"Finn, this Jack and Ilsa Shovelton, ruling lord and lady of the Dwarf Nation," explained Anders.

Behind them, Finn could see several more figures who Anders introduced in turn. There were Dagfinn and Dagmar Fjellen, representing the other giant families. They were in full giant form and stood nearly twenty feet tall each of them. Dagfinn's face was hard, with a stringy white beard extending to his chest and his left eye was milky white with a deep scar running through it. Finn couldn't see how the eye was of any use, but something about it made him uneasy. Just a still white orb peering directly into him. Anders explained Dagfinn was Finn's grandmother's older brother, making him Finn's great uncle, and that Dagfinn hadn't spoken to Anders in decades because he blamed Anders for his sister's abduction. Standing next to him was his wife, Dagmar. She had long salt and pepper hair and her face was as hard as her husband's and void of any emotion.

Neither one said much except Dagfinn, who looked down his nose at Finn and snorted. "He's kind of small for a king."

"Kind of ugly for a noble," thought Finn to himself.

Finn had already met the Edons, Aaron and Edna, and then finally he was introduced by Mick to Ed and Dotty Nightfeather. Ed was Mick's uncle and he and his wife were there representing the Troll Alliance. Dotty ran up and gave a

Finn hug so tight that he thought he would lose consciousness. Since she was in full troll form, that was a definite possibility. She released him about the time his vision dimmed. Both of them stood about twelve feet high, and Ed looked at Finn and just grunted.

"Don't mind him, dear. He's just grumpy because he had to leave our mountain. He doesn't take being summoned very well," said Dotty.

"Well, now that everyone is acquainted, can we get this Thing started? I'm hungry, and the food is getting colder all the time," grumbled Dagfinn.

"Oh, hush your avalanche hole! You know I enchanted the food to never cool or rot," said Dagmar, slapping Dagfinn on the arm. He faked a wince at the strike and turned to walk to the back of the garden.

It was then Finn noticed something he hadn't noticed amidst all the introductions. Towards the other side of the garden there was a ring of thrones made from stone, twelve of them to be exact.

"What are those?" he asked Anders as they approached the ring.

"That is the court of Midgard. Each of the five families has a pair of thrones and they make here all major decisions concerning the realm. There is a smaller one in the Keep for day-to-day use," explained Anders.

"So what is my role in the court as King?" Finn asked.

"Well, mostly you as king will determine what happens, but for wars or serious criminal cases or things that threaten Midgard as a whole, the court may convene and review your decisions," explained Anders.

"If it works right, it can prevent Rathgar from rising to power," added Mick.

As Finn approached the ring of stone chairs, he saw they were all smooth and devoid of ornamentation except for the family's crest etched into the back of each chair. They were all different heights and widths. For example, Finn's seat was enormous and made him feel like a small child. Finn felt the uneasy weight of being king return to the all too familiar knot in his stomach. He wished Einar was there to encourage him somehow. The Shovelton's seats were wide but low to the ground. On the floor was an etching in the shape of Thor's hammer, Mjolnir.

"There are twelve seats, but only ten members of the court if you count me. Who are the other two for?" Finn asked.

Lady Lily responded, "The one next to me would be for my husband, Lars, but sadly he was killed during the battle of Rathgar's second coup." Her voice trailed off, and she seemed to be lost in a memory. She blinked rapidly, breaking her trance, and turned to Anders. "Would you do me the honor of taking Lars's place as long as no one objects? It would be a proxy position only. You wouldn't have voting power, but it feels wrong to leave it vacant."

Anders' eyes went wide. "I would be my honor, my lady."

"So, is the empty seat supposed to be for my queen? Because I'm a little light in the queen department," said Finn.

"I'll do it," said Tallis. "I'll be your queen for a day." She grasped Finn's hand.

Finn swallowed hard as he stared directly into her bright green eyes. The dim light of the garden made the golden flecks in her eyes dance. "Okay," he finally said.

"Very well, everyone, please take your seats and the rest of you can go to the banquet table and enjoy yourself. This is a closed meeting only court and proxy court members allowed." said Aaron.

Finn Stonefist

"Woohoo food!" shouted Arna as he bolted towards the tented area.

Heidi rolled her eyes and headed over when Ed spoke in a loud, gravelly voice. "I think the Huldre should attend this council. I think she could provide some excellent information."

Heidi stopped in her tracks and lock eyes with the old troll. "What could I possibly know? I am a victim of Rathgar's lies." She tried to look as innocent as possible.

"We agree, the Huldre should be questioned. She was in Rathgar's inner circle for decades," growled Dagfinn.

Finn looked at Heidi and said, "They have a point. You could be very helpful."

Heidi sighed and went to stand next to Finn and Tallis. The rest of the group headed towards the table. Mick gave Finn two thumbs up and mouthed "you've got this" as Lorelei shuffled him off.

The court took their respective seat when Heidi asked, "Just where am I supposed to sit?"

"I can handle that," said Dagfinn. As he gripped the armrest of his chair, the symbol in the floor split open and another, much smaller chair rose out of the cavity until the base was flush with the ground.

Heidi marched toward the chair and sat with an indignant air about her. Finn and Tallis took their own seats. Then everyone looked at Finn like they were expecting him to say something.

Tallis leaned over and whispered, "Call the meeting to order or something."

"Oh, right? I call this court to order," he stated loudly.

All at once the others shouted "Skaal!" and pounded a fist on their respective arm rests. The sound echoed through the garden and caused birds to flutter from their resting places. Finn's heart was pounding.

"King Finn, if I may, but it is customary that those who can be in true form should be. That includes the king," said Lady Lily.

Finn gave Tallis a nervous look and took a deep breath. Then he shifted into his full giant form, standing thirty feet tall. He reached into his backpack and grabbed the King Stone and donned the Guardian's Armor. In a flash of light, he was clad from head to toe in shiny silvery armor.

He looked over at Dagfinn and asked, "Am I still too small?"

Dagfinn sat back in his chair, staring in awe.

"That's better, my king. Now have a seat and we can begin," said Lady Lily with a wide grin on her face.

Finn cleared his throat. "As the one who convened this Thing, I believe Lord Edon should conduct this meeting."

"Skaal!" the others chanted in unison, striking their arm rests again.

Aaron rose from his seat. In his true form, he was nearly seven feet tall, with pointed ears and slightly angular features. He stepped towards Heidi at the center of the ring and addressed the court. "King Finn, Lords and Ladies of Midgard. I convened this Thing because we are presented with an opportunity that we haven't had in many years. The Gods have removed their favor from Rathgar and restored it to the rightful king. Thor himself has visited our king on this very mountain top and gifted him and his friends with rare and powerful gifts. It is my belief that he would not have done this if he did not think we could bring Rathgar's reign to an end."

"How can four teenagers, three of which can't even shift yet, hope to defeat Rathgar and his army? No offense, my king," said Dagfinn nervously.

"They can't," said Aaron. "That is why I called all of you here. To recruit help. With our five families' combined resources, I believe we have a chance. When the Norn attacked me, I saw Rathgar's plan."

"We know his plan: to amass the magic of Midgard for himself," growled Ed Nightfeather.

Aaron shook his head. "That's what we all thought, but when the Norn accidentally broke my mind spell, I remembered what I had learned just before we dismantled the Staff of Jotunheim. It was the reason such drastic measures were taken."

"What, pray tell, is that, oh learned one," scoffed Dagfinn.

"Hey! Respect, man!" growled Finn at Dagfinn's flippant comment.

"Sorry, my king," said Dagfinn quickly, as he sat up straight in his seat.

"Please continue, Lord Edon," said Finn.

"Thank you, my king. Rathgar's goal has always been the same, but it is not to amass power for himself," Aaron paused. "It is for Loki!"

A shiver moved down Finn's spine.

"Now, according to the ancient texts, after the fall of Jotunheim, our people realized they weren't able to get back home," Aaron said. "Odin sealed all the portals leading from Midgard to the other realms so no one would suffer the same fate as Jotunheim, and as punishment, Loki was stripped of the staff and locked in a cell at the heart of Midgard. It has had many names. Some of them are Tartarus, Outer Darkness, Hell. He was completely alone and unable to communicate with anyone . . . or so we thought. I believe Loki has somehow influenced Rathgar from within his prison, and it is Loki Rathgar is using the staff to release."

"If Rathgar knows it was Loki who trapped our people here, why would he help release him? That would make Rathgar subject to Loki, and he doesn't strike me as the subject kind," said Ed.

"Loki is a master manipulator and has probably promised Rathgar rule of this world if he helps him escape his bonds. The gem of the staff is a chunk of the heart of Jotunheim and made of the same material Midgard's heart is made of. The Staff is the only thing with enough power to tap into the heart of Midgard and focus it on the cell containing Loki," said Aaron.

"I get why Rathgar wants him out, but why does Loki really want besides freedom?" asked Finn.

"Domination. Loki wants to be king of the Gods and he will do anything to achieve it and if he can't have the throne, he figures no one should have it and he will destroy everything. I am sure his malice has only grown over the thousands of years in that cage," said Lady Lily.

"This is where the Huldre comes in. It was a Huldres magic that was used to seal the cage. Your magic," growled Dagfinn.

"That's impossible; I wasn't even around then," Heidi retorted.

"No, but we know from the ancient texts that your mother was," said Aaron.

"My mother? That's impossible. She had no love for the Gods, but she liked humans even less. Why would she do anything to help this pitiful world?" Heidi spat.

"As you know, pure Huldre children are rare because Huldre men are all but extinct and the ones still around are mostly sterile from years of inbreeding. The texts say little except that she struck a deal with Odin, that if she sealed the cage with Loki in it, he would grant her a pure Huldre child to raise and take her place as high priestess of your people. That child was you, Heidi," said Aaron.

Heidi looked stunned, like someone exposed to a deep, dark secret.

"It is your mother's magic that runs through you. Haven't you ever wondered why Rathgar picked you to be his lieutenant? It wasn't because he liked you, it was because he needed to use you. Your magic is the power source for his spell," said Dagfinn.

Was she really just a tool to Rathgar? Heidi always knew he was no good, but she recalled Rathgar speaking of a key element. "So why am I here now?"

"What we need to know is where your loyalties lie. You were in his council for many years and had appeared to have his complete trust," said Aaron.

"True, I trusted him with everything. He was like a brother to me. I had faith in his plan to rule Midgard, but that all changed the day my father refused to attack a human town. Rathgar had him killed and my town burned. I saw him then for the monster he truly was, and I ran as far as I could until I found Finn and his crazy family. Then I swore an oath to Finn. I bear a ring of the king's guard."

"You swore an oath to Rathgar!" yelled Aaron, getting nearly nose to nose with Heidi.

"Rathgar broke that vow the day he killed my people," said Heidi through gritted teeth.

Aaron smiled and turned to the rest of the room. "I am satisfied that she is trustworthy."

Finn stood, having been silent throughout the interrogation. "I agree. She has done nothing but help since we met."

Starting with Lady Lily one by one, the members of the court struck their chairs and answered "Skaal," the last being Dagfinn, who paused for a moment and studied Finn's face.

"Skaal!" he finally bellowed.

"You may go," said Aaron to Heidi.

Heidi jumped out of the chair and wasted no time getting away.

As soon as Heidi was clear of the court, the chair in the middle of the room sank back into the floor and the etching of Mjolnir covered the floor once again. Finn sat and let out an enormous sigh. He was already exhausted, and they hadn't even planned the attack yet.

"So, if we have two parts of the staff and the Huldre child, why do we need to depose Rathgar?" asked Ed.

"Because if we don't stop him, he will unleash his army on the world to retrieve the scepter and Heidi. We have to take the fight to him to protect the human world," said Anders.

"And how are we going to stop Rathgar?" asked Dagfinn. He was certainly the skeptic.

But Finn said, "I actually have a thought about that. We are going to do a quarterback sneak."

"Is that some tactic you learned from the humans?" asked Lady Lily.

"It's a play one can do in the game of football. You make your opponent think the ball is in one place when in reality it is in another, and you score before they realize we have duped them."

Finn Stonefist

"So, you propose to trick Rathgar?" asked Aaron.

"Look, from what I've been told, the Keep is a mountain fortress nearly impenetrable. So that means we need Rathgar to come out of the Keep."

"What could cause him to leave the safety of the Keep?" asked Ed.

"This," said Finn, and he reached his enormous hand into his backpack and produce the Raven's claw scepter with the sapphire of Jotunheim still in its grasp. Gasps could be heard throughout the room.

"By the Gods, I never thought I would see that thing again," said Aaron.

"That will definitely lure him out, but it may also land right into his grubby meat hooks," said Jack in a gruff voice while he stroked his long beard.

"I don't plan to let this out of my sight. What we need is a forgery good enough to fool Rathgar," said Finn.

"No one can do that," said Dagfinn.

"Jack and his dwarven forge could," said Aaron.

The room got quiet, and everyone looked at Jack, who sat back in his chair. "I don't know if I could do that kind of work," he said.

"Oh, sure you could, dear," encouraged Ilsa, his wife. "Why, back in your less reputable days, you did work that could have fooled Odin himself."

Jack paused for a moment as he quickly contemplated the challenge put before him. "Well, it wouldn't have any powers and it would only look good from a distance. As soon as he touched it, he would know it's a fake, but I think I could make something passable."

"Great! How long do you need?" asked Finn.

"Well, normally a job like this would take two to three weeks," said Jack.

Aaron said, "Unfortunately, we don't have that long. Magic of this magnitude will require a large astrological event to draw on the power of all the realms and, unless I am wrong, there is a solar eclipse happening on the summer solstice this year. That will mean all nine realms will be aligned, including the sun. That would be more than enough cosmic juice to jump start the spell."

"That's five days away!" said Jack.

Finn looked over at Jack, who was white as a ghost. "Can you do it?"

Jack huffed and puffed and stammered. "By Odin! If I don't sleep or eat or crap for five days, I might be able to get it done. It won't be nearly as pretty, it being a rush job and all."

"He will suspect we want something in return," said Dagmar, who was now standing to be heard better.

"I have an idea," said Lady Lily. "We shall ask for the dark shifter Tove to stand trial before this court for her crimes against Midgard and its citizens."

"Rathgar won't give up his greatest weapon," bellowed Dagfinn.

"He would for a better weapon," stated Ed.

"I agree!" Finn shouted above everyone, causing the room to shake. "I agree. That is the best trade. We must believe that his lust for the Staff of Jotunheim will outweigh any price."

And so it was agreed. They spent the rest of the meeting counting the number of soldiers the court could gather on such short notice. The Nightfeathers and the Shoveltons said they could gather as many as a hundred trolls and a hundred dwarves willing to take down Rathgar, and Jack said he could supply weapons from his forge. The Stonefists had one hundred and fifty kin who were keen for a fight. The Edons said there were only about twenty-five to thirty elves they could think of that would help with tactical magic and healing. Lady Lily said she could provide about ten scouts and two hundred and fifty heavy infantry units from their army without leaving their kingdom too undefended. That brought the army to a maximum of just over six hundred strong, plus whatever Heimdal could muster from his feathered brethren. It was decided that while the army distracted Rathgar with the fake scepter, Finn and the others would portal into the underground cavern where Rathgar was assembling his machine and steal the shaft to the staff and portal out without being noticed.

Finn was more nervous than he had ever been. For the first time in his life, actual lives were in his hands. People may actually die for him, and that scared him to think about.

After the planning and all parties agreed to the plan, Aaron stood and raised his hands to get the attention of the room. "My King, if it pleases you, I suggest we adjourn until the eve before the siege, at which time we should meet at the foot of the Keep with our forces and prepare for the attack."

That made it all sound so official. There was no stopping this wave from moving forward. "That sounds good to me," said Finn.

"Does that mean we can finally eat?" asked Jack eagerly.

"I adjourn us," announced Aaron.

The court members made their way to the large feast table where much of the food had already been consumed, but with a clap of Lady Lily's hands, the food was refreshed, like it had just come from the kitchen. They sat and enjoyed a lighthearted meal as they spoke of the battle to come and their hopes and dreams. After the meal, they said their goodbyes and Talon opened a portal back to Troll's Rest.

Back in human form and laying in his bed that night, Finn thought about everything that had happened in the last hours and realized he had held an actual royal court meeting and created a battle plan. His thoughts drifted from battles to come to his parents, and he thought of his father trapped in the cave and his Mother who was trapped by the lies of Rathgar. He vowed to himself that he would save them as he drifted into a restless sleep.

...

Chapter 16

A few hours later, Finn opened his eyes to the very distinct feeling he was being watched. He rolled over, only to be greeted by two large, identical, and very bearded, smiling faces. Finn jumped back and fell off the other side of his bed. When he peeked back over the edge, he again saw two smiling bearded men staring back at him. They were of average height, but Finn certainly recognized the face, even in human form.

"Jack?" asked Finn, still confused why there were dwarves in his room.

"Oh good. You're awake, my king," said Jack.

"Am I seeing double?" asked Finn.

"No, my King, allow me to introduce my brother Orlyn. We're twins if you can't tell," said Jack.

"You don't say," said Finn as he pulled himself up to sit on the edge of his bed. "So why are you in my bedroom?"

"Well, Anders said it was time to get you up, and we volunteered because we are here to offer you a rare opportunity," said Jack.

"What is that?" asked Finn.

"Well, my Lord," began Orlyn, "I was your parents' best friend and when I heard you had no official training, I thought what better way to help my friends than to make sure their son is properly prepared to take on Rathgar."

"How do you plan to do that?" asked Finn. He'd never say so, but he was skeptical of what a dwarf could offer in training to a giant.

"Before the coup, Orlyn was head of royal guard training. He can help you harness and control your abilities as an ice giant and control your inner fire ogre," stated Jack.

"Right," Orlyn said. "I wasn't there when Rathgar attacked all those years ago and I couldn't protect your parents, but I am here now and I couldn't think of a better way to help now than to make sure their son had the best training possible and that is what I can give you."

Finn thought hard about the offer. He agreed he could use some help in the training department. He definitely couldn't be any worse at battle training than he is now and something about Orlyn made Finn innately trust him, so he accepted Orlyn's offer to train him and followed the dwarves back downstairs where Hilde had a large bubbling pot of grits going. The smell of cooked bacon nearly overwhelmed Finn with hunger. He had just wolfed down an enormous plate and was heading for seconds when Orlyn interrupted him.

"We should get started, my King," said Orlyn.

The dwarf was right. The coming battle would not wait for breakfast. Finn set his bowl down grudgingly and went upstairs to get dressed. He returned a few minutes later in sweats and an old football tee-shirt and sneakers.

"What are you wearing?" asked Orlyn.

"My workout clothes," said Finn.

"We aren't lifting weights at a local gym. We are training for a life and death battle. Put on the clothes from Thor and bring the King's Stone. You must learn to train in full armor."

Finn huffed and went back upstairs to change.

Orlyn waited until Finn was out of sight when he approached Anders, who had been sitting at the table sipping his coffee and reading the morning paper and trying not to act too interested in the goings on around him..

"Anders, I couldn't help but notice the staff you carry these days. The Norn's staff?" said Orlyn.

"That's right. Since I got it, my leg feels stronger, I feel stronger. Like the old days," said Anders.

Finn Stonefist

"Well, you should, considering that was the staff that cursed you to begin with," said Orlyn.

"What are you saying?" asked Anders

"I'm saying when the Norn was killed, and the staff passed to you, the curse that crippled you was broken. I dare say you could truly be your old self again," said Orlyn, touching the side of his nose.

Anders tried to process what Orlyn was saying. "Are you saying—?"

Finn reappeared dressed in the shoes, jeans and tee-shirt he had received from Thor and the King's Stone in hand.

"Better?" Finn asked.

"Much. Now go outside and shift into your true form with armor and weapon. I will be there shortly," said Orlyn.

Finn nodded and went out the backdoor to the yard.

In the backyard, Finn was in full giant form with the Guardian's Armor on and his battleaxe in hand. He was busy throwing it into the woods and catching it as it flew back to his hand when Orlyn approached him.

"Alright, Finn, let's get started," Orlyn said.

"Finn? What happen to my King?"

"Oh, I forgot to tell you," said Orlyn. "In training, there are no titles. No kings or lords or ladies. Just people with only what they have. In battle, your enemy won't care about your social status as they hack you to bits, Rathgar, least of all. Out here you do as I command when I command it. You must trust and listen to me. Rathgar has had a lifetime of training from the best, including me. I have five days to teach you enough to keep you from being killed. Now let's begin. I think we will start by assessing how good you are in a fight."

"Who do I fight?" asked Finn.

A wry smile crept across Orlyn's lips. "Me." Just then, Orlyn grew. He continued to grow until he was eye to eye with Finn.

"How did you do that? I thought dwarves were, uh, you know, uh...." said Finn.

"Dwarves are what? Short? True, we are, but you're not the only one with fancy toys from Asgard," said Orlyn. He then produced an amulet in the shape of Mjolnir. It was simple and ornamentation, but Finn could sense a very strong aura from it, almost like it was watching him. "When I was made Battle Master by your grandfather, I was gifted this amulet that has been handed down from one master to the next. It allows me to mimic my opponent's abilities and shape. Comes in very handy when you're short," said Orlyn.

"I'm still not so sure—" said Finn.

Without warning, Orlyn struck him in the chest with an enormous fist.

Finn felt like Mjolnir had plowed into him. He stumbled backwards and nearly lost his footing, but steadied himself. He looked at his chest and saw a dent in the shape of a fist directly in the center of his chest. "Ow! You dented my armor!" he bellowed.

"The enemy will not care if you are ready or if it's a fair fight," instructed Orlyn.

Finn looked at his armor again, but the dent was gone, despite the throbbing in his sternum.

"You want to dance, let's dance," said Finn as he gripped his axe and charged Orlyn at full speed. Orlyn didn't flinch until the last second when he grabbed Finn's axe and, using Finn's own momentum against him, he spun Finn and kicked him in the butt. Finn stumbled this time and landed face first in the grass. Finn picked himself up and turned to face Orlyn, who was standing with Finn's axe in hand.

"Lesson number two, you ain't all that, football boy. Assume the enemy knows all your moves because he does and more. A cocky warrior is a dead warrior," said Orlyn, as he tossed the axe back at Finn.

They spent the rest of the morning with Finn attacking Orlyn and getting promptly tossed or knocked or thrust into the dirt. When Hilde appeared on the deck with a stack of sandwiches for them, Finn was dirty, tired, and very discouraged. He hadn't landed a single blow against Orlyn. They both returned to human form and ate their food in silence until Finn finally spoke. "How am I supposed to survive an actual fight when I can't even knock you down in practice?"

"In the beginning, I told you to listen to me," Orlyn said.

"But you're not saying anything. You're just tossing me around like a rag doll," said Finn.

"I may not be saying any words, but if you watch your opponent, they will show you what they will do by how they hold themselves. Their eyes widen just before they strike or block. Their attacking side will naturally be faced away from you for protection. Look for the little things. Even I can't hide all my tells. My body is talking to you. Just listen to it. Pay attention and you will see what to do next. Also, trust the King's Stone. It will guide you. Some have even said it speaks to them."

"I have had the experience like it knows what I need and how to give it to me," said Finn, staring at the stone in his lap.

"I would suggest you listen to it and let it teach you," said Orlyn.

"I will try, I promise," said Finn.

"Should we get back to it?" asked Orlyn as he finished the last sandwich.

"Oh, I guess," groaned Finn.

Back in full form, Finn squared up to Orlyn and swung his axe straight at him. Orlyn easily deflected the blow and swept Finn's legs out from under him, landing him flat on his back.

"You're not listening, you're just attacking," said Orlyn as he helped Finn to his feet.

This time, Finn paused and studied Orlyn. He was standing practically square to him, but Orlyn's left foot was cocked just a little to the side. Then a thought came to him that Orlyn will strike from the left this time. Finn swung his left hand with the axe at Orlyn, which he quickly deflected and just as Finn had thought, Orlyn responded with a left-handed round house punch. Finn ducked, avoiding the blow, and saw his opportunity to strike back. As he stood, he caught Orlyn's chin with a full uppercut punch. Striking him with everything he had. His fist connected, and the blow knocked Orlyn backwards, causing him to stumble. Finn took this opening to hook Orlyn's leg with the blade of the axe and pull his feet out from under him; much like he had just done to Finn. Orlyn landed with a great thud in the grass, causing dirt and debris to fly everywhere. Finn immediately went to Orlyn and offered him help up when he noticed Orlyn was laughing, loudly.

"Are you okay? I didn't mean to hit you that hard. I am so sorry," said Finn.

Sitting up and catching his breath, Orlyn wiped a little blood from his lip that was already showing signs of swelling. "My boy, I haven't been hit like that since I worked in the Keep. Let's go again."

Finn helped Orlyn to his feet, and they sparred for the rest of the afternoon with Finn landing even more blows. In the end, both were bruised, sore, and exhausted when Hilde appeared on the deck. "If you boys are done beating each other senseless, I have dinner ready."

Orlyn looked at Finn and said, "I think he's had enough for one day."

"I've had enough. You're the one with a fat lip and a one heck of a shiner on your eye," said Finn.

Both returned to human form and limped into the house. After dinner, Tallis came over and applied salve to both Finn and Orlyn. Their bruises and cuts healed quickly, and they both felt much better. Hilde made a tea for their sore muscles and prescribed lots of rest.

Orlyn stood and said, "I need to go, but I will return in the morning. We have something special to explore tomorrow."

"What's that?" asked Finn.

"Tomorrow," was all Orlyn said, and he said his goodbyes and left out the front door.

That night, after a long hot shower, Finn lay in bed reviewing the lessons he had learned that day from Orlyn. His thoughts turned to the King's Stone, and he retrieved it from his desk. He turned it over in his hand and stroked the family crest etched into it. It hummed when he did this, almost like a cat purring.

"What are you trying to teach me?" he asked the stone.

There was no response.

"Great, I'm talking to rocks again," he said out loud, placing the stone on table next to his bed. Finn's eyelids grew heavy, and he drifted into a dreamless sleep. The sleep that only comes after pure exhaustion.

Finn woke to his cell phone's alarm clock screeching in his ears. He sleepily slapped at it until he finally connected, and it shut off. It was only then did he realize that every muscle in his body felt like it was on fire. He had never felt this sore, not even after spring training for football. He stiffly made his way downstairs, where Hilde had a breakfast of eggs and pancakes waiting for him.

It wasn't long before Finn was enjoying a plate full of delicious pancakes and eggs and a large mug full of hot, healing tea when the rest of the house woke up.

A sleepy Arna appeared and said, "Pancakes!"

Hilde slapped his hand away. "Those are for Finn. Yours are in oven staying warm."

Arna pulled his hand back quickly and grumbled as he served himself a plate of lukewarm pancakes. Finn just smiled at him with a mouth full of pancake and egg. There was a knock at the door. Hilde answered it and there stood Orlyn, right on time.

Finn groaned at the sight of his teacher. "I'll go get ready," he said, gulping down the rest of his tea and grabbing one more pancake for the road. He returned a few minutes later, already wearing his armor. "The backyard then?" he asked.

"Not today. Today we go on a brief trip," said Orlyn. He then produced a small, round metal disc about the size of a drink coaster with a mountain etched into it.

"What's that, a giant nickel?" asked Arna with a smile.

"Not exactly. This is a Vei Mynt or a Road Coin. It can take a person or persons to a specific set of coordinates by simply placing it on a door. The etching on it is where you want to go and the spell takes you to within a hundred feet of that point, give or take," he explained.

"A Road Coin is a rough way to travel if you aren't specific enough," said Anders, who had appeared behind Orlyn.

"Well, I made this one, so you can blame me if it's bumpy," said Orlyn.

"You know about these Road Coins, grandpa?" asked Finn.

"Oh, sure I do. It was a common way to travel back in the day. I haven't seen one in a long time. I was never very good at making them, so I didn't use them often. Ended up twenty miles off my target inside a tree one time. It took me two days to get out of that tree. After that I traveled the old-fashioned way, by foot," said Anders.

"Inside a tree?" Finn asked, glancing at Orlyn.

"Don't worry, Finn. I have made dozens of these, and I almost always hit the mark," Orlyn said. "Anyway, we are going to the top of Gunsight Mountain today and that is a mighty large target, so we'll be fine." He turned and placed the Road Coin flat against the front door. It seemed to hold itself in place. Then he stepped back and cleared his throat.

"I would travel to the top of Gunsight Mountain, Alaska," he said clearly. Then he tapped the coin once with a stubby, hairy finger. Nothing seemed to happen. The coin just dropped to the floor with a clank. Orlyn retrieved the coin and replaced into his pocket.

"Did it work?" asked Finn.

"Open the door and see," said Orlyn.

Finn carefully opened the door. There was a swirling vortex on the other side. It immediately pulled on Finn, drawing him in. He grabbed the doorknob and clung to it for dear life.

"Just let go and jump in like this," shouted Orlyn over the roar of the vortex. Then he jumped into it yelling, "Yahoo!."

The dwarf disappeared into the vortex. Finn closed his eyes, held his breath, and let go of the knob. The force of the vortex immediately grabbed him and pulled him through the door. Finn dared to open his eyes and found that he was swirling in great loops as he was pulled along the current of the vortex. He felt like he was falling from a great height and could feel his speed increasing. At the other end of the vortex, he saw a familiar sight. The mountain top he was aiming for. He couldn't believe it, but it worked. Then, just as he was about over the flat spot on the top of the mountain, the vortex disappeared completely, and Finn found himself falling to the ground. He was sure that he was about to go splat on the side of the mountain. The ground rushed towards him at an alarming pace. He did the only thing he could think of. He closed his eyes and waited for the impact. Then, nothing. No impact, no searing pain of broken bones, not even the rush of falling anymore. He barely opened one eye and saw that he was hovering over the ground about ten feet up like some looney tune character. Then, THUD! He fell the last few feet and hit the rocky ground. After catching his breath, Finn got to his feet. To his dismay, he was about a third of the way down the mountain. He had to climb. He shifted into giant form, knowing the longer legs would make shorter work of the climb. As he reached the top, he saw Orlyn sitting on a boulder, smoking a pipe.

"Well, it's about time," said Orlyn.

"What was that? It just crapped out on me and I nearly died!" said Finn.

"Ah, but you didn't die, and that's what counts and the only reason you fell is because you waited too long to jump in. Otherwise, you would have floated in like a feather," said Orlyn.

Finn Stonefist

Finn noticed the rock dust all over Orlyn and figured neither one of them floated in except like a lead weight. Finn found a boulder big enough and sat to catch his breath.

Finn looked around the mountain top and noticed it looked just like he remembered it did from his encounter with Thor. The garden was gone, and the top was flat with two tall sides and broken boulders scattered about.

"So, what am I going to learn here, oh wise one?" asked Finn.

"You see the rock you are sitting on? Pick it up," instructed Orlyn.

The rock Finn was sitting on was about the size of a minivan and probably weighed as much. Finn doubted he could lift it, but stood and wrapped his arms around the enormous boulder, anyway. He lifted with everything he had, but the stone didn't move an inch. Finn let go and stepped back, huffing and puffing from the strain. He was dismayed that even in giant form, he couldn't lift it.

"That thing probably weighs a ton. There is no way I can lift that," he said.

"Sure, you can. Don't think about how big the stone is, just think about lifting it. You are an Ice Giant from your father's side and but on your mother's side you have Stone giants. You can command stone and earth. So tell the stone you wish to lift it and you will," explained Orlyn.

"Just that simple, huh?" said Finn.

"Just that simple," said Orlyn.

Finn again wrapped his arms around the stone and in his mind, he plead with the rock that he could lift it. Finn strained against the weight of the rock, with the same result as before. Then all at once, the rock moved and lifted from the ground. Every second it felt lighter and lighter until he was standing up with the boulder wrapped tightly in his arms. He released the boulder, and it dropped to his feet with a great crash, sending dust and debris in every direction. Once the dust settled, Finn could see Orlyn watching him with a look of awe on his face. The dwarf clapped his hands together.

"Well, done!" he said. "I honestly thought we would be here all day. Now, do it ten more times."

"Ten more times!?" Just the thought exhausted Finn.

"Yep. You need to command stone and earth with a thought, but to do that, you must have the earth's respect. The earth only respects strength which you need to build. Once you are powerful enough, the earth will become your ally and even your friend. I understand from your uncle you had an experience close to here where the earth protected you from the eagles of Rathgar. That tells me the earth knows who you are and already has an inherent trust in you. Now, trust yourself,"

Finn hefted the great stone ten more times with each lift getting easier instead of harder. By the end he could lift the stone over his head with no problem at all, at which point Orlyn yelled, "THROW IT!" Finn did. He threw the great stone nearly across the top of the mountain.

"Now, the next thing I want to try is very advanced and few giants have ever been able to do it, but you being a Sammeloper and us being short on time, you might have it in you. As a stone giant, you may have the ability to take on the aspect of stone on your skin," said Orlyn.

"I can turn into stone?" asked Finn.

"Not exactly. You can cause your skin to become as tough as stone. So just focus in your mind on what that would feel like to you and picture that covering just one of your hands."

Finn closed his eyes and pictured the only thing he could: Einar turning to stone in the cave. He pictured the stony film covering his hand and then felt something on his hand. He chanced a peek and sure enough, the same looking stony film was slowly covering his fingers, then his palm and up to his wrist.

"Okay, that's enough for our purposes. Tell it to stop," instructed Orlyn.

Finn thought the word "stop," but the film didn't stop. It continued to climb his arm and its pace was growing.

"Finn, you need to stop it before you turn to stone!" panicked Orlyn.

"I'm trying, but it won't stop!" howled Finn.

The stone skin continued to climb Finn's arm. His panic grew with each second. It climbed all the way up his arm and across his chest and down the other arm, and then it seemed to stop. Both of his arms were completely covered in the stone skin. The only problem was Finn couldn't move. Then suddenly he felt something, he felt heat. Starting in the pit of his stomach and traveling up to his chest. He could see red veins form on his arms. They were hot, but they didn't burn him. The sweat on his body steamed off and Finn could feel himself getting hotter.

"Orlyn! What do I do!?" pleaded Finn in a strange voice. It was low and gravely.

"You have somehow sparked your inner fire, and it's trying to release the fire ogre within you. Your emotions are too high. You need to calm down and get control of your fear!" said Orlyn as he took cover behind a boulder.

"And if I don't?" panicked Finn.

"You'll either turn into a raging fire beast or you'll explode," said Orlyn from behind his boulder.

Finn's skin on his arms was a molten red color and heat waves could be seen coming off him.

"Get a hold of yourself, Finn," Finn said to himself. "Calm down. Breathe, focus on your breathing." He closed his eyes and tried to breathe slowly in through his nose and out his mouth. His breath was hot and tasted of sulfur. He ignored this and focused. He could feel himself calming down. He felt a cooling sensation flow over him, and he opened his eyes. It hadn't worked. It had changed, though. Now his arms were lit up with blue flames, but they didn't burn him, and he could move his arms. He waved his arms around in punching motions, then tried something. He turned and faced the boulder Orlyn was hiding behind and smashed it with a blue fiery fist. The boulder shattered into a hundred individual pieces, leaving Orlyn exposed.

Orlyn dusted himself off and inspected Finn's new form. He was still thirty feet tall, but his arms were covered in blue flame.

"Ice fire," muttered Orlyn.

"What?" asked Finn.

"Ice fire or Is Fir in the old tongue. It is a rare and powerful gift. It combines the destructive force of fire with the strength of pure stone and the purity of ice. I have only ever read about it in the old stories from Jotunheim. No one on Midgard has ever done it," said Orlyn.

"I feel strong. Almost invincible," said Finn.

"Yes, well, it is an extremely powerful ability. Maybe we should call it a day. Return to human form and we will go," said Orlyn.

"But I feel like I just got a hold of this," insisted Finn.

"No!" shouted Orlyn,

"Why? Are you scared?" argued Finn.

"It can consume you! That feeling of power you have right now . . . in the old stories, those who had this gift eventually succumbed to their dark sides and were destroyed. So, no, we are finished for the day and that's an order!"

Finn became silent and shifted back into his human form. The stone skin and flames were gone. He was his old self again. A feeling of relief washed over him.

"Orlyn, I'm sorry for arguing. I didn't know," started Finn.

"I know, my boy. I am sorry for yelling at you, but what I haven't told you is that your father and mother weren't my only friends. Your uncle was my friend as well, but when he learned to create the stone skin and got a taste of the power, it consumed him and destroyed the person I knew. Rathgar became cruel and twisted in his mind. I swore I would never let another trainee become that again."

"I am not my uncle or my parents. I am my own person," said Finn.

"That you are, my boy, that you are," said Orlyn, clapping Finn on the arm.

Just then, a portal opened in front of them and Arna came stumbling through.

"Arna! What are you doing here?" asked Finn.

"Mom says you both need to come home now. There is something going on and I have something to show."

The three of them made their way quickly through the portal and found themselves in the barn. Finn could see a group of people surrounding a figure that was sitting on the ground. Finn stepped toward the group when Anders appeared in front of him.

"Finn, take a moment. This could be a trap," said Anders.

Finn pushed by him and made his way through the crowd. He noticed Heimdal sitting on the workbench. He looked tired and his feathers were missing in patches. Corvax clacked in her cage and flapped her on good wing. The group comprised people Finn recognized. There were Mick and Anders and Erik, but there were also Jack and Lady Lily. Finn was shocked to see them until he saw who they surrounded. It was his mom. She was bound and gagged.

"What is she doing here?" asked Finn.

"My scouts reported a creature in the woods near Saxman Village that seemed to shift into any form," Heimdal said. "I went to investigate when I found her wandering through the forest. She wasn't making any sense, and she kept shifting between different forms, from Fae to giant to troll and back to this form. That is when I recognized her. It took a lot to subdue her, and I lost good men in the fight, but we were able to get her here where Arna was able to bind her with his rope from Thor. As I understand it, it can bind anything in the nine realms so it should hold her."

"You didn't subdue me. Your buzzard brigade outnumbered me, and you caught me off guard. Something that will never happen again," said Tove, who had pushed the gag out of her mouth. Her face was bruised and scratched.

Finn wanted to pity her. He wanted to hug her and tell her everything that had happened over the last few weeks. But he knew now was one of those times Jimmy spoke of where he had to be a king.

"We don't have time to deal with this. For now, keep her here until after the battle," said Finn, and he turned to leave the barn.

Tove laughed. "Quite the little king they have turned you into, my son."

Finn stopped in his tracks and came back to face Tove, eye to eye. "What did you call me?"

"King or son," Tove sneered. "You think you can stop him? He will win and he will amass the magic of Midgard and he will destroy you all."

Finn stared at Tove hard. "Uncle Erik, you, Mick and Grandpa workout a guard schedule, everyone else to the house now."

Chapter 17

At the house, Finn barely noticed that Aaron and Edna had arrived. He stood at the fireplace, staring into the flames. His mind was on the prisoner in the barn and the fact that in only a few days, he was expected to lead hundreds into battle. He turned and faced the group of family and friends that had joined him. No one spoke. They knew what was coming and now there was a real chance Rathgar knew they were coming. What were they supposed to bargain for now? They had their prize. She was tied up in the barn. After what seemed like an eternity, Finn finally spoke.

"Once, during a playoff game, we heard a rumor that our coach's play book had been leaked to the other team. That meant they possibly knew all our plays and could counter anything we threw at them. We have a similar situation here and I will be honest with you. I don't know if our plan will still work. I don't know if any plan will work. I am scared of failing. I am scared to lead others into battle. I'm scared to be king, but this is the only plan I have, and I have to get the last part of the staff to save my father. So, if you and your people want to back out, I will not hold it against you, but I need to go through with this."

Heidi was the first to step forward. "I know I am the last person any of you ever thought would be here tonight, but Finn, you have trusted me from the beginning. Even when you learned of who I was, who I am, you still put your faith in me. You made me a member of the royal guard and have hidden nothing from me, which is more than I can say for Rathgar. I made an oath to you and this kingdom and this crazy family, so as for me I am here to stay, and I will help in any way I can." Then she sat back down.

Finn Stonefist

"Well, a dwarf has never backed down from a challenge no matter how hopeless, so we are with you, boy," said Jack.

"The Fae made a promise to aid you and we never go back on our word," said Lady Lily.

Finn listened as each family spoke and swore their help. Anders spoke for Dagfinn and the giants and Mick for trolls. Each clan promising to go forward with the plan.

"We have to tell the council of these developments, and you may lose their confidence, but Edna and me, we are with you," said Aaron.

"And you will have my talons and fellow brethren, my King," said Heimdal.

Finn was overcome as one after another pledged their allegiance.

"Well then, I think we should proceed as if nothing has changed. Rathgar may not know we have Tove, so we should still ask for her in exchange for the fake scepter," said Finn.

"Where should we stage the army?" asked Jack.

Mick stood and said, "I have an idea for that," and he produced a rolled-up map of Alaska. "Here on the northwestern slope of Mount Denali. There aren't any human towns and the tundra is vast, so there is little chance of surprises."

"How am I going to get into the keep if Rathgar can see us coming?" asked Finn.

"Since you can't portal straight into the keep without being vaporized by the wards, you will enter through the original entrance that was carved by the ancestors. It lies here in a small town called Peterville on the southeast slope of the mountain range. Through the old mine, you can travel up to the great cavern. It was maintained as an emergency escape for the royal family, but it will still be miles of rough going," explained Jack.

"That's where I come in," said Arna proudly.

Everyone stared at Arna like he was crazy.

"Jack, can we show them please?" asked Arna.

"Absolutely," said Jack. "If everyone will join us in the backyard for a little demonstration."

With that, everyone exited to the backyard where Arna was nearly busting with excitement.

"So, I spent the day playing with my horse and learning all about him from Jack," said Arna as he held out the tiny jade horse figurine he had received from Thor. Arna set the figurine on the ground and stood back up. He was about to say something when Jack interrupted him.

"Remember, just like we practiced," said Jack.

Arna nodded and took a deep breath and shouted, "Sjleipnir, I need you!"

Everyone watched the figurine. At first, nothing seemed to happen. Then the little horse jumped into the air and, with a loud crack of green light, an actual horse appeared in its place. Only, this was no ordinary horse. It is larger than any horse Finn had ever seen, and it was blacker than the blackest black. Even its hooves shone like obsidian in the dim light. Its eyes were a bright blue, and they seemed to glow in the evening light. The oddest thing about the horse was that it didn't have four legs or even six, but eight legs. Each as strong as the next. The horse snorted at the group and stomped each of its hooves.

"Everyone, I want you to meet Sjleipnir!" announced Arna like a proud father. "Jack told me he is Oden's personal steed and an Asgardian horse. He is faster than any other horse in Midgard. He should be able to get us up the tunnel in no time flat. And he can see in the dark no problem, so even if we can't see, he can. He also already knows his way through the tunnel."

"How does he know that?" asked Talon as he carefully moved towards the giant equine.

"Legend has it that Odin himself came to the coronation of the first king and queen and he rode his noble steed, Sjleipnir. At that time, there was only one entrance to the keep," explained Lady Lily.

"I've never read that legend," said Mick.

"Really? I guess you had to be there," said Lady Lily with a sly smile on her face as she moved forward to pet Sjleipnir's muzzle.

Finn was in awe at his cousin as he watched everyone carefully approach and take turns petting Sjleipnir, who seemed to enjoy all the attention. Arna was explaining all he had learned about his new friend and the history surrounding Sleipnir.

"Just one question. How do we ride him?" asked Finn.

"Oh, that is the craziest thing. After I summoned him the first time I was in the barn looking for a rope to use as a lead when a saddle just appeared in the barn sitting on top of the old tractor," said Arna and he pulled back a tarp that Finn hadn't noticed before. Under the tarp was a saddle, but not just any kind of saddle. It was longer than any saddle Finn had seen before, and it had four seats, each with their own saddle horn. It looked like someone had taken four saddles and joined them end to end. It was made of a dark brown leather with a Nordic knot etched into the edges and the horns all resembled the shape of Mjolnir.

Arna, with the help of Talon and Finn, hefted the great saddle and lifted it as high as they could, but Sjleipnir still had to kneel for them to reach his back. Once saddled next, came the reins and bit. They were enormous, with the steel bit feeling more like a dumbbell as Arna hefted it. Sjleipnir lowered his head and easily took the bit into his mouth. While the boys finished tacking up Sjleipnir, Tallis noticed something else under the tarp that the boys had not seen.

"Arna, you're going to want to see this," said Tallis.

They're laying on the ground neatly displayed were two items. The first was a large metal helmet that was obviously for Sjleipnr and a very large breast plate that looked like it would only fit a giant horse. It shone like chrome in the evening sunlight and had a large etching of Mjolnir in the center. Tied to the breastplate was a rolled piece of parchment. Arna retrieved the roll and opened it.

"What does it say?" asked Finn

"It's a letter from Thor!" said Arna and he broke the Mjolnir shaped wax seal and he read it aloud.

Arna,

This is Sjleipnir. He is a genuine gift of the Gods. He has served for many years with the royal guard of Asgard and is now assigned to you as your companion. You will never have a more loyal friend than an Asgardian steed. You will find that you will quickly form a bond with him that goes beyond man and beast. Treat him well and he will never fail you.

SKAAL!

Thor

P.S. Tell Finn he has the favor of the Gods and the faith of Odin that he will succeed.

"I would dare say that Finn isn't the only one with the favor of the Gods," said Anders.

"In all my long years, I have never seen the Gods put so much faith in someone so young, let alone four young ones who can barely even shift yet. You are all chosen for a great destiny, and I believe you will do great things beyond the coming battle. With this, I have no doubt that we will be victorious," said Aaron.

"It is getting late," said Finn. "I suggest we get some rest and continue training tomorrow. We have three days until we will meet at the rendezvous point at first light and we will end this. I am not one who is good at speeches, but this occasion seems to need one. I am new to all of this. When I started this summer, I never thought I would end it with a life-or-death battle or that I would find out my entire family history is just that, history, and not crazy stories for children. As I look around, I don't see friends or subjects or giants or Fae or any other race. I only see family. A crazy and out of this world family, but a family none the less. Despite our differences, we are brought together by a common purpose: freedom. We all desire to be free from fear and oppression. So, tell your people that in three days we don't fight for a king, or a boy or a savior, or even for the staff. We fight for freedom from tyranny. We fight for freedom to exist as we are and to be who we are and what we are. Rathgar would control us and the human world. He would have us bow to his tyranny, but I am here to tell you that no one I know will ever bow to fear mongers and hate. Be them man, giant or god, we will not bow. We are a free people and free we will remain! SKAAL!"

In a resounding cheer, the entire group chanted "SKAAL!" repeatedly until the surrounding woods echoed with the sound of cheers and battle cries.

They broke up and began doing their individual jobs. Talon got together with Mick and Lady Lily and began sending messages with the battle plan through small portals to the different faction's headquarters.

After all the messages were sent, Talon approached Finn and asked, "So you have your armor and axe and you can shift, but the rest of have no weapons to defend ourselves. What should we do about that?"

Overhearing the conversation, Orlyn approached the two boys and said, "I have a solution to that problem. If you will permit me a quick trip home with Talon, I will return with what you need."

Finn agreed, and Orlyn and Talon disappeared through a portal. A while later, the portal reopened and Orlyn and Talon emerged. Talon was carrying three sheathed swords under his one arm, and Orlyn had three round wooden shields wrapped in his burly arms. They approached Finn, Arna, and Tallis.

"That place is amazing. If we survive this, you will have to go visit!" said Talon.

"I would be my honor, but for now, this should do. These are dwarven swords and shields. They are crafted with intuitive magic. So essentially, you think of the move and the sword or shield will move in that way. They are great for novices in a pinch such as yourselves," explained Orlyn.

Talon, Tallis, and Arna each selected a shield and sword and within minutes they were sparring throughout the backyard. The new weapons felt light in their hands and moved with the greatest of ease. Tallis attacked Talon and in an instant he could parry and block the blow with his shield like a well-seasoned battle master. Parries and thrusts and the clang of swords and shields filled the night air.

"Those are great!" said Finn.

"Thank you, my King, but the magic in them is temporary and will only last a few days, less if they use them more. Unfortunately, it was the best I could do in a pinch, but this I could take more time on and it came out much better than even I thought it would," said Orlyn as he unwrapped another package.

Finn Stonefist

Inside, Finn saw something that made his heart skip a beat. It was the false replica of the scepter. It looked identical to the real one. Complete with a gem grasped in a raven's claw. Finn picked up the replica and immediately could feel the difference. It wasn't nearly as heavy, and the magical aura that radiated from the real one was much stronger than the aura being put off by the fake.

"You were right. He will know it is a fake the second he touches it," said Finn.

"I think we can sell it though, my King. It only has to hold his attention long enough for you to get inside and get the shaft and get out," said Lady Lily, who had noticed the two talking about the replica. She asked to hold the scepter, and Finn handed it to her.

"It's lacking something," she said.

"Yeah, more time to do it better," scoffed Orlyn.

"No, I think it needs... this," said Lady Lily, and she closed her eyes. Suddenly, the fake jewel glowed brightly and dimmed.

"There now, when it is held it will shine just like the real one and that should add more curb appeal to our little ruse," said Lady Lily.

Jack, who was helping the others spar with their new weapons, saw the scepter and came straight over. "It's not my best work but not bad for a short notice job."

"It will work perfectly," reassured Finn, clapping Jack on the shoulder. "Now, if you will excuse me, I wish to have some fun with my friends before the battle."

Finn then shifted into full giant form with armor and axe and had the other three attack him, where he could easily deflect their blows. He was impressed by some of their moves that their new weapons gave them. Sjleipnir also got in on the fun and charged Finn, planting two hooves into his chest knocking him backwards. It didn't hurt, and it was fun for Finn to spar with someone closer to his size. This sparring game continued for a couple of hours and resulted in an exhausted Sjleipnir and four exhausted teenagers. Finn shifted back to human form.

"We had better save some of this for the battle. I need some time to think, and you guys should get some rest," said Finn.

The others agreed and Finn left them breathless and laying on the ground. Finn's thoughts wandered all over the place, but he kept coming back to the prisoner that was tied up in the barn. He finally decided he needed to talk to her. This could be the last time he would the chance.

In the barn, Tove was still tied to the post. She was busy shifting from one form to another in an attempt to escape her bonds, but it didn't matter what size or shape she took. The Asgardian rope that bound her shifted with her. She was the size of a large bumblebee when she noticed Finn enter the barn. She quickly shifted into her giant form, nearly hitting the rafters with her head.

"Calm down! I'm not here to hurt you. I just want to talk. I want to get to know you a little before... you know," he said.

"So, you worry you won't survive the coming battle. That's good; fear can keep you alive, but not for long. Rathgar will win. You can't hope to outnumber or outwit him. He is a trained killer and an expert tactician. What could you possibly learn from me that would help you and your pitiful rebellion?" said Tove, looking down at Finn from the rafters.

"Do you mind?" asked Finn, gesturing for her to return to human form.

Tove rolled her eyes but complied and shifted into the form of a dark-haired woman with bright blue eyes. Something about this form made Finn feel comforted. Like he was looking at someone he had known his whole life, but only in a dream.

Finn approached closer and could see that the ropes had chaffed her wrists and they were red and irritated. He took a stool from the work bench and sat in front of Tove.

"They say I am Sammeloper like you. I don't know, I can only take giant form. How did you learn the other forms?" he asked.

Tove quit struggling against her ropes and looked deep into Finn's eyes like she was looking for the deception, but found none.

"I was never very good at it when I was growing up" Her gaze was distant and her voice was soft. A small smile threatened her lips. Like she was thinking of happier times.

"Then, Rathgar took me. Every day for years he would demand I shift into this form or that form and if I couldn't, he would torture me until I did it out of desperation to make the pain stop," said Tove.

"How did he torture you? You are clearly more powerful than him," asked Finn.

"After he took me, the first thing I remember is waking up in the Keep in a cell. Memories flooded my mind. Memories of losing control and attacking Einar. I can remember there being a lot of fire as we fought. I struck a wall with my fist and a large stone fell and crushed the crib you were in. After realizing what had happened, I turned on Einar and caved his skull in with a stone. So, you see, you can't be my son. I watched him die," she said.

"But you never saw my body. You were just told I was there and obviously I wasn't. From what I am told by Uncle

Erik; you got us here safely. The night we arrived, Einar was sent to take you and me, but he only got you. You know what he remembers? He remembers losing control somehow and accidentally releasing his inner fire ogre and burning you and me alive. So, you see, you have the memory of killing each other and me, but it never happened. I am alive, and so is Einar," said Finn.

"Even if this is true, I have still taken innocent lives for him," spat Tove.

"Yes, but it was all because of a lie. I can tell you are fighting the mind spell Rathgar used on you. Which tells me there is still good in you. My mother still lives," said Finn.

"Since the fight at the village when I was knocked unconscious, I started having confusing dreams of a blonde baby boy and an old truck. I traveled a long distance with the baby. I have memories of a battle in the keep and me and Erik escaping as Einar stayed behind, but when I focus on them, it hurts and the old memories of your death come back. I don't know what's real anymore," Tove said.

"If I were you and I was as confused as you, I would search my heart and it will tell me the truth. You can lie to the mind, but the heart will always know the truth," said Finn. Anders had given him the same advice, and it had worked for him.

Tove looked up at Finn and met his eyes. A small smile crept along her lips. "He sounds like a wise man."

"The wisest," said Finn.

As Finn turned to leave, Tove said, "He knows you're coming, you know?"

Finned turned back and faced Tove and said, "I'm counting on it."

Finn Stonefist

Then Tove said, "If this is real and you are my son, I would say may the Gods be with you and to look for the unexpected, if you were my son that is."

Now that was progress. Finn smiled and left the barn.

Orlyn filled the next few days with intense training. Finned learned how to shift faster and faster and became more comfortable using his war axe and producing the shield when he needed it. Arna, Tallis, and Talon trained just as hard with Orlyn and their dwarven weapons. The third day was spent going over battle plans and practicing the last few moves that Orlyn had to teach them for fighting airborne foes, such as eagles and falcons.

As Finn stood outside, the air was cool and crisp. Morning was coming and butterflies filled Finn's stomach. It was time to enact his plan. It was now or never. He joined the gathering in the house. No one had slept that night. It was the same way before a big game. This was the biggest game ever. As he entered the house, it was quiet, with only hushed conversations being held in the kitchen. Finn saw that Ed and Dotty had arrived and were talking with Mick and Lorelei.

Anders spotted Finn and came up to him. "How are you, my boy?"

"I'll be better when this is all over. I don't see Dagfinn or Dagmar," said Finn.

"They sent a message that they and those fighting with them will meet us at the rendezvous point. Otherwise, everyone else is here and waiting for you to give the go ahead," said Anders.

Finn approached the group and cleared his throat to get their attention. The room fell silent. "You all know where to go and what we have to do. We just have to hold them long enough for us to get in, get the shaft and get out. Now, all of you return to your forces and let's move out."

With that, people gathered their things and disappeared through portals to their respective meeting places until it was just Finn, Tallis, Talon, Arna, Erik, Hilde, Anders, and Heidi.

Heidi approached Finn. "I would like to come with you and the others. I want to help; I want to fight. I need to fight."

Finn studied her face hard for a moment, then said, "I would be honored to have you fight by my side. Do you need a weapon?"

Heidi then produced her long cow like tail and whipped it back and forth. "I'll be fine."

With that, Arna hugged his parents. Tallis and Talon gave tearful goodbyes to their parents. Finn turned to Anders and didn't know quite what to say.

"Hell of a summer, am I right boy?" said Anders awkwardly. "I have never been good at sending family into danger. If I could, I would do it for you just to keep you safe."

"I know, grandpa, but you will keep us safer the longer you keep Rathgar distracted with the fake scepter," said Finn.

Finn and Anders embraced like it could be the last time they would ever see each other. Finn suppressed a wave of tears and turned to the office at the end of the hallway. In there was a safe that held the true scepter. Finn retrieved the scepter; he studied the scepter in his hand. It seemed strange to him that something so beautiful could be the root of so much destruction. Battles had been fought, lives ended, worlds changed forever just for a chance to wield it. As Finn stared deeply into the gem clutched tightly in the raven's claw, it hummed, then the hums turned into screams and cries of torment. It caused Finn to nearly drop it. He snapped out of the trance and stuffed it in his backpack. He turned and saw Heidi standing in the doorway to the office.

"How long have you been there?" Finn asked.

"Long enough. You can hear the screams, can't you?" said Heidi.

"What are they?" asked Finn.

"They are the screams and laments of all those who have suffered at the power of the staff. They haunt it forever and will never rest until we finally dismantle the staff, and the stone returned to the heart of Jotunheim," said Heidi.

"Why am I only hearing them now?" asked Finn.

"It can sense the coming battle and it laments for the souls that will be lost," Heidi said.

"You make it sound like it's alive or something," said Finn.

"Why not? Jotunheim had a heart. It was a living, growing entity and it was attacked and had its heart broken for the gain of evil. That day Jotunheim died and the only thing that can bring it back is that gem," said Heidi.

"You sound like you were there," said Finn.

"No, but my mother was, and I grew up hearing the stories of Jotunheim."

"Let's do this right then, and maybe we can make the past right too," said Finn, and they exited the office to join the rest of the group.

Upon returning to the living room Finn said, "Grandpa, Talon will open a portal for you all to meet the army at the rendezvous point. Once you are through, we will portal to our entry point or at least as close as we can get without being vaporized."

In the backyard last goodbyes were said, and Talon opened a portal to the army. Through the portal was a congregation of all kinds of creatures, from dwarves heavily armored with axes and battle hammers to full grown giants armed with clubs or spiked bats. The Fae were interspersed, armed with swords and lances and shields. The portal settled next to Lady Lily, who was staring at them, beckoning them to come through quickly. Though they couldn't hear her, they could see she was worried. Once the adults were through, Finn could see Anders gesturing for them to look in front of the army.

"Talon, can you adjust the portal's view?" asked Finn.

Talon swung the view to the front of the army and what Finn saw made his blood run cold. It was an army just as big as his, already staged and battle ready. It looked like it was mostly goblins and imps made up the infantry along with dark elves who were posted as archers. Ogres brought up the rear flanks armed with stone clubs and some were covered in a stony skin or flames like Einar's. Then Finn saw him. Standing high above the opposing army on a balcony carved out of the mountainside was a giant standing over twenty feet tall and clad in full battle armor. With a grin on his face like he had already won the battle, Rathgar looked over the battlefield with certainty. The sight of Rathgar made Finn feel sick to his stomach, but he knew there was no turning back now.

Chapter 18

As Finn passed through the portal, the air became crisp and cool. The smell of pine and snow was heavy in the air. Finn took a deep breath and allowed the cool mountain air to calm his nerves. Sjleipnir passed through the portal with Tallis, Talon, Arna, and Heidi onboard. Talon got them within a mile of the mine's entrance so they would have a short hike, then into the tunnel. Finn's thoughts turned to his family on the other side of the mountains. They had little time to get inside the cave, so he motioned for the others to stay mounted on Sjleipnir and follow him and to keep quiet. Finn remained in human form to reduce the sound he would make in the woods as they approached the mine. After about ten minutes into the hike, Sjleipnir became nervous and stopped dead in his tracks. Arna couldn't get him to move despite all his nudging with his heels.

"What's wrong with him?" Finn asked quietly.

"I don't know, but he feels nervous, like danger is close," Arna whispered.

Finn shifted into giant form and panned the surrounding area. About a hundred yards in front of them, Finn saw what made Sjleipnir nervous. Two creatures were posted as centuries near the mine's entrance. Each creature was ten to twelve feet in height and clad in armor that didn't quite fit them. They were each armed with a long wooden club with knobby spikes. To top it all off, they had long tusks that had been sharpened to a point. Finn told the others what he saw, and Heidi jumped down off of Sjleipnir and climbed a nearby tree for a better look. After a minute, she came back down and told them that the creatures were Dark Trolls. Orcs. Very tough, but not very bright.

"I think the direct approach is needed here," said Heidi, looking at Finn.

Finn understood what she was saying. He turned and charged the two orcs, who were sleepily guarding their post. Both orcs were taken by surprise when a full-sized giant came charging straight for them. They had no time to react. Finn knocked their heads against one another, leaving them unconscious in a heap on the ground. Finn drug the orcs off into the woods and signaled for the others to join him.

"Nicely done, cousin!" said Arna.

"Yes, very direct," said Heidi.

"I'll stay in this form. Then I can keep up if the rest of you ride Sjleipnir," said Finn, helping Heidi back into the saddle.

"Are you sure? It's a long way, and giants aren't known for their stamina," said Heidi.

Finn grunted. "I'll be fine." In truth, he didn't know if he could keep up, but he didn't want to be caught unawares by whatever may be in the tunnel.

"Alright, let's get going. We're losing time," said Arna as he slapped the reins on Sjleipnir's neck. Sjleipnir took off at a blinding pace and Finn ran at almost full speed, just to keep up with the giant steed. The others held onto the saddle horns for dear life, and Arna let out a "YAHOO!" as they entered the tunnel.

On the other side of the mountain range, Anders and the others faced an army of goblins, imps, orcs, ogres, and dark elves. They were howling and roaring at a deafening volume that made the perma-snow on the mountainside threaten to come crashing down on them. Anders locked eyes with Rathgar, who was still standing on his perch, preening like a peacock.

Finn Stonefist

Rathgar raised his hands, and his army fell silent. "I see you have come out of hiding, Father. What do you think of all my friends I have literally made? I helped every soul here turn to their dark nature, their true nature. Now, tell me why you have assembled an army on my doorstep? Not exactly the reunion I had imagined," he said in a loud, bellowing voice.

"Tell me, Rathgar, how did you know where we would be?" asked Anders.

"Oh, say a little bird told me," responded Rathgar as he gestured towards the sky.

It was then that Anders and the others noticed that the dark clouds above the mountain were actually a great flock of birds above them circling the mountain top.

"Now, tell me why you are here father!" roared Rathgar.

"We have something to trade for the traitor Tove. We have heard she is with you and she needs to stand before the people to answer for her crimes," responded Lady Lily.

"What could you possibly have to give that would cause me to give up my best weapon?" Rathgar asked.

"This!" said Lady Lily as she hoisted the fake scepter. The gem glowed just as she had enchanted it to, and the entire field fell silent.

"How did you come by such a relic?" asked Rathgar, shocked at the sight of his one desire.

"That is not important. What is important is whether we have a deal. We can either trade or we can come in and get Tove. Either is fine with us," said Anders.

"I will need to inspect it for treachery first," said Rathgar.

Rathgar waved his hand and a small, slender dark elf appeared in the front of Rathgar's ranks.

~ 235 ~

As the dark elf approached, Lorelei gaped at the sight of him. "Mir?"

"Yes, that is my name," the dark elf replied.

"It's me, Lorelei, your sister! I'm here with mama and papa." Aaron and Edna made their way to Lorelei's side.

"Son, you're alive! Come home with us and leave all this craziness," pleaded Aaron.

"Father! It is good to see you. I have your old job. Are you proud?" said Mir coldly.

Aaron and Edna were silent. They didn't recognize the being in front of them. It looked and sounded like their son, but something was missing. He seemed cold and detached. Mir approached Lady Lily and stretched forth his hand to receive the scepter for inspection.

The tunnel was dark, and Finn had nearly collided with the ceiling more than once. He was growing tired, and he lagged farther and farther behind. He finally signaled that he needed a break. Sjleipnir came to a sliding halt, and that nearly dumped his passengers off their saddles.

"I just need a few minutes, then I'll be good to go," gasped Finn.

The others were glad for the break as well and slid off of Sjleipnir. Tallis and Talon retrieved water bottles from the saddle bags. Finn shifted to human form to drink and downed all the water in his bottle almost without breathing.

"Slow down, Finn! You'll make yourself sick," urged Tallis.

Finn finally came up for air, though he felt as though he could drink an entire lake and still not be able to quench his thirst. He had never run so far, but he felt okay. He knew if he stopped for too long, he would not get going again. The fatigue was real, and Finn could already feel his muscles cramping.

Finn Stonefist

Arna shone his flashlight up and down the tunnel; the light disappearing into the thick darkness that surrounded them. "How far do you think we have gone?" he asked.

"We're close," said Finn, shifting back into giant form.

"How do you know?" asked Arna.

"I don't know, I can just feel it, and there is a smell now," said Finn.

"What kind of smell?" asked Talon.

"Water. We're really close; mount up and be ready for anything," said Finn, and he helped Tallis and Heidi onto Sjleipnir.

They set off again, but this time Finn felt more nervous. Their goal was close. The tunnel widened and there was a cool breeze. Sjleipnir seem to sense the group's emotions as they got closer and slowed down just a little. Suddenly, the tunnel gave way to a huge open cavern. Finn and Sjleipnir came to a sliding stop and everyone stood in awe. It was just as Talon had shown them in the Way Finder. The cave so high you couldn't see the top. They pulled out flashlights and scanned the cave. It was empty except for the forge that seemed to be abandoned and nearly cold, sitting silently next to the large lake in the middle of the cave floor.

Outside the mountain, Mir waited impatiently. After a moment's hesitation, Lady Lily handed the scepter to the diminutive elf, who grasped it greedily. Mir hefted the scepter and scrutinized it. The gem glowed brightly, and the metal was cool in his hand. Suddenly he hoisted it high above his head like a trophy and a great Golden Eagle snatched it from his grasp. It was Talax. He took the scepter and flew it up to Rathgar and dropped it into his waiting hands. Rathgar turned it over in his hands and studied every inch. Then his expression changed to a pinched snarl, and he smashed it against the stone rail of the balcony he was standing on, causing the gem to shatter into hundreds of pieces.

"It's a fake!" roared Rathgar from his high perch. "Kill them all!"

Talax soared down to his now enraged master.

"Take your forces and get to the cave. I have a feeling they have deceived us while the enemy was going for another prize," ordered Rathgar.

Talax called to his brethren, and the cloud of birds ceased their circling and followed Talax into the mountain. The army below charged forward towards Finn's army, waving spears and clubs.

"Shield wall!" shouted Anders.

The front infantry quickly formed a near solid wall with their round shields just as the enemy forces crashed into them like a wave on the rocks. The battle was on. A horde of imps and goblins poured over the shield wall, armed with spears and small swords. The Fae fended them off as best they could, but there were just too many. The dwarves moved in armed with war hammers and axes and began swatting large swaths of imps and goblins clear of the shields. Just then, a volley of arrows came in from the opposing side, raining down on the modest force with deadly accuracy. Dwarves and Fae alike fell to the rain of death from above. The trolls and giants took this as their cue to move in. They charged forward with shields and clubs and blew through the first line of enemy defenses with ease. They quickly reached the dark elf archers and dealt them in sweeping blows. It looked as though they had Rathgar's army on the run. That was until his ogres and orcs moved in to meet the trolls and giants toe to toe. This stopped their advance cold on both sides. The battle was brutal, and losses were getting heavy on both sides.

Finn Stonefist

"We have to get into that mountain and help Finn before there aren't any of us left on either side," cried Lady Lily over the clang of swords and shields. Just then, a shadow covered the battlefield.

Arron looked up. "The eclipse has begun!"

Rathgar had noticed the same thing. He ordered the army to retreat to the keep, and he disappeared back into the mountain top. Anders knew it was now or never. While deflecting blows from a group of goblins that had set their sights on him, he ordered the army to press forward as Rathgar's forces began their retreat. This seemed to embolden Finn's army, and they rushed forward with a great cry. Just then, in a last-ditch effort, a group of imps attacked Anders. Using his new staff, he fought them off the best he could, but they just kept coming. He yearned to get to the cave to help Finn, so he swung the staff over his head and slammed it hard into the ground. It hit with such force that the ground shook and an invisible wave came from the staff, knocking all the imps clear of Anders. They turned and joined their fellows in the retreat to the keep.

Anders grasped the staff with both hands and focused on what he looked like as a giant. It had been so long since he didn't know if he could even picture it. Then he glimpsed it in his mind's eye and he clung to that image with everything he had. He felt a rush of wind and when he opened his eyes; he was high above the battle and the imps and goblins at his feet were scattering in fear. Then he saw his feet were enormous. He was enormous. He was a true giant once more! The staff in his hand had grown with him and now resembled a bare gnarled tree. Magic coursed through his body. Someone clapped him on the shoulder. He turned to strike whoever it was, only to stop short when he saw it was Dagfinn.

Dagfinn had a big smile on his face. "It is good to see you again, old friend. Now let's finish this!"

They charged forward side by side, easily clearing a path through the goblins, imps, and dark dwarves in their way. When they got to the archers on the wall, the arrows fell with no effect, and the archers quickly retreated. The last line was the ogres and orcs who, when they saw the giants heading straight for them with no resistance in between them they dropped their clubs and spears, and some ran for the keep while others just ran. Those who ran for the Keep were quickly overtaken by the Anders and the others. With them out of the way, the path into the Keep was clear and wide open.

Deep in the Keep in the cave of the ancestors, Finn and the others made their way in the dim light of the now dormant forge and what light their flashlights gave off. It wasn't hard to find their goal. There, suspended over the center of the lake, was a long shaft of interconnected rods extending from the darkness of the ceiling. Finn imagined it extended clear to the mountaintop. At the end of the shaft, one rod differed from all the others. It was slightly longer and gave off a faint aura of blue energy. As Finn got closer, the lake's edge the scepter in his hand hummed and the jewel glowed brightly illuminating the water in front of him. Suddenly, the runes on the shaft glowed a bright blue, and the scepter pulled towards the center of the lake. In giant form, the pull wasn't great, but Finn imagined that in human form it was enough to drag him into the water. Finn waded into the lake towards the pull of the scepter.

"FINN! What are you doing?" said Tallis.

"I can feel the pieces calling to each other. It's like they want to be joined," replied Finn.

Finn Stonefist

He continued into the lake. Even in full giant form, the water still reached Finn's armpits. The water was dark and ice cold. The lake bottom was soft and covered in silt. The water made Finn shiver, and he could feel the silt filling his shoes with every motion, making his steps heavier and heavier. He reached the center where the shaft hung with its glowing runes and near deafening hum. It hung about eye level to him as he reached a shivering hand out to grasp it.

Suddenly his other hand, which was holding the scepter, jerked forward, and the scepter flew from Finn's grip. Finn swiped in vain to reclaim the scepter, but it flew through his hands and attached itself to the bottom of the shaft. There was a loud clang as the pieces met. Finn gripped the shaft and pulled with everything he had. The rod above the shaft began to bend and give way to Finn's enormous force when he suddenly heard a voice that made his blood run cold.

"I wouldn't do that if I were you nephew!" roared Rathgar from the beach.

Finn spun around. There was a cloud of birds holding Tallis, Talon, and Arna high off the ground. Rathgar had Heidi by the throat and lifted her off the ground. Finn could see Heidi struggling to get free of Rathgar's enormous fist.

"Now, come back here and I'll let them go unharmed," said Rathgar.

Finn didn't know what to do, but he knew Rathgar could not succeed.

"I know what you want, or should I say who you want. I also know that you need Heidi to activate the staff so you won't hurt her," shouted Finn, still gripping the shaft tightly.

"And who is it you think I want?" asked Rathgar.

"Loki!" shouted Finn. The name seemed wrong in his mouth and an icy shiver came over him different from the cold of the water. "But I can't let that happen no matter the cost and if you ever loved anything, you wouldn't let him out, no matter what he has promised you. You have to know it is a lie."

"You are but a boy who would be a king. You can barely control your first form. How could you possibly know the mind of a god? Now, come here or I order my eagles to pull your friends apart."

Finn looked up at Tallis, Talon, and Arna as they struggled against the immense eagles that had them stretched out. Rathgar raised a hand and Talax gave a caw that caused the eagles to increase the tension on the limbs of the others. They hollered out in pain. Finn released the shaft and put both hands up.

"Okay, okay I'm coming. Just let them go!" Finn trudged through the water back to the shore. Rathgar lowered his hand, and the eagles loosened their grip but did not let them go. Back on shore, Finn stood toe to toe with Rathgar. He bent ever so slightly so his nose nearly touched Rathgar's and growled, "Let them go."

Rathgar smiled and said in reply, "NO! You're big, but still a boy. I will let them go when you ferry little miss cow tail here out to the shaft, and she activates it. If you don't, I will have my eagles pull your friends apart."

Finn looked up at the others hovering above him. "It'll be okay, guys. I am sure we can find a way out of this." He looked pointedly at Talon, who seemed to understand what he was saying. "Give me Heidi and I will do as you ask."

Rathgar placed the near purple-faced girl on Finn's shoulder. Heidi quickly gripped Finn's neck and gasped hoarsely for air as she rubbed her chaffed neck.

"Now go," instructed Rathgar coolly.

Finn Stonefist

Finn turned and waded back out into the lake. About halfway out, Heidi leaned close to Finn's ear and said, "You can't let him release Loki. No one is worth letting that monster out."

"Just play your part and leave the rest to me," whispered Finn.

They reached the shaft in the middle of the lake. "Alright, do your thing," urged Finn.

"The problem is I don't know what my thing is," said Heidi.

"Just try touching it or something before the others get ripped apart," said Finn.

Heidi took a deep breath and reached out a trembling hand towards the shaft. She gripped it and the runes glowed and hum loudly. The gem glowed brightly, and a beam of light extended from the gem into the murky water below. Suddenly, the water around Finn and Heidi swirled in a clockwise motion like someone had pulled the plug on a great sink of water. The force of the water nearly swept Finn off of his feet, but he maintained his footing as Heidi gripped the shaft with her hands and Finn's neck with her legs and tail. Finn looked back at Rathgar, who seemed mesmerized by what was happening in the lake and had completely forgotten about his hovering captives. Just then, the lakebed shifted under Finn's feet, and he could feel himself rising out of the water. He looked down to see a great round platform rise from the depths. In the center was a figure chained to a large stone. The figure looked up at Finn and locked his fiery red eyes with Finn's.

Something suddenly filled Finn with dread. "Heidi, let go of the shaft!" he shouted.

"I'm trying but it won't let me go!" shouted Heidi desperately.

Finn grabbed the shaft and pulled with everything he had. The rod snapped free and the entire staff came free. A roar could be heard as the stone pedestal sank back into the lake and the swirling stopped.

Finn looked back at the shore and roared to Talon. "Now!"

With that, Talon managed to get an arm free and grabbed the Way Finder from his pocket. He immediately produced a portal below him, Tallis, and Arna. Pulling the portal towards them, they quickly found themselves on the floor of the cave and free of most of the eagles. The three of them bolted for Sjleipnir and retrieved their weapons amongst slashes of talons and the beating of wings. With swords and shields in hand, they fought back, bringing many birds to a bloody end, but there were too many for them to handle. Rathgar roared from the beach. Finn took the Staff of Jotunheim in hand and pointed it at his now enraged uncle. A shaft of energy came from the staff and struck Rathgar in the chest, knocking him clear into the wall behind him. Finn made quick work back to the beach to help his friends. With staff in hand, he laid a now weak and nearly unconscious Heidi on the shore and went to work scattering and eliminating the remaining eagles and falcons.

Suddenly Finn was struck from behind, nearly knocking him senseless. He turned to see Rathgar standing with a hammer from the forge in his hand and a scorch mark on his now bare chest where the staff had struck him. Finn used the staff to block another blow from Rathgar's weapon. He pushed Rathgar back far enough to give himself enough time to retrieve the King's Stone from the saddlebags. In a flash of light, Finn was covered head to toe in the Guardians' Armor, complete with his double-edged war axe.

"You are a thief! The King's Stone is mine!" Rathgar roared.

"Not anymore. The Gods have chosen a new king. I don't want to hurt you. Just stop this and face your punishment," pleaded Finn.

Rathgar roared and charged Finn. Rathgar slammed his hammer into the ground, throwing sand and debris into Finn's eyes, blinding him for a moment. Finn reeled backward from the flying debris, but not fast enough. Rathgar swung his sledgehammer in a sweeping motion and caught Finn square in the chest plate, but in his blinded state Finn couldn't compensate for the force of the blow and it knocked him into the cave wall. Then everything went dark for Finn.

"Finn!" screamed Tallis, and she ran to his side, coming to a skidding halt next to his head.

Blood dripped from his mouth, and he was out cold. She did her best to lift his enormous head into her lap, but Finn was clearly down. She watched as Rathgar smiled and turned his attention to Talon, Arna, and Heidi. They let out a battle cry and attacked Rathgar in an aimless frenzy. Rathgar easily disarmed Talon and Arna and tossed their swords into the lake. He then grabbed them both, one in each hand, and squeezed. They let out a strangled scream, then both boys went limp. He dropped them to the ground in a heap. Heidi attacked but was quickly knocked unconscious by one of Rathgar's fists. Overcome, Tallis jumped to her feet and charged Rathgar with just her sword. She sliced a clean cut through his calf before he turned around on her. He roared out in pain and swung an enormous fist at the frenzied girl who was swinging her sword at anything that moved. Tears filled Tallis' eyes as she furiously swung at the giant. Just then Rathgar connected a blow, but it just glanced off of her head. It wasn't enough to knock her out, but it knocked her to the ground, causing her to lose grip of her sword. Tallis hit the ground hard and could feel the blood coming from the new gash in her head. Her vision was blurry, and her ears rang, but she could see Rathgar coming her way. She looked around for her sword, but couldn't find it in the dim light of the cave. The ground shook as Rathgar got closer, ready to finish her. Finally, he stood directly over her and, with a smile on his face; he raised his foot like he was squashing a bug. Tallis met Heidi's eyes. The Huldre had managed to get next to Talon and Arna. Tallis prepared for the final blow. She looked once more at Finn's face and braced for the final impact.

Finn opened his eyes and first felt the deep dent in his chest plate. He had at least two broken ribs. He looked right, then left and saw Rathgar with his foot raised, ready to squash Tallis, who laid on the ground near unconsciousness. Finn tried to sit up, but the pain in his chest was severe. In frustration, he punched the cave floor and roared to get Rathgar's attention. This had two effects. One, it got Rathgar's attention, secondly it caused a chunk of the cave floor to rise and strike Rathgar in the bottom of his raised foot, knocking him off balance. He stumbled backwards and fell to the ground. Rathgar quickly recovered and jumped to his feet.

"Now I end this!" roared Rathgar and ran straight for Finn with fists balled and murder in his eyes.

Finn frantically struggled to his feet just as Rathgar got to him and swung a fist straight for the dent in Finn's chest plate. Rathgar continued to pummel Finn repeatedly. With such ferocity and speed that Finn could do nothing but hold his arms up and deflect as many blows as he could. Finn was against the wall and was running out of energy. He looked down and waited for the final blows when he heard Orlyn's voice in his head.

"Study your opponent," the voice said.

Finn Stonefist

Finn looked down and saw Rathgar's feet were far apart, which meant he was coming in for a heavy hit. A head shot, he thought. Finn, without thinking, ducked just in time to feel Rathgar's fist glance at the top of his helm and heard it crash into the wall behind him. In his crouched position, Finn had a clear shot to a very sensitive spot on any male of any race. It was a low blow, but his life depended on it. Finn swung his fist straight up and connected squarely with Rathgar's family jewels. Rathgar howled in pain and stumbled backwards, holding himself.

"Nobody steps on my girlfriend," said Finn.

"I was going to kill you quickly, but now I am going to stretch this beating out," said Rathgar, as he began another volley of blows.

This time Finn felt more focused and could deflect more of the blows. He pushed Rathgar backwards, giving him a little space between them and a chance to focus his mind on the one thing he thought could save him: The Ice Fire he manifested on the mountain top. He closed his eyes and focused on the feeling he had on the mountain top. It came to him quickly, and he latched onto it and allowed it to grow. He could feel Rathgar charging towards him and just as Rathgar raised a fist, Finn opened his eyes and blue fire filled them as he met Rathgar's gaze. He caught Rathgar's fist in mid-swing with his own fist of blue fire. Finn now appeared completely covered in blue flames from head to toe. Rathgar struggled in vain to free his hand from Finn's stony grip.

"We are done!" said Finn in a calm voice that made the air tremble with authority. Finn raised a fist and struck Rathgar in the face, knocking him backwards. Rathgar stumbled and fell to the ground, unconscious. Finn then turned his attention to the birds that still hovered nearby, ready to attack. He clapped his hands together, sending an enormous ball of blue flame towards the flock. Whoever it didn't cook instantly, it scattered and sent flying to all corners of the cavern. With the battle appearing to be over, Finn closed his eyes and returned to his normal giant appearance. The chest plate had repaired itself and his ribs already felt better. He quickly ran to Tallis's side. She was pale and unconscious.

"What do I do?" Finn begged, but Tallis was silent. "Heidi, get her salve now!"

Heidi scrambled to find Tallis's salve and ran as fast as she could to Finn's side. She applied some to the gash in Tallis's head. At first, nothing seemed to happen. Then the wound glowed bright blue and closed on its own, but Tallis didn't wake.

"Tallis! Wake up, please wake up. I need you. Wake up!" roared Finn, causing the whole cavern to tremble.

"Finn, you stay here." Heidi ran to Arna and Talon. Since there were no visible wounds, she did the only thing she could think to do. She took a heaping finger full of the sticky salve and jammed it into each of their mouths, forcing them to swallow. Suddenly, they both coughed and sputtered.

"Ugh! That stuff is awful. Death might be better," sputtered Arna.

Heidi laughed and threw her arms around his neck, sobbing that she was so happy he wasn't dead. She hugged Talon, and they quickly got to Finn's side, who was still holding a lifeless Tallis.

"Why won't she wake up?" asked a teary-eyed Talon.

"I don't know," said Finn.

Just then Anders, the Nightfeathers, and a large contingent came bursting into the cavern, ready for a fight. Anders surveyed the scene and found the group of teenagers huddled around a figure. Anders turned to Dagfinn and ordered him to take troops and secure the Keep and the cavern. Dagfinn immediately turned and started barking orders to the ever-growing throng of creatures entering the cavern. Anders followed the Nightfeathers over to Finn and the others. As they got closer, Mick and Lorelei recognized the figure on the ground and ran over. At Finn's side, they dropped to their knees in human form, and Lorelei cradled Tallis's lifeless body in her arms. She wept uncontrollably and Mick embraced them, both trying to stay strong. But it was no use.

"We tried everything, but she just won't wake up," explained Finn between sobs.

"That's because she isn't there," said a deep voice from behind the group.

No one had noticed the stranger. The group turned at once.

"Thor! What are you doing here and what do you mean, she isn't there? Is she... dead?" sputtered Finn.

"I am here to deliver a message from the All Father, Odin. He is pleased with the bravery and valiance you and your party have shown in battle. You have proven your character as the bearer of the King's Stone, and you have all used the gifts you were given with wisdom and skill. As far as far, your friend is concerned—" said Thor.

"Her name is Tallis!" shouted Finn, causing the air to shake.

Thor smiled a toothy grin. "As far as Tallis is concerned, I will let her talk to you."

"You can heal her? You can bring her back; I mean, you are a god?" asked Lorelei, almost frantically.

Thor moved towards Lorelei and Mick and kneeled beside them. He pushed a lock of hair from Tallis' face and looked deep into Lorelei's eyes. "Oh my dear Lorelei, I do not have the power over life and death and her body is too broken to bring your dear one back to you, but she can explain everything." He put a caring hand on Lorelei's shoulder. He then looked up, which caused everyone to look up. At first, they saw nothing except the darkness that was there before. Then they heard a flutter of wings and then saw a glint a gold in the distance. Then another glint, only closer. It seemed to circle the group. As it got closer, they could see the glint was actually a breastplate of gold color worn by a woman with great white wings. She soared towards them in a great circle and she eventually came to light next to the still kneeling Thor.

Thor smiled and stood. "I see you made the journey okay," he said to the woman, who silently nodded.

Finn couldn't believe what he was staring at. Even from his great height, she looked tall and muscular. She was clad in golden armor from head to toe. Her helm had wings on it, resembling those on her back. On her back, Finn could see the hilt of a sword that was nearly as long as the woman was tall.

"Finn, come down here. You are going to want to see this up close," said Mick, who was now standing with a look of shock on his face.

Finn returned to human form, but still clad in his armor with his axe in hand. He stepped forward and scrutinized the woman. She was as tall as him and glowed with a very distinctive aura that seemed to light the surrounding air. Then it hit him like Rathgar's fist. This woman was Tallis! He looked back and forth between the woman and Tallis's body, which still lay on the ground.

"Tallis?" said Finn with a shaky hand, reaching out to touch the woman's face.

"It's really me, Finn, I'm okay," said Tallis, taking his hand.

Finn Stonefist

"How are you here if you are there?" asked Finn, still swiveling between the girl on the ground and the woman standing before him.

"Well, the brief answer is that I died," said Tallis

"You what!" said Talon.

"I died, sort of. Let me explain," said Tallis and continued. "When I battled Rathgar, I was so focused on avenging my family I didn't see the fatal blow until it was too late. After I was struck, I don't remember much except a woman at my side telling me everything will be okay. She scooped me up, and we flew through the top of the cavern and into the stars. After what seemed like a long time, I was brought to a golden city and laid on a table. They gave me some juice to drink, and it immediately restored me. I was healed and feeling great. I wanted to get back to you all, but the woman told me that my fight was over, and my mortal body was beyond repair. I was scared and angry all at the same time. Then the woman explained that because of my valiance in battle, I had been chosen by Freya to receive a gift rarely given to mortals, let alone someone as young as me. They offered me a place among the Valkyrie! This meant a new body and new responsibilities. I am to ferry the souls of fallen warriors to the afterlife. Time moves differently in Asgard, and I spent what felt like weeks training and learning what it meant to be a Valkyrie. It also meant I could come back to you and say goodbye," she finished.

"Say goodbye? You can't leave, we just got you back. I just got you back!" Finn choked up on this last part.

"Finn, my boy, she has been called to a higher purpose by Freya herself. There is no greater honor than to be chosen by the Gods, you know this. Yes, it hurts, but she isn't gone just working somewhere else," encouraged Anders.

This did not comfort Finn at all.

Just then Lorelei walked forward towards Tallis and placed a hand on her cheek. "Are you happy with this choice?"

"I am mama, and it's not like I can't come visit and the Valkyrie have agreed to let me stay on Midgard to finish my human school to keep up appearances, but for now I have to attend more training on Asgard," said Tallis.

Just then, a low groan was heard from behind the group. It was Rathgar waking up. With Thor and Tallis, the group and nearly forgotten about the unconscious giant. Finn quickly shifted into giant form and prepared for a fight.

Tallis put a hand on his leg and said, "Let me handle this."

She walked over to a groggy, barely conscious Rathgar. He looked up at her at first, not realizing who she was.

"Have you come to take me to Valhalla?" he asked in a low voice.

"No, you're not dying today and you sure as hell aren't going to the All Father's great hall. Look a little closer, you tyrannical bastard," spat Tallis, crouching closer so he could see her face clearly.

Rathgar sat up a little closer and a look of shock replaced his hopefulness.

"That's not possible! I killed you!" he said, trembling.

"Yes, you did, but I'm back to bring you to face the All Father for your crimes against the nine realms," said Tallis.

Before Rathgar could stand, Tallis had the great giant flipped over face down in the dirt. She bound his wrists with a rope that looked much like rope given to Arna. She then flipped him onto his back and kneeled beside him, and pressed her lips against his forehead. When she stood again where her lips had touched Rathgar, there was a binding rune like one used on Heidi, except it glowed gold in the dim light of the cave. Tallis then drew a great sword from its sheath on her back and drove it straight into the ground. Suddenly the ground surrounding Rathgar disappeared, and a portal opened directly under him into which he fell, screaming curses until he could be heard no more. The portal closed, and it was quiet again. Tallis let out a relieving sigh and returned to the group, who were watching in awe.

"That was incredible!" said Finn, returning to human form.

"Now that is taken care of, there is one more thing that needs to be dealt with," said Thor in a very official tone.

"What would that be?" asked Finn.

"Anders, step forward," commanded Thor.

Anders, now in human form, seemed surprised and took a couple of careful steps towards the god of thunder.

"Yes, sir?" said Anders.

"You have done something that has never happened in the history of history. You have taken the place of a Norn," said Thor.

"I have?" asked Anders.

"Yes," Thor said. "When the Norn joined forces with Rathgar, all those years ago. She perverted her purpose and abandoned her sisters in Yggdrasil, leaving the fates of thousands hanging in the balance. When you accepted the staff from Finn, Yggdrasil recognized your heart as pure and chose you to take her place as a Norn. You are to return with me to Yggdrasil to join the other two Norns and bring balance back to the fates of many. The staff you bear is an actual branch of Yggdrasil gifted to each Norn to connect them to the nine realms. You are connected now. That's why you can shift again. You will, over time, learn the full power of the Norn as you study with your new sisters. It may also help you find your beloved."

Anders stood, mouth gaping open. "I don't know what to say except I didn't kill the Norn that was Finn. Why isn't he being offered this?"

"The Norn's staff must be given, not taken. When Finn killed the Norn, he technically took the staff in combat, but he gave it to you," explained Thor.

"Grandpa, this is the best news you could hope for. You're whole again and now you can look for grandma!" said Finn.

"Well, okay then, put me in coach. I'm ready," laughed Anders, with tears in his eyes.

Thor let out a thunderous laugh. "Well, it is time for us to leave, but before I go, I would speak with Finn alone."

Finn and Thor stepped over to edge of the lake where they were out of ear shot of the rest of the group. Thor's face got very serious as he turned towards Finn.

"Finn, you have a lot of work to do here as the king, and I know I am taking the two most important people to you away for a while. You may feel alone, but trust me when I say you are not alone. I look around at the noble family you have brought together under one cause. You got all the great clans to work together for the first time in years. These people have fought and died for you and will continue to do so as long as you treat them well. You stand at a tipping point of things. You can return to the old ways or you can make something completely new. Just know that whatever your choice, you have the confidence of the Gods as long as you are a fair and just ruler. The day that you are not, our trust will be taken from you just like Rathgar, and another will be chosen to take your place. Now, concerning your parents; taking the staff to the cave will set your father free but both your father and mother will still be dark shifters, but our magicians on Asgard have come up with a potion that will negate the false dark shift if they take it every day without fail. The only thing is they don't know how it will affect a Sammeloper like your mother."

Thor then produced two vials from a pouch on his belt. They were made of crystal with a clear fluid that had a faint blue glow to it. "These vials are enchanted to refill once every day with the needed potion." He handed them to Finn.

"Do you really think I have what it takes to be king?" asked Finn.

"I do, and so does the council of the Gods. That is why we gave you the King's Stone, but more importantly, you have to believe it. You will do just fine, my friend. Now let's get back."

Returning to the group, Tallis and Anders took their places next to Thor in preparation for their journey.

Anders then turned to Thor and asked, "My Lord, you are asking us to leave our loved ones at a very dangerous time. Could we please say goodbye before we go?"

"Of course. I will meet you in halls of Asgard when you arrive. Tallis can you handle taking a passenger with you?" asked Thor.

"We'll be fine and thank you," said Tallis.

With that Thor turned to the others and said, "The Gods are with you," and he lifted Mjolnir high above his head and, in a flash of lightning, the great god of thunder disappeared as fast as he had appeared. As soon as everyone had recovered from the blinding light, hugs and kisses commenced as the family bid farewell to Tallis and Anders. Tallis tried to reassure her parents that she would be fine, but this only caused Lorelei to sob even harder. Anders hugged Hilde and Erik and Arna and turned to Finn.

"Who would have thought this summer would have turned out like this, eh old man" said Finn, trying to lighten the mood. Inside, he was terrified of Anders leaving.

"My boy, your feelings betray you. You will do just fine and as a Norn I think I will keep an eye out for you. Know that I am always watching, and I will return when I can. Now is time for you to become king and rule with honor and justice. Our people deserve it and I know you can do it. I have always known you were destined for great things even if you couldn't see it," said Anders.

Finn was afraid if he spoke, his emotions would overtake him, so instead, he just hugged his grandfather with everything he had. Anders hugged him back just as hard. Then it was Finn's turn to say goodbye to Tallis.

"I don't know what to say. You look so different and the same all at once. I wish I could have protected you. Then you wouldn't have to leave. Tallis, I need you here to be with me, to be my queen. I love you," said Finn with a shaky voice.

"Oh, Finn, this was always my fate. I see that now, but that doesn't mean we can't be together. I will always love you and we can make this work. Just think of it as the ultimate long-distance relationship. Plus, I'll be back in a few weeks for school," encouraged Tallis.

The two kissed like it was their last kiss and embraced one more time before Tallis turned to Anders.

"We should go. It's not good to keep the Gods waiting," she said.

Anders and Tallis stood where Thor had stood and Tallis drew her sword. She held it high above her head and with one more longing look at her family and lastly at Finn, she spread her great white wings and said in a loud voice, "To Asgard!"

A faint glow emanated from her and it grew in brightness until Finn and the others couldn't see either Tallis or Anders. Then all at once it faded out, and they were gone like smoke in the wind, leaving Finn and the others in the dim light of the cave. Mick appeared behind Finn and placed a fatherly hand on his shoulder.

"They will be fine, and we will see them again soon, but for now we need our king to tell us what is next," said Mick.

Next? What is next? Finn hadn't even thought about anything beyond beating Rathgar. Finn thought fast and tried to recall what Anders would have done. He turned and faced the group of waiting faces, took a deep breath, and gave out directions, just like on the football field.

"Uncle Erik, I need you and Auntie to go home and check on my mother and our other guests. Lady Lily, please take what troops are left outside and round up any stragglers from Rathgar's forces and put them in the dungeons for now, and then make sure the surrounding area is clear of enemies for at least fifty miles in all directions. Mr. and Mrs. Nightfeather, can you, Dagfinn, and Dagmar stay here and coordinate securing this whole place, including the tunnel we used to get in."

With orders given and people making their way to securing the keep, Finn turned into the darkness and made his way along the shoreline of the lake until, in the darkness, he nearly stepped on it. The Staff of Jotunheim laid in the sand, faintly glowing. Finn lifted it and was surprised at how light it felt in his hand, although it stood nearly a head taller than him and had a football sized jewel on it. The staff had a faint glow about it and hummed quietly, almost like it was purring. Finn was eager to get to his father, but he knew he needed to help secure the keep and round up any of Rathgar's forces that remained.

Finn spent the next few weeks traveling between Troll's Rest and the Keep in an effort to secure both locations and to get to know his mother. Late one night, Finn gave his mother the same binding rune given to Heidi and Einar. After pulling the brand from her shoulder, she handed the brand back to Finn and promised with an oath to behave. It would be two more weeks before she agreed to take the potion. She felt the dark shift was her penance for all the terrible things she had done.

"If I take this, it could cause the wrath of the Gods to come upon me," argued Tove when Finn offered her the potion.

"Mick tells me that if the Gods were angry with you, you would sit next to Rathgar wherever he is and would not have been offered this potion. Besides, what do you have to lose in trying it?" asked Finn.

"I could lose my life, but even that would not be an enormous loss. Give me the potion. You haven't lied to me yet and I don't know why you would lie to me about this now," said Tove.

Finn gently handed her the small crystal vial with the potion in it. Tove accepted the vial and looked it over skeptically, then popped the top.

"Skaal," she said as she poured the fluid into her mouth and swallowed. Her face made a puckered look, and she nearly dropped the vial. Finn caught it mid-air and put the top back on it. Tove suddenly doubled over and wrenched with pain. She collapsed onto the nearby sofa and clenched her stomach. Finn called for Hilde, who quickly appeared at his side.

"What's happening? What do we do?" Finn asked frantically.

"I don't know. We can only wait and see. This is magic way beyond me and my herbs," replied Hilde.

Suddenly Tove got to her feet. "I'm going to shift!"

"Not in here, you're not! Outside!" ordered Hilde and helped Tove to the backyard.

In the backyard, Finn was at Tove's side trying to help.

"What do you need?" he asked Tove.

"Space! Back up!" Tove yelled.

Just then she shifted into full giantess form, standing at least twenty feet tall. Then, she grew a little and was clearly an ogre. Then she arched herself backwards and shifted into something the size of a large bee. In her current fairy form, she zipped up and down in the air as she hollered in pain, then all at once she fell to the ground in human form. As she sat up straight, Finn and Hilde couldn't believe what they saw. Gone was the dark Sammeloper and before them stood a woman with short dark hair and bright blue eyes. She was slender in her features and had a kindness in her bearing.

"Mom?" asked Finn, nervous that she wouldn't recognize him.

"Finn? Is it really you?" cried Tove as she embraced Finn with everything she had.

Finn pushed back from her embrace. "Do you really remember me, like really remember?"

"I do, my son. My baby boy. I remember everything from the day you were born to my entire life. It has all returned. I remember Einar! Einar! Is he alive like you said?" said Tove.

"Well, mostly, but now that you are back, I plan to go get him as soon as I can," said Finn.

"If you are done shifting, we can go back inside, and Finn can fill you in on everything that has been going on," said Hilde.

Back in the house, Finn told Tove everything that had happened. He explained she would need to take the potion every day without fail to keep the darkness at bay.

"I plan to make amends," Tove said. "I know I have a long road to redemption, but with my family I believe I can do it."

Finally, early one morning Finn rose and gathered his gear and collect the Staff of Jotunheim from the large family safe in Anders' office. He had kept it close all these weeks for fear one of Rathgar's minions would try to reclaim it, but today Finn had only one thought on his mind. Today, he would get Einar from the cave. Today, he would bring his family back together for good. Hilde and Tove met him at the bottom of the stairs.

"I wish I could come with you, but this binding rune won't allow me," said Tove as she gently touched the scarred rune on her neck. "Just be safe and keep the King's Stone handy."

"I know, and we will deal with that rune when I get back. I promise," said Finn.

There was a knock at the front door.

"That would be my ride," said Finn.

He opened the door to see Talon standing on the porch.

"Are you ready to go?" asked Talon.

Finned looked back at Tove and Hilde and said, "I am."

Chapter 19

As Finn passed through the portal and the cold crisp air of the forest replaced the warmth of his home. Finn surveyed his surroundings and being satisfied he was alone, he signaled for Talon to close the portal. He would signal Talon via his ring when he had Einar and was ready to come back. Finn filled his lungs with the cold air and took in the scenery. It had changed some since they were last there. The air was colder, and the leaves of the birch trees were yellow, like large drops of gold dripping and covering the forest floor. Finn could see a squirrel rushing around collecting pine nuts to prepare for the winter that threatened to come any day. The sky was clear, and the sun was warm on his face. Finn began his hike to the cave's entrance. With the Staff of Jotunheim in hand and the weather on his side, Finn felt good for the first time all summer. He could see old salmon trying to making their last-ditch effort to get upriver. In the distance, a moose chewed lazily on the tall grass and didn't pay any attention to Finn.

Finally, standing at the cave's entrance, it looked just as they had left it. It was quiet and seemed hard to believe that just inside was a great stone giant. Finn made his way into the cave and the staff hummed loudly, like it knew where it was and what Finn was about to do. The staff began vibrating hard and Finn stopped and examined the staff. It was like the staff was saying, "I don't want to be here!"

"Stop it!" ordered Finn. "Understand, this is the safest place for you and the only way I can get my father back," he said, feeling silly to be having a conversation with an ornate stick.

The staff ceased its vibrating and returned to a dull hum. Finn continued on and entered the cavern. Einar was right where he left him. Sitting on his stone throne completely encased in stone. His face looked peaceful, and Finn hoped he wasn't in pain.

"Father!" he said and ran towards him, but quickly remembering the two giant stone fists and the curse guarding Einar. Suddenly, the staff stopped dead, causing Finn to come to a screeching halt. At first he was confused, then he realized where he was. He was directly in front of one of the stone fists. He quickly backed up to the staff and caught his breath.

"" he said to the staff. The staff hummed in acknowledgement.

Finn looked around the room but could not see any place the cave had for the staff. The room was empty except for the fists and Einar and his throne.

"Okay cave, now what? I brought the staff in trade for my father. Where do you want it?" hollered Finn into the room.

His voice echoing off the walls. At first nothing then, a low rumble shook the floor enough to make the small pebbles on it dance around Finn's feet. Just then, Einar and his throne slid backwards as if by invisible hands. Where he had been, a small hole appeared in the floor. Finn carefully stepped towards the hole and examined it. It was slightly larger than the diameter of the staff.

"This is your great idea to keep it safe, a hole in the floor?" Finn asked the room.

Just then, the giant stone fists shifted ever so slightly towards Finn, which cause Finn to take a giant leap backwards in fear of being crushed like the Norn.

"Not funny!" he said. "I get it, you can keep it safe."

He stepped forward again towards the hole and held the staff just above.

"Welcome home," he said and planted the shaft into the hole. It slid about a third of the way down and hit a solid bottom, bringing the jewel to about eye level with Finn. The hole closed around it, clamping the staff into place. Finn quickly stepped back and waited for a change in Einar, but nothing happened.

"Okay, you got what you wanted. Now give me my father!" said Finn.

Nothing. The room was silent. Einar was still encased in stone. Finn slumped to floor and sat cross legged staring at Einar.

"I've got nothing to do all day. I can wait!" he yelled to the quiet.

Finn retrieved two sandwiches Hilde made for him and devoured one. He hadn't realized how hungry he was and soon devoured the second one. Just as he finished his sandwiches, he heard something. It sounded like gravel moving or eggshells cracking. Finn jumped to his feet and grabbed the King's Stone from his pack just in case he needed to shift quickly. He looked around, but he seemed to be alone still. The sound happened again, this time louder. Finn couldn't see anything or anyone in the cave with him, but the third time he heard the sound, he could tell where it was coming from. It was coming from the Einar statue. Finn looked closely and that when he saw the source of the sound. It was Einar's fingers they were moving slowing. With each movement, the stony shell crumbled away to the floor. Soon Einar's hands were completely uncovered and moving freely. Cracks were now visible all over Einar's body, and Finn could hear grunting from under the stone mask.

"Come on, Dad, you've got this!" encouraged Finn, careful not to step between the fists.

Suddenly, Einar gripped the arms of the chair and let a loud grunt out. He then opened his eyes and Finn could see the bright red fiery eyes of the fire ogre. Einar strained against the stone shell and forced his legs free. The shell was crumbling into bigger pieces now, and there was a pile of rubble at his feet. Then, with one last grunt, Einar stood from the chair, causing the remaining stone to fall from him in a pile of dust and rubble on the floor. Einar shook himself, and small bits of rubble and dust flew from his shoulders and hair in all directions. Once the dust settled, Einar looked up and locked eyes with Finn.

"I take it we won," said Einar with a huge toothy grin.

"And then some Dad," said Finn, and he carefully made his way between the staff and the fists to get to Einar.

They embraced, and Finn helped Einar off of the pedestal. Just as they were both clear of the fists and the staff, the throne where Einar was sitting sank back into the floor from which it came, and the staff slid into the very center between the fists and hummed quietly like it was comfortable with its new home.

Suddenly, Einar doubled over like he was in pain.

"Dad! Are you okay?" said Finn, but what he saw scared him.

Red veins could be seen working their way up Einar's arms and neck. His eyes were red as fire.

"Run Finn! I can't stop the shift," yelled Einar in a deep voice.

Finn had forgotten that Einar was in the middle of the dark shift just before he sat on the throne. Then Finn remembered the potion Thor had given him.

Finn Stonefist

"Hang on, I have something, I can fix this," said Finn.
"WHAT?" roared Einar.
Finn ran for his backpack and quickly found the second of the vials Thor had given him. He ran back to Einar and popped the top on the vial.

"Here quick, drink this," urged Finn, putting the vial in Einar's hand.

Einar looked at the vial skeptically for a second, then tipped it back and drank the fluid. Instantly, his insides felt cold and he could feel the fire ogre within fading from the surface. The red veins on his arms and neck glowed blue and faded. The pain stopped, and Einar felt like he could breathe again. He stood up straight and looked at Finn, who had a stunned look on his face.

"What's the matter? How do I look?" asked Einar.

Finn couldn't believe what he was seeing. All traces of the fire ogre were gone. Before him stood a tall man with broad shoulders and a muscular chest and arms. He had sandy blonde hair and deep blue eyes, just like Finn.

"You look like me," said Finn.

"Actually, you look like me, my boy. I feel like my old self again. I feel strong and in control for the first time in decades. I think it's time you fill me in on what has happened since I've been gone," said Einar.

Finn told Einar every detail of the last few weeks, including the news about Tallis and Anders' new callings in Asgard. When Finn finished, he slumped to the floor next to Einar and caught his breath. Einar just looked at Finn in amazement.

"What?" asked Finn.

"Oh nothing, just sitting in amazement that you Finn Stonefist, Sammeloper, conqueror of tyrants, friend of the

Gods, brother, King and most importantly my son; has faced every challenge head on and defeated every foe in your path. From the day you were born, I knew you were going to do great things, but you have surpassed even my imagination and the crazy thing is you have barely started your journey. I am so excited to watch you grow into the Giant and king, I know you are destined to be," said Einar.

Finn had no idea how to respond. "Come on, let's get you home so we can help mom." Finn jumped to his feet and offering a hand to Einar.

Standing outside the entrance to the cave, Finn stopped and looked back into the tunnel.

Einar stopped when he noticed Finn standing still. "What is it, son?"

"There is one more thing I have to do to make sure no one, man or beast, can ever get the Staff of Jotunheim until we know what to do with it," said Finn.

"Shouldn't the wards be strong enough?" asked Einar.

"They let us and the Norn in," said Finn. He then spread his arms wide and closed his eyes. He took a deep breath and focused on the Is Fir deep within him. He felt it grow and when he opened his eyes, he was completely covered in stony blue fire.

"That's incredible!" said Einar.

"Just watch this," said Finn.

He then kneeled down and dug his hands deep into the earth at his feet. He closed his eyes and focused. From Einar's perspective, Finn looked as though he was kneeling in prayer when a low rumble came from deep in the ground. It started directly below Finn and rolled with a deep growl towards the cave entrance. Once the rumbling reached the cave, it got much louder and the sides of the cave shook, and rocks began to fall.

Finn Stonefist

Fearing it would bury them in a rockslide, Einar got to Finn's side and tried to arouse him from his trance, but to no avail. Seeing this was futile, Einar hunkered down next to Finn and dodged and deflected as many rolling boulders as he could. The rumbling grew more intense and cracks could be seen in the stone around the cave entrance. Suddenly, Finn jerked and drove his hands deeper into the ground. He then yanked two great fists of dirt and underbrush out of the ground. The cave tunnel collapsed from the inside out. When the last rock had fallen, and the dust settled, Einar crept from behind Finn, blinking the dust from his eyes. At first all he could he see was dirt and gray dust in the air, but after a minute he could see where once the cave opening was stood an enormous pile of large gray boulders. The cave was completely gone. Einar turned to Finn in total amazement just in time to see Finn shifting back into human form.

"There are not words for what you just did!" said Einar.

"Now the staff is buried under a mountain's worth of rock and the tunnel to it is completely filled in. There is just one last touch it needs," said Finn, scanning the forest floor.

He found what he was looking for near to where he had kneeled. It was a single boulder about the size of a basketball. It was unremarkable except for the deep rune etched into that Finn recognized as the rune for danger. The rune was glowing green and humming. Finn hefted the rock and quickly climbed about halfway up the pile of rubble that was the cave entrance and firmly placed the stone squarely with the rune facing out towards to forest. Once in place, the glow and hum faded away, like it was comfortable in its new station.

"That should keep the wards powered just in case someone gets a wild hair to dig it out," said Finn.

"You know, a rumble like that will get the human's attention. By tonight, this place will be crawling with geologists and earthquake geeks," said Einar.

"That is why we need to leave," said Finn, touching the gemstone on his King's Ring.

It glowed brightly, and a moment later a portal opened just in front of them. They could see the house and everyone Finn loved surrounding the familiar dinner table. Finn thought he could smell Hilde's famous chili. His thoughts drifted first to Anders and then rested on thoughts of Tallis. He fought the emotions and told himself it would only be for a few more weeks and with that and a sharp clap on his shoulder from Einar, he cleared his mind and followed Einar through the portal.

Glossary and Pronunciation Guide

Asgard – As-gard - Home of Aesir Gods in Norse mythology

Midgard – Mid-gard – Planet Earth, home of humans

Jotunheim – Yo-tun-hime – Home of the giants

Sammeloper – Som-uh-luh-per – a confluence or convergence.

Made in the USA
Columbia, SC
28 July 2023

a6c5b6de-47cf-44e5-854c-8227d434cfa3R01